High praise for

LOUDMOUTH

by Robert Duncan

A SONIC WAIL of a tale about the youthful beginnings of one of the Mount Rushmore "heads" of rock 'n' roll journalism. I loved it.

JOEL GION, musician, Brian Jonestown Massacre

INTELLIGENCE AND GRACE . . . entertainingly larger-than-life.

PUBLISHERS WEEKLY

LOUDMOUTH IS, as advertised, a loud and brash trip that takes you through the hellish halls of childhood and adolescence before delivering you to the sweet salvation of rock 'n' roll music and all that rides alongside it. The story is majorly compelling—funny, tender, and very very honest. Read this book immediately if you like truth, drugs, generation gaps, guitars, and lifelong quests for freedom and kicks.

CRAIG FINN, singer/songwriter, The Hold Steady

THIS PICARESQUE, COMING-OF-AGE novel, about a boy who looks for answers in rock 'n' roll, but finds them in the love of an extraordinary woman, is sad, serious, funny and, in the end, ridiculously moving.

SYLVIE SIMMONS, *New York Times* bestselling author, *Face It: Debbie Harry* and *Serge Gainsbourg: A Fistful of Gitanes*

IN PROSE THAT'S beautiful, when it's not hilarious, this noisy, nostalgic novel tells how an excitable boy from a darkly conservative family survived childhood and then rock 'n' roll. It's a wild ride with some amazing characters—including a few you might recognize—and I'm in awe.

JAAN UHELSZKI, former editor, *Creem*; writer, producer, *Creem: America's Only Rock 'n' Roll Magazine*

LOUDMOUTH

LOUDMOUTH

A NOVEL

ROBERT DUNCAN

THREE ROOMS PRESS
New York, NY

Loudmouth
BY Robert Duncan

ISBN 978-1-941110-92-8 (trade paperback original)
ISBN 978-1-941110-93-5 (Epub)
Library of Congress Control Number: 2020936039

TRP-083

Publication Date: October 06, 2020

BISAC category code
FIC043000 FICTION / Coming of Age
FIC069000 FICTION / City Life
FIC041000 FICTION / Biographical
FIC060000 FICTION / Humorous / Black Humor

COVER DESIGN:
Jen Kellogg, www.duncanchannon.com

COVER PHOTOGRAPH:
Nick Rorick

INTERIOR DESIGN:
KG Design International, www.katgeorges.com

DISTRIBUTED BY:
PGW/Ingram: www.pgw.com

Three Rooms Press
New York, NY
www.threeroomspress.com
info@threeroomspress.com

For Roni

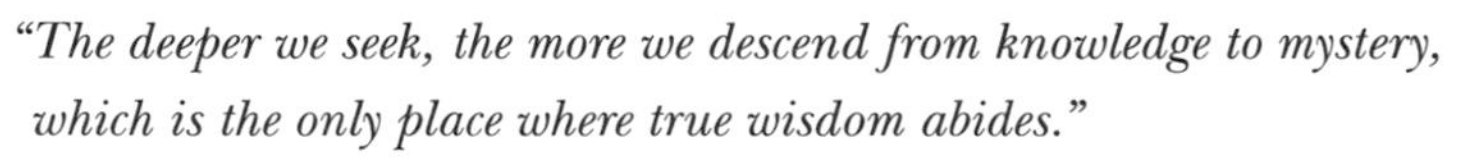

"The deeper we seek, the more we descend from knowledge to mystery, which is the only place where true wisdom abides."

— Nick Tosches, *Where Dead Voices Gather*

"Unscrew the doors themselves from their jambs!"

— Walt Whitman, "Song of Myself XXIV"

LOUDMOUTH

CHAPTER 0
Cuyahoga

Towing a long, black veil of unabashedly leaded exhaust, the Fairlane swung by Swingo's, Cleveland's famous-for-calling-itself-famous Celebrity Inn, and we climbed in. Me shotgun, Bruce in back. Bruce, when he was scrawny and wispy-bearded, hanging over the front seat, like a boy in a Bruce song. My friend Charlie, slouching in the driver's, was here to show us the sights: A dive bar Charlie liked. A dive bar his band played before they threw him out for being drunk all the time. A dive bar next to a radio station—"Allen Freed," Charlie tossed out, by way of history lesson, as we rattled past. A dive bar Charlie liked to hang, by the record store he liked to hang. And here he snatched his fingers from the wheel to count down the righteousness within—"Ayler. Ornette. The 5. Stooges . . ."—before plugging another Camel in rubber-band lips, another homemade cassette in the dash, and drifting into focus and out.

It had started with a handwritten note on a pink square of paper, "While You Were Out" pre-printed in black at the top. On the message line it had said: "Come to Cleveland." In the "From" space, the raspy-voiced caller had asked the receptionist to write: "B.S." But even a short-term temp from Squaresville knew what those initials stood for, a week after simultaneous covers of Time *and* Newsweek.

I couldn't help but wonder if the invitation was actually the ploy of a manager who used to be a critic, trying to make sure all the contrarians—and our magazine was a hotbed of them—had come aboard.

"Hey, Bruce," I could hear him saying, "why don't you invite that Creem *kid to the Cleveland show."*

Maybe I'd gone cynical—a credulous Midwesterner curdled, at 22, by too long in New York. Or maybe Bruce, a credulous kid from the Midwest of the East Coast, wide-eyeing the towers across the river, actually thought he'd found someone who knew the feeling. I don't doubt a bond was forming. We'd shared a few adventures in Detroit and New Orleans, and the couple times we'd run into each other in New York, good feelings seemed to be mutual and genuine. So, let's just agree that the "Come to Cleveland" summons was all Bruce, spontaneous and real and even, beneath the characteristic offstage reserve, wildly exuberant. Either way, the guy was enough of a star that enough of a starfucker went.

Called Bruce back, said I'd get my friend Charlie to show us the real Cleveland. He would love Charlie. Cleveland born and raised, Charlie was a poet, songwriter, out-of-tune guitar basher, squiggly-voiced singer, Lou Reed apostle, pal of Lester Bangs, implacable evangelist—in the columns of Creem*—for all sorts of rock insurgencies, pill popper, syrup sucker, boozehound, bad dancer, blood donor, world's most skeletal life-model, mama's boy and nothing if not a "bird"—which, I explained, is what my father called people he didn't know where to file.*

Like me. Probably like you, Bruce.

Charlie was also a sweetheart. And through a long, perfectly odd—and perfect—afternoon, he swerved his wobbly junker all over Cleveland's crumbly streets and pockmarked highways until I thought it might fly off its springs. He slowed down, sped up, scraped off his last hubcap and kept going, screeched to a halt and, after roaring back into freeway traffic, dove under the dash for a dropped cig. Missed the exit and backed up on the shoulder, abruptly leaning across the front seat to flip open the glove compartment.

A pistol fell out, with not a "Shit" or "Fuck" from Charlie, who kept scratching around, scattering gum wrappers, crumpled Camel packs, band flyers, parking tickets, expired registrations and assorted detritus of an outmatched attempt at citizenship, until finally, with bony fingers and long, dirty nails, he extracted three .45-caliber bullets. He gave one to Bruce, one to me and held one, for ceremony, in the palm of his tremulous hand. And then—I'll never forget—Charlie from Cleveland said to me and Bruce:

"This is how we'll remember."

Part I

CHAPTER 1

Oral

GOT A MOUTH ON ME. BEEN at the root of most of my troubles, most of my days. It's not just that I'm making up for being a wimp—mute, fearful and frequently bloodied—in grade school. Or that, shortly after grade school, I became fond of drink and getting rowdy. Or that my grandmother, who was fond of drink, was an opera singer before amplification, and volume—apparently—is inherited. And, yes, I have a tendency to get carried away. But it's not that either, not entirely. Mostly, it's technical: faulty calibration of the oral-aural feedback loop. I hear everything fine—except myself. Which is why, all my life, it confused me when people held a finger to their lips—as they did, regularly, friends and strangers alike—and made me mad.

I'm not loud, I'd think. It's Mother who's loud.

"Yoo-hoo!" she'd call across the restaurant, in that time-stopping alarm my little brother and I had come to dread. A millisecond later, before any mere mortal could react, she'd do it again, louder, angrier.

"YOO-HOO!"

And repeat it, over and over, with rapidly rising stridency, wildly waving her napkin or banging a spoon on her glass for superfluous emphasis, while Roger and I gripped our ears and scanned for the nearest exit.

Mother wanted her Tabasco. Now!

But even her dinner table chit-chat had a way of flying off the handle. If she recognized someone at a nearby table, she'd give them a polite nod-and-smile and immediately start expounding, in what she imagined were discreet tones, on their private illnesses or unsightly infirmities or the all too obvious—"Just look at them!" she'd yell, even as you were pleading with her not to—disabilities of their grandchildren. After just enough of a pause to make you think the outburst was over—a classic false ending—she would burst out again, with no basis in fact, let alone civility: "They're *retarded*!"

No denying Mother had a mouth. If its tongue was substantially more acid, there was still something eerily familiar. I couldn't help but wonder: wait, this is me?

As socially disagreeable as it may sometimes have been, the family loudness, as pure physical feat, could be positively Olympian. Never more so than on a post-midnight lark to the City Hall environs, early in my abortive college career, following reports an old department store had been transformed into Manhattan's most banging disco—three vast stories of shrieking synths, sucking hi-hats, and bowel-emptying bottom at the far frontier of Dr. Richter's scale. I didn't take a hemisemidemiquaver of it seriously. But as I flaunted that disrespect, unleashing a barrage of antisocial ribaldry (something about being ravished by the Tyrolean sprite in platinum pigtails who terpsichored nearby), the black-clad, earplugged muscle on floor one was roused to action, bounding up two sets of escalators before roughly dragging me back down and unceremoniously heaving me out. Outside, leaning close, he blasted my prostrate form with what appeared to be the best an angry normie with a fully functioning feedback loop—and not a drop of mezzo-soprano blood—could manage:

"YOU'RE TOO FUCKING LOUD!"

He was pretty fucking loud, I'll grant. But as a recovering wimp with overenthusiasm issues, I wasn't about to surrender. Sitting up on the sidewalk, I replied, hand cupping ear, attitude matching amplitude:

"WHAT?"

Loud that way, too.

* * *

THE OTHER THING ABOUT MY MOUTH is it won't close, even when nothing's coming out. That's not the thing that makes me loud. Sometimes it even makes me quiet. Because beyond my improperly tuned neuro-laryngeal apparatus, it's true: I'm shy.

Now I know every ham claims he's a wallflower, and every axe murderer's mama says he'd never hurt a fly, and anyone who's ever known me has commenced to rolling eyes. But get a load of this: a 3-by-5-inch color portrait of a boy of eight in St. Olaf's uniform—white short-sleeves and short red tie, its halves overlapped into a ribbon-like cruciform. See how the head sinks below the shoulders—blocked from disappearing into his shirt only by the strange tie—eschewing the blandishments of the picture-day photog, mortified to be scrutinized, let alone immortalized, black eyes locked up and away, anticipating the rest of today's whupping at recess. Look how, immediately in front of that desperately fleeing mien, scrabbling for comfortable stowage, but always in the way, is a pair of oversized, overbiting, irredeemably awkward front teeth. The description "buck teeth"—even said of someone else—would make me squirm. As with more hateful epithets, it was surprising how often it came up, dropping the trapdoor to shame, resentment, and a sense that, no matter how much I might try to compensate, I would forever remain the spaz, chicken, freak who spurred bullies to brutality and a father to shame.

* * *

FATHER WASN'T LOUD. NOT WHEN HE didn't want to be. Mostly he was quiet, because he was hundreds of miles away. In any event, it would be a misapprehension to think the pillar of the quotidian in our family was ever someone named Mother or Father. No Atticus Finch, Pa Walton, or Homer Simpson for this household. No Ma Joad or Mrs. Miniver or Marge either. Not even a Betty Draper. Instead, there were maids (that was the word Mother used). So, as children, Roger and I were expected not to bond to one specific caregiver—there were too many, an unknowable procession, all women, a few old, most young, most white, one Black; from Yugoslavia, Ireland, Peru, Belgium, Sweden, France, Brazil, Martinique—but to the whole bounteous system, the magnificent transnational combine that produced for America's upper-middle class an unending supply of underprivileged, underpaid, fundamentally faceless domestic labor. Imported, interchangeable mother-figures tasked with cooking, cleaning, shopping, serving, picking up, dropping off, answering phone and door, taking shit, and—near the bottom of a ballooning portfolio of responsibilities, judged by billable hours—taking care of the kids.

The maid wasn't only the engine of our home. She was the engine of Mother's life away from it. Father had business trips. Mother had luncheons, dinners and, best of all, cocktail parties. That was where this worthy spore of the Southern oral tradition and fount of Southern history—white Southern history—would blossom anew, unfurling her meticulous, bourbon-infused froth of history, genealogy, and gossip, shot through with rhetorical barb and razor-edged aphorism and delivered in an enchanting, half-speed drawl. The Yankees would chortle and say she was a "sketch" and invite her everywhere. Glimpsed in that context, it was easy to understand why Mother felt she'd been miscast. This was no prim keeper of the mid-century homefires. This was a fire-starter, a flirty, tart-tongued Southern Belle, last of the Memphis debutantes, in the last days of Jim Crow (official Jim Crow), Scarlett O'Hara before Sherman's March—but more erudite. Easy to see why, at home, with us, she could become so irritable and bitter and go so berserk. Why it was, for her, such an interplanetary disaster, with gulping lamentations and sulfuric recriminations, when the system stumbled, when a maid quit—which they did on a regular basis, generally in a huff—and the supply chain couldn't immediately deliver a replacement part.

It's also why, one remarkable Sunday morning, with the lady of the house oversleeping a post-maid hangover, our prodigal Father got pressed into unprecedented service readying the children for Mass. As he manhandled us into our Sunday best, brushing our hair with a striking motion this side of assault—like an overgrown mean girl attending to her favorite doll—yanking our pants up so hard we dangled for a wincing moment inches above the wall-to-wall, overtightening our big-boy ties till we coughed, it became clear Father's was not a teaching method. On his knees to jam my feet into lacerating new shoes, he leaned back to admire his handiwork—whereupon, with an exasperation verging on contempt, the Tucson High School wrestling captain blurted:

"Shut your mouth!"

He wasn't talking about talking. Because I wasn't. He was talking about teeth. Not *only*, I knew. It was about the whole un-wrestling package.

"Shut!" he said, chucking his little dud under the chin.

But I couldn't. Nothing to do with recessive psychology. My choppers simply didn't line up. As much as I dreaded going to the dentist, I secretly looked forward to the day the guy would tell Mother my big, buck teeth needed braces. Bastard told her I'd grow into them. And absolutely no one said anything about getting them knocked out at the biggest rock club in the littlest state.

CHAPTER 2
Liverpool

WHEN I FIRST CAME UNDER THE spell of rock 'n' roll and Mother would tell me it came from Memphis, I assumed she was full of shit. I'm sure I thought rock 'n' roll was invented in Liverpool. Anyway, Mother was usually full of shit. You wouldn't put it past her to say rock 'n' roll was invented in Memphis just to get you back there for another summer without a fight. Not that we ever had anything to do with the native noise. In 14 summers and a dozen Christmases we never even drove past Graceland—a feat in that small city—let alone Beale Street, still hanging in there as the Home of the Blues. We had nothing to do with music of any kind, on the radio, the phonograph or elsewhere—even though my grandmother, before being subsumed by her demons, had indeed been a professional singer of some repute, feted in the opera houses of New York, Chicago, Philadelphia and the Continent, often paired, onstage, with the celebrated violinist, Jascha Heifetz, who, offstage, pursued her ardently. Among the photos I would unearth in Papa's guestroom was a spectacular one, captioned "May, 1917," of Mama standing on a small stage, on a crowded pier, wrapped head-to-toe in the red-white-and-blue, singing the dough-boys off to war—with Heifetz sawing away over her shoulder.

* * *

When it comes to Mother, Memphis is always the place to start. It's where she started. More than a memory box, it was her lifelong Mecca, her sacred fountainhead of equanimity, as well as the universal standard, the Greenwich Mean time—morally, sartorially and otherwise—for the planet's pale and well-bred. It was also home to her parents, my grandparents: the scowling Southern Gent we called Papa; and Mama, the erstwhile prima donna.

Charles Carroll McKenna—Charlie to family and servants—was Papa's name until the age of 10, when he was abruptly re-christened by his new stepfather Col. Thomas Bailey Walker, the Scotland-born coal magnate who donated the polar bear enclosure at the Memphis Zoo. Thomas Bailey Walker II was Papa's new name—Tom to family and servants. If the transformation from Charlie to Tom was dispiriting, those weren't the days a kid could complain.

Anyway, that's how I became Thomas Walker Ransom.

If Mother went home seeking calm, Memphis mostly seemed to rile her up, stirring memories that were painful and strangely vivid—chief among them the Confederate States of America, disbanded half-a-century before her remembering began. To her, the Confederacy stood for youth, beauty, privilege, honor, courage, her beloved Papa and a City of Memphis soon to be no more. Not long after we had emigrated to the Yankee stronghold of New York from the Yankee outpost of Minnesota, our parents returned late at night from the El Mocambo club, and Mother teetered into the room where Roger and I were sleeping, plopped down at the end of my bed and, without salutation or preamble, commenced to punch the mattress.

"I'm not raising no damn Yankees!" she repeated, as Roger and I startled awake—first, deeply alarmed, soon, deeply ashamed, and, finally, not at all sure what to do. Owing to Father's jobs and

Mother's damnable luck, Roger and I had been brought up entirely in the Union. I was born in Manitowoc, Wisconsin, a factory town by Lake Michigan, moved at six months to Des Moines for a year, then Chicago for two, and came to consciousness in a hilltop colonial-cum-ranch looking down on Deephaven, Minnesota—before being evacuated, in fourth grade, to the polyglot multiverse of New York City. It wasn't just points on the map, all of them well north of the Mason-Dixon. It was point of view. And ours—mine and Roger's—was definitely Yankee.

How could it not be?

In the Catholic institutions of Minnesota and New York, we were love-bombed by the vintage socialism of a longhaired pacifist Jew named Jesus. And after church and class, in bedrooms, basements, and Florida rooms, we were showered with the chiming progressivism of the blossoming pop culture—Beatles, Dylan, Stones, and, soon, the Summer of Haight in *Life*—after which we were bustled off, beyond the reach of hippies, Negroes, pot pushers and Commie agitators, to deepest, damnedest, abolitionist New England—me to a Protestant boarding school called Harkness, a long way from the Mid-South Mecca.

* * *

MINNESOTA, WHERE I STARTED SCHOOL, WAS a particularly rough ride.

"Your mother's not from around here," they'd taunt, in the nasal singsong that instantly distinguished them as off-course Norsemen—"not from around here" centuries ago. By the time we got to Deephaven, I had figured out that anywhere we went was a long way from where Mother was from, that she was different, that we, by inescapable extension, were different. Mother reveled in it, never more so than when she drove me down the hill to St. Olaf's.

Though I pleaded with her to drop me around the corner, she insisted on piloting the broad-beamed, rocket-finned Eldorado directly into the parish parking lot—which, by the common usage I frantically tried to remind her of, had long before been turned into the school's playground. Brandishing a forbearing Southern Belle smile, amid superfluous toots of the horn, she would promenade through the assembled nuns, priests, altar boys, lunch ladies, janitors, truckers' wives, and tradesmen's, through sacramental-tchotchke salesmen, Knights of Columbus conferees, and sundry courtesans of this provincial Papist realm. Not unlike when, after granting asylum to the country's despised dictator, President Eisenhower dispatched a shiny, new Cadillac and Richard Milhous Nixon, the VP he didn't much care for, on a "good will" tour of Venezuela. Mother—like Ike—knew how to give a seething mob what it wanted.

And that human sacrifice was me.

CHAPTER 3

Wet

WIRY, LEATHERY AND, IN HIGH-WAISTED TURQUOISE clam-diggers, demonstrably bean-bellied, Ginny Gustafson fished a pack of Salems from a wicker bag embroidered with a golfer, scooped the golf ball-dimpled lighter from the coffee table, fired up a smoke, and slipped behind the bamboo bar to pour drinks—one for her, one for Mother—even as she shouted the magic word.

"Kristin!"

Ginny's daughter was our next-door neighbor in Deephaven, and I wanted her, body and soul—though at seven-years-old, I had not a clue why. Big-eyed, shorthaired, long-limbed, and headstrong, not only smart, smartass, and fundamentally disinclined to the frou-frou, Kristin lit me up like a Salem. As she bounced into the Florida room of the Minnesota split-level with a curt "Hi," I was fully engulfed—crimson cheeks to quivering knees—and, at the same time, thoroughly crushed, stubbed like a lipstick-stained butt in her mother's sand trap ashtray.

"Show 'em, Kris," Ginny cajoled, with a hacking laugh.

As her mother cranked open the louvers and switched on the overhead fan the nine-year-old obediently propped open the big oak record cabinet and, without a word, dropped the needle on a

45. And we watched—Ginny on a wicker stool at the bar, me, Mother and baby bro Roger on the jungle-print couch—as, spiraling up and down in her white stockinged feet, lifting one foot and leaning back and the other, leaning forward, wiggling her bottom and jiggling her shoulders, Kristin Gustafson worked out to Chubby Checker. For 150 heaven-sent seconds, the love of my fledgling life cycled, deftly and earnestly, through every combination and permutation of the new dance craze she had memorized from *Bandstand,* not showing off, just showing. When I first came under the spell of rock 'n' roll may have actually been then and there.

I resisted, at first. Something felt wrong, and fed into the nasty little civil war heating up inside me. Instead of Blue vs. Gray, it was Down vs. Up. Down the hill was St. Olaf's Church, with five days a week of low Mass, one of high, alongside its wholly-owned subsidiary, St. Olaf's School, featuring moral instruction beneath the bootheels of the Sisters of Notre Dame. Down was Father Demetrios stopping the service to angrily call out a buck-toothed first grader for silliness—"*You!*"—thereby granting playground bullies permission. Down was busting a gut waiting for bathroom break—because Jesus is about suffering, children—and sent home from a classroom of jeers with a pantsload. Down was rosary beads and frankincense. Up, cultured pearls and My Sin by Lanvin. Down, ancient Latin. Up, salty English. Down, amid the dire nuns, vengeful priests, and resentful progeny of carpenters, garbagemen, plumbers, and deputies: whupped cur. Up, within the emerging hilltop subdivision named Highcroft, in our colonial-cum-ranch one lot from the Gustafsons: horny dog.

Saturdays, Sundays, I'd bolt from bed and, before bike, church, or Cocoa Krispies, dial her number. My goal: to cock-block her existence.

It was hard. Kristin was a champion diver, starting softball pitcher, and five-handicap who could more than hold her own on the links with grownups. Weekends, summer, after school and sometimes before, Kristin was booked solid—for practices, meets, games, or, all of July, golf camp. She'd tell me she couldn't play—"Maybe later"—and hang up. I'd call right back to say, "Call me when you get home." I'd call again: "What time did you say you'd be home?" I'd even do it once more, with nothing more to add. Weekends and summers, I'd get up and call Kristin three or four times in a row. If phone-love was all it could be, I was determined to have it all.

No surprise that Kristin wearied of my attentions. I suppose her mother could have collaborated with mine on a fix. But Ginny was alcoholic and Mother was busy: hair appointments, Junior League lunches, doubles at the club, thank-you notes, and afternoon bourbon. So, as a first-string right-hander who knew how to take care of herself, Kristin took care of herself. Wrote me a letter. And because one of my only chores was to retrieve the mail, it landed in my tender fingers with nary a cushion.

The pink envelope was addressed to me in a florid, multi-colored script, orbited by stars and flowers, executed with every ounce of uncharacteristic girly whimsy, all in an attempt—transparent even to a child—to soften the blow. The painfully obvious sugarcoat of the envelope carried to the perfumed stationery inside, where the body of the letter, impeccably tailored to my reading level, reaffirmed how much she liked me as a friend and how she just wanted to ask one teensy-weensy thing.

Kristin knew it was going to hurt.

"It's not that I don't want you to call ever," she began.

As an alternative to the ceaseless telephonic harassment, her note went on to suggest a fun-packed, two-call-a-day schedule. Two, any day, any time, any season. It was generous, graceful, compassionate, and jaunty to a fault. And it killed me. I don't think in a lifetime of romantic injuries I've had any more devastating. Even as all that erotic longing was starting to surge—however aimlessly—so apparently was my capacity to suffer. Shame spun with anger, despair, loneliness, and unsortable frustration, and left a Minnesota second grader, however improbably, singing the Mississippi Mean Woman Blues.

I got over it. By that, I mean months later Kristin and I started talking again—though never on the phone (an object of terror ever after). I began to love her again, or at least to ache in the hollows where love had once been. A decade or two later Kristin was still percolating in my brain, and on one round-number birthday, I asked my big half-sister Connie—who'd married into a solid Viking family and stayed in Minnesota when we left—if she ever got wind of our sweet old neighbor.

"Wouldn't it be fun to invite her to my party?" I said. "Wouldn't that be a blast!"

My sister replied that last she'd heard of Kristin Gustafson, she was living in Oregon.

"Kristin's a lesbian," Connie said, in that overzealous way she has. "And I hear she's gained a lot of weight."

None of that would matter, not with Kristin. What Connie didn't know was that one historic blue afternoon, Kristin returned from a game or meet or camp and did not duck inside. Out the window of the bedroom Roger and I shared, I could see her, alone, in her yard. Knowing better than to call, or even call out, I scrambled, barefoot and panting, to her side.

"Hi."

If it felt a little strange at first, she didn't seem unhappy to see me. For the first time in forever, for 20 or 30 euphoric minutes that will play in memory till the end of memory, Kristin and I played anew. Earnest and open and joyous children's games.

Racing, tagging, jumping, falling, joking, laughing, pretending. Kristin, in knee-length Bermudas and white sleeveless blouse. Me in . . . who cares?

A sprinkler was sweeping the lawn, like a home version of the Dancing Waters show that had enchanted us—me and Roger and, as it happens, her—at last summer's State Fair. I don't remember if it was Kristin who'd turned it on, or me, or it was just on. The sprinkler was dispersing great refreshing weaves of H_2O. The air was hot, Midwest summer-hot, and 10,000 lakes-sticky. Our skin gleamed with sweat.

I felt guilty. I always felt guilty, which was understandable. When I wasn't sitting in a church, under the tutelage of the bombastic Demetrios, whose bushy black brows and flowing grey beard were the embodiment of the guy in the catechism illustration, I was sitting in a classroom 50 yards away, under the tutelage of a sternly doctrinaire, fishbelly-complexioned Sister. These dedicated servants of the Lord—one a dead ringer for God the Father—had made it clear as heavenly light that the peril to your immortal soul came not only from acting sinfully, but thinking. If you wanted to purify your soul, you also had to purify your thoughts. Still, when you started thinking about thinking—antiseptic thinking on this inexorably septic plane—you headed straight down a Minnesota gopher hole. Because every motive is mixed. Every clean thought, to some degree, dirty. Then there are the actual dirty ones. When you're a devout seven-going-on-eight-year old, you eventually figure out that the only way to get on the safe side of Judgment Day is to assume you're guilty of everything. So you can confess to everything and make everything right, whether it was wrong or not. Like the terrified suspect who admits to the crime he never committed, it becomes easier to say you did it all.

Mea maxima culpa.

Sure, I was there. And, yes, it was skin-gleamingly steamy. And of my God-given free will, I did open my yapper and from the other side of the sprinkler call out for my best friend, love of my embryonic life, to run, run, run through the spray. Then I looked away. But before I looked away, I looked. And what I saw was Kristin in a soaking white blouse as she came to a distressing realization, crossed her arms over her now visible chest and, from beneath a dripping pageboy, shot me a look—embarrassment maybe, but, in my hemorrhaging guilt, I could see only daggers—before run, run, running away.

CHAPTER 4

Ivanhoe

FAITH HAD ALWAYS BEEN A CURIOUS thing in our family, no matter how deeply felt. Father didn't feel a thing. Never went to church, any church. Never even said the word church. Sabbaths when he wasn't on the road, he was sealed in his study, brutalizing an old gray Smith-Corona—a single digit protruding from each hairy fist—pounding out the next cost-cutting diktat or manhandling the lever on a bread-box-sized Burroughs Model 7 to tote up the savings. To Father, grace was money. Heaven was Elmira.

But he was an Episcopalian.

I think.

More peculiar, Mother didn't feel anything, though she was the one—Irish on her mother's side, Notre Dame Prep, St. Agnes College—who'd insisted on piety. Yet her sole role in our worship was to steer the Caddy to the church house door—until we were old enough to get there on our own, when she abandoned involvement entirely.

A real-life mystery of faith. More than perplexed, I worried for my mother's soul.

"Why don't you come in?" I'd ask every Sunday morning.

And every Sunday morning, as she shoved me and Roger out of the car, Mother would answer, "I can't."

If in the schoolyard, with knees of beef tartare, I longed for a tad more of His tender mercy here on Earth, that's not to suggest I didn't believe, heart and soul, in His Kingdom in Heaven. Actually, *believe* implies a choice. Transubstantiation, resurrection, multiplying bread baskets and seafood platters, the unatoned in forever fire—that was simply my world. And, just in case I was tempted to stray, that world was watched over by a cloud-based, trinitarian Godhead—three pairs of eyes, all of them all-seeing. It was my unabridged faith made me consider what vile iniquity might deter a believer from the comfort of hers. Especially with absolution readily available—indeed part of the game. What could be the unconfessable? Eventually, having sifted the entire known sludge of Catholic transgression—or as much of it as a sharp-eyed eight-year-old with a well-thumbed catechism could—there came a shattering epiphany:

Mother had murdered.

I never breathed a word of my suspicion. Not to Roger. Not to Kristin. Not to the priest behind the confessional screen. I held close that dark knowledge—knowledge, I'd decided, no longer suspicion—in secret, in sorrow, in shame, in fear, and in sin. I assumed there'd been good cause. I assumed she'd had to fend off a marijuana addict or one of those "deranged Negroes" she was always telling us about. Did she not know self-defense was forgivable? Or could she not forgive herself? Or due to trauma, not speak of it? Could she not bear the remembering? Or not fully remember? Was she afraid of the police? I wore those anxieties like a hair shirt, when not carrying them like a large wooden cross, and two or three years passed. Then, one sweat-lodge summer afternoon—before the mercies of residential AC were bestowed on the Bluff City—I stumbled on it.

* * *

I STARTED TO GROW A SOCIAL conscience around the same time I learned to lie. But I would call them white lies and found the designation—technically, not a sin—to be powerful. The biggest whopper was when I told Mother on that sweltering day I'd decided to forgo the cool of the Memphis Country Club's Olympic-sized wateringhole in favor of academic pursuits. With fifth grade only months away, I explained, I needed to get a jump on summer reading. If it was preposterous, she wanted to buy it, and did. What had really happened was her first-born son—whose unreconstructed grandfather had plied him with a child-sized Rebel uniform from FAO Schwarz at Christmas and on birthdays dispatched kiddie books about Robert E. Lee, Stonewall Jackson, and the Southern prototerrorist, the Gray Ghost—had taken a second look.

Where once I had embraced the family's racial animus, now I found myself embracing the fraternity of man. Where I had been amused when the kids in the pool, instead of responding with "Polo," shouted a racial slur, now I shuddered. I began to question whether Jesus really would sanction the killing of a Black man or drug addict. And every night, anxiously fidgeting with the rabbit ears on the snowy black-and-white, I stared into the cavalcade of times-that-were-a-changing on Walter Cronkite's TV news—Black students dragged from a Woolworth's counter in North Carolina, Police Chief Bull Connor opening the firehoses on marchers in Alabama, NAACP leader Medgar Evers cut down in his Mississippi driveway by the KKK, which a few months later would blow up four young Black girls in their church. I chewed my fingernails to a bloody pulp. I had become exactly what Mother feared most: a damn Yankee.

With not the slightest intention of cracking a book, I hid out at Papa's from the junior Johnny Rebs of the club, rambling through the stairless manse, idly swinging open closets and sliding out drawers, until in a back guestroom, bottom of a built-in cabinet, I happened on a stack of photos. They were formal portraits, black-and-white, nested in tissue within linen-lined folders, and they started in the wayback of the family:

Papa in his World War I uniform.

Mama, when she was a well-known diva, serenading the troops.

Cousin Mae, the sweet spinster who shared our Memphis holidays, looking old-fashioned even 30 years ago.

Then the pictures jumped ahead.

There was Mother—early twenties, I guessed. I'd seen other pictures of her in her twenties—there was one where she's holding me as a baby (Roger liked to joke that I looked scared). In this photo, a gauzy formal portrait, she was dressed in a white gown, smiling stiffly, as Mother did, being sensitive about a freckle on her front tooth, and gazing into the eyes of a Naval officer in dress-whites. Between them was a tall white cake. I lifted the photo from the drawer. Tough to square the father I knew—big belly, receding hairline—with this starched young officer. I knew parents in old pictures looked alien, but my father had never been in the service. He'd spent the war as a factory manager in Lapeer, Michigan, supervising the manufacture of rocket launchers (I'd shown Johnny Shannon the Top Secret clearance I'd found in his office, much as Johnny, son of an MD, had shown me the naked lady with elephantiasis he'd found in his dad's). No question, this was a picture of a wedding. Must have been my aunt's, where Mother was maid-of-honor. But the squared-off sailor in the photo bore not the slightest resemblance to the gangling, bespectacled Uncle Arthur. Why would the maid-of-honor help cut the cake? Overcome by something like the Memphis heat, I flung the picture in the drawer, scrambled back to my room and, with throbbing brain and heaving chest, opened to the middle of *Ivanhoe*.

I fretted about that photo for years. If I had asked Mother, she would have thought I was impudent and wild for going through her things. If I had asked Father—well, I never would. Then one ordinary midweek evening—almost a decade after we'd resettled in New York—with the family breadwinner off winning bread in some remote, clanking factoryville and his bride relaxing in our old brownstone in the shadow of the groovy, gray 59th Street Bridge (then being immortalized on the radio by Simon & Garfunkel), out of nowhere, apropos of nothing, with a flick of a Viceroy and clink of Kentucky bourbon, as flatly as you can say in an opulent plantation drawl, my mother tossed in the general direction of her two teenage sons what remains in my personal and professional experience the most stupefying independent clause in the annals:

" . . . but that was with my first husband."

There was shock, as one longtime suspicion was confirmed—accidentally or incidentally or whatever you want to call such an echt-Mother moment—and a more devastating one put to rest. Yes, she had sinned, sundering the bonds of holy matrimony and laying with the infidel—punishable, I knew, by automatic excommunication. But she hadn't murdered.

Not yet.

CHAPTER 5

Deuce

We knew Father had been married before. That didn't matter because he was a heathen. What did matter is that Father had other kids. My half-sister, Connie, and half-brother, Sandy.

I met them first as fugitives in black-and-white. In contrast to the professional, linen-sheathed artifacts in that out-of-the-way drawer at Papa's, this was a snapshot, an informal gray square from a Brownie, tossed into the back of a half-filled photo album under the living room bar. Three figures faced the lens on a tree-lined, summer sidewalk. Father in the middle—pleated slacks and stubby tie, shoulders back, chin down, smiling stoically—holding the hand of a neat little blonde girl, neat little floral dress, shoulders back, chin down, smiling stoically. Other side, corkscrewing from Father's grip, a boy in short pants, drooping socks, newsboy cap, flapping shirttail and a clenched face you might reasonably describe as surly.

Though Mother had explained, curtly, the who, what, where of the photograph, after explaining, no less curtly, Father's prior marriage, it had left me—to grossly understate—intrigued. Which made me afraid I'd never get the rest of the story, that showing too much interest in the photo might set Mother off. Or something else would set her off, and she'd take it out on the photo. Or she'd decide that all our ridiculous mooning over that silly picture had upset Father (who, between banging on his Smith-Corona, going to Elmira and not giving a rat's ass, would never have noticed), and we'd wake up the next morning and the album would be gone. Not hidden—unless you mean in the garbage can around the corner—gone for good. Mother had a thing against photos anyway. She said they made her feel old. I think it was more that she didn't like someone else telling the story, whatever story, and didn't like us—especially Father, a man of steely reserve, who took a rare open joy in his first-born "baby girl"—paying attention to others, even in pictures. But I was entranced these phantoms were my flesh and blood and horrified they'd been left behind.

* * *

FATHER PICKED UP OUR NEW 17-YEAR-OLD sister at the airport one sunny afternoon, installing her in the room next to his and Mother's. Along with two suitcases and a steamer trunk, Connie arrived with a pink portable record player, on which she liked to play "Tom Dooley," "Charlie of the MTA" and other folk favorites. Meanwhile, on the top, in big white letters that danced with black sixteenth-notes, the machine proclaimed: "Rock 'n' Roll!" A few weeks later, Connie's baby brother Sandy, the thing incarnate, showed up in a taxi with a gym bag in the black of a Midwest winter night and, during one of those catastrophic lacuna when no maid was in residence, was assigned to the maid's room in the basement. Connie, in pastel sweaters and a tight blond halo of hair, may have sneered at her trio of brothers—new and old, half and full—but she was positively chirpy with the country club youth, who quickly clutched her to their cashmere bosoms. Sandy—15-going-on-19, in his white t-shirts, rumpled jeans and greased hair that would have been long, were it combed down, but instead eddied about his head like a stormy golden sea—was nothing but surly. While Connie was swept into the Deephaven social whirl, Sandy kept to himself, at first, mostly sacked out in the cellar. Some mornings, puffy-eyed and tempest-maned, he would plod up the stairs and, as Mother howled in protest, guzzle milk from the bottle. One day, while glug-glugging breakfast, he spotted the milkman arriving and, with no explanation, before or after, slipped out the side door to commandeer the truck. As Sandy peeled off down the hill, the middle-aged man in white hat, white coat and black bowtie scrambled back to the driveway, bouncing up and down and shouting, before turning utterly befuddled to the mother and two little kids, not one of whom knew what to say. Ten minutes later big brother roared back from the joyride with a grin, and Mother loudly assured the apoplectic milkman that, when Father got home, the boy would be dealt with severely, so no need for cops. It was a harbinger of anarchy to come.

Later I came to understand that the merriment had less than merry roots. Father's ex—mother of Sandy and Connie—was a drunk. Not like the dainty auto-destructs of the dysfunction-chic era, more like Mother's mother—an alcoholic in the unironic first flowering of cocktail culture, when you had to be a bed-pissing basketcase to even raise an eyebrow. She was a rich drunk, too. That's how a townie loading freights got his big break. They met as teenagers in Tucson, where her mother had taken her for asthma, and Father's friend had dragged him to a dance. Soon she'd dragged him to an altar in Milwaukee and a job managing a factory floor for her moneybags dad. After the divorce, as the young floor manager, a shoulders-back wrestling captain who never tapped out and never ran, hightailed it west, the mother took off east, to New York, with the kids, where she surrendered to the big-city anonymity that wouldn't register if one more divorced mother of two stayed out every night and slept through most days, not alone. The apartment, off Park, next to the Blake Hotel, was big enough to get lost in, and their mother wouldn't mind if the children did. Connie escaped to boarding school, soon as she could get her aunt to write the tuition check (her mother being nowhere to be found), while Sandy simply escaped—from school, from everything—hanging out in the cellar with the doormen, who taught him about five-card stud, Irish whiskey, and the high-priced prostitutes two doors down.

* * *

TWO DOORS DOWN, THE THIRTY-SOMETHING WOMAN who answered took one look at Sandy's fresh-faced pal, another eighth-grade hooky player from the block, and told him to scram.

"You're okay," she said to my brother.

It was my favorite of Sandy's incredible true-life tales. He told it when I was undergoing the hormonal indignities of eighth grade. Even more than the titillating milieu, what got me was the grace, the balls, and the inviolable authenticity of a 13-year-old—exactly the brother I had come to know. So the prostitutes—sisters—ushered him in and he never left. They gave him breakfast, lunch and dinner. Let him watch their TV and didn't peep if, from time to time, he grabbed a Schaefer from the fridge. Once or twice, long before the hippies, they even let him try their pot. They never had sex with him, wouldn't. He never asked. Days he did make it to school—almost always at their urging—he'd come straight back afterwards, and they'd feed him a snack and bug him to do his homework and if, when sitting at their kitchen table, he was struggling, the older one would put on her glasses and help. When Sandy was in residence, they never let a man up. Unlike his mother.

Sandy never wondered what the angle was with the sisters. He knocked on that door because there was nothing and no one he was afraid of. And no one he measured. The sisters became his family, their apartment his home—until the private detective figured out where he was living and told the divorce lawyer, who told the deputy, who knocked on the door, flashed a court order at a misty sister and escorted a smirking Samuel Russell Ransom, Jr., and the gym bag that fit everything, to Idlewild and the next flight to Minneapolis-St. Paul.

* * *

SAMUEL RUSSELL RANSOM, JR., WHO EVERYONE called Sandy. He got your attention, this ancient teenager. If I would grow up to be a combustible mix of Yankee and Rebel, spiritual and secular, loving and hating, Mother, Father, Roy Rogers, and Curly Howard, with bits of Iowa, Minnesota, Illinois, Tennessee, and New York thrown in—it was him I really wanted to be.

A six-foot rail with pale blue eyes, a sleeve-roll of Lucky Strikes and blond Medusa pomp, it wasn't only that he *looked* different. Soon he'd got his hands on the husk of an old Ford, rusted and patchy-gray from not a drop of paint since 1932, and he and a buddy at the DX station had turned it into a hot rod. Not all chromed and anal like the rides of the ponytailed coots at the Chamber of Commerce Dream Cruise, but a real Deuce Coupe, with racing slicks and a big, dirty engine, that was too fast even for Sandy. *Rebel Without A Cause*—except this wasn't playacting. The filling station guy, with a souped-up ride of his own, invited my new brother to join the gang. If the Kings weren't the biggest or baddest outfit in the Midwest, a half-dozen bored-out V-8s cruising county road, just across the tracks, could still fill a small town with an alarming noise. It wasn't long before Sandy had ascended to gang president—king of Kings—and the gang had taken up arms, or their president had, and the three-car Deephaven PD, already on edge that the youthful hordes of 50s B-movies and yellow journalism might be headed thisaway, had assigned a man.

Clomping through the country club in engineer boots, glower melting to crooked smile, he caught the eyes of the ladies of the golf terrace, no less than the beehived vixens of the Oasis, Deephaven's notorious drive-in diner. You didn't have to be a bad girl to know Sandy was sexy. Or a good girl praying for more from life than boys in Banlon and golf spikes. You could be a little brother.

Part of it was danger—actual danger, not the danger of beauty. Having largely raised himself, largely in the big city, the guy was a veritable beast of the urban wild—acute powers of observation, quicksilver reactions, independent moral compass. But he wasn't always fun to be around—not at first. And not what you wanted in a babysitter, especially if you were the "baby." Nonetheless, from time to time—when another irate maid had stomped off and Mother was due at the Embers for cocktails with "best friends in the whole wide world" we'd never heard of—it happened.

"Feed the boys," she directed, handing Sandy a five, "and send them to bed."

With Roger and me flopping around in the hot rod's tiny back seat, brother Sandy slammed it into R, 180'd out the driveway, blew through the stop sign and caught air over the tracks, before hanging a screeching louie across oncoming traffic—microseconds ahead of the too-slow, too-polite and, now, totally pissed-off—into the last open slot at the Oasis.

Actual danger. Generating, in one little brother, actual fear. Forever joined with that other danger pumping from the coupe's dash, a racket almost as headlong and reckless as Sandy. Not so much a song as a terrible illness, mental illness: a Memphis crazyman screaming about a dog.

With the hot rod at a menacing idle, Sandy shouted over Elvis for us to speak up, so he could give the order to the girl on skates, who tendered a wrinkly-nose to me and Roger, before shifting her winsome blond regard, with the barest smirk, back to brother. If Sandy's danger was not fake, we were still a chink in it. By the time the waitress rolled back with the order, our babysitter was losing the patience he never had, tersely handing out food with the command to shut up and eat. First, I had to arrange my dinner on the rear dash. Hot dog. French fries. Coke. Finally, I ripped the tip off the straw wrapper, shot the paper out the window, and jabbed the straw in my cup.

"*Root beer!*" I cried.

Then I cried.

"*Drink your goddamn pop!*" the president of the Deephaven Kings shouted into the rearview. A moment later, enough was enough. As the car fishtailed onto Lake Street, my cup of root beer flopped, emptying its contents onto the back dash. I shrieked. Never taking his foot from the gas, Sandy swiveled his pompadoured head to spray invective, convinced I had dumped the drink—now sloshing around under the rear windshield—on purpose. Back home, he dragged me out of the backseat by the armpit, into the house and, from six feet away, slung me onto the bed.

"You little shit."

My new big brother slammed the bedroom door. I sobbed into the pillow, mostly out of shame, entirely out of ignorance.

Within months, bad girl at his side, he'd wrapped that hot rod around a telephone pole, and somehow at a time seatbelts were just stuffed into the seat and forgotten, they survived. Later, in the company of another small-town wanton, he would go off a cliff, head-first, driving Mother's copper Eldorado. This time a cushion of swamp saved their lives. Next day our maid of the moment, a devout older lady with firm ideas about a good object lesson, marched Roger and me down to see the wreck, stashed behind the DX where the Deuce had been born. If the bigger moral was lost on us, there was no arguing the car was a sight: front bumper jammed halfway up the hood, a two-foot-thick core-sample of Minnesota swampland—bulbous vines, lily-pads and a still oozy bog—filling the rectangle where the windshield used to be.

But no surliness or danger could keep me at bay. When Sandy was home, I followed him. When he wasn't, I snooped in his room. If I didn't discover any more black lace undies, I did find the cool guns he'd stashed under the bed: a pistol, a rifle and, coolest of all, a machine gun. When I presented the only one I could carry, the pistol, to Mother—who seemed to harbor some mollycoddling notion that a kid raised on cowboys wouldn't know how to handle it—she screamed. But I did know, and showed it to her by pulling the trigger. Click. A Deephaven police sergeant, case officer for the Kings, stopped by later for a chat with big brother. The judge railroaded him into enlisting. And over a four-year hitch, the Navy beat it out of him. The surly, not the danger.

CHAPTER 6
Boot

DADDY WAS A HATCHET MAN. THOUGH that's not how Mother would ever describe it. When new friends, or her mystified children, probed about Father's hazy and peripatetic line of work, she painted him as a kind of American business Jesus, dedicated to the miraculous resurrection of dead companies. I for one was impressed and wondered why in the world he didn't just run for president and fix everything.

I came to realize later he was an old-breed cost-cutter—brilliant enough, in his barbarous, industrial way—called in to hack outdated enterprises back to whatever droplets of profitability could yet be squeezed. But when you're the hatchet man, you often get the hatchet yourself. Which only makes sense: dirty work done, blood in the water—eyes turn toward the hatchet man, by definition an outsider and nobody's friend, cousin, or uncle. Father getting axed always meant big changes for us. By the time I was ten, I'd moved six times, as the family wended its way among the just-hanging-in-there factories of the soon-to-be Rust Belt. The next move turned out to be most discombobulating of all, psycho-culturally: from the wilds of Minnesota to the wilds of midtown Manhattan.

* * *

My New York school was St. Ignatius—S.I. to those in the know—on the Upper East Side. If, as the family of a corporate hatchet man, we ranked among the gentry at working-class St. Olaf's, in the rareified environs of St. Ignatius, we were barely serfs. Housed in a grand Beaux-Arts mansion—once the pied-à-terre of a nineteenth-century robber baron—S.I. was a new idea in Catholic education: not a parochial school, with narrow-minded ecclesiasticals overseen by a retrograde archdiocese, but a private boys school where sophisticated Catholic laymen could deliver a rich variety of Catholic instruction to the spawn of New York's most politically, socially, culturally, and commercially eminent Irish and Italian:

- *John-John Kennedy, America's heartrending toddler, escorted to kindergarten by his unexpectedly freckled heartthrob mom.*
- *Dec Murphy, the fearsome, square-jawed police commissioner's anxious, slack-jawed son.*
- *Ottavio Maginnes, scion of a world-famous soprano (pointed out by my opera heiress mother).*
- *Ralph Torino, Jr., the cherry-cheeked roly-poly—who in summer, like a half-dozen other classmates, would ship out with me to Great Pine camp—whose roly-poly, cherry-cheeked dad owned Torino's Twisted Taffy, a relentless Soupy Sales advertiser, and who between his family's TV fame and the canny dispersal of sweets, managed to surmount his own prickly persona and chronically sweaty upper lip to achieve surprising popularity.*

If morning worship at S.I. was less solemn than at my old school, with the 20 minutes of modern-English hoodoo not even rising to the level of Low Mass, if the students at S.I. were not assigned uniforms—like the kids at St. O's—and the teachers, almost all men, in rep ties and elbow-patched tweed, were less severe than the Sisters, if the New York school was, on paper, less hidebound, there was nonetheless a formality—religious and academic, cultural and couturial, formal and informal—that struck a boy from the sticks as bizarre. The kids were just odd. Miniatures of their masters, in blazers, ties and gray flannels, they addressed the teachers as "sir" and referred to them in absentia as "my sir"—as in, "My sir says I have to do better on my next Latin vocab test." In fifth grade, I would read *Goodbye, Mr. Chips,* and all that would make more sense. But this wasn't 1914 England. To an émigré from the Midwest provinces, where black-hooded wraiths terrorized boys and girls within walls of brown cinderblock, while the sons of plumbers and garbagemen schooled sissies and infidels on the macadam beyond, it seemed downright, well, sissy.

* * *

NEW YORK WAS AN EDUCATION, IN and out of the classroom. By seventh grade, three years in, I had learned plenty and made a fascinating new friend who would teach me more.

Gray Turner wanted to be James Bond—we all did. But Turner was a boy of action. He mail-ordered a 007-style Walther PPK and a shitload of ammo, and the gun store promptly sent it to him. His fourth-grade brother, who was wild, certifiably nuts even, who the year before had thrown the family cat out the sixth-floor window, clomped down the hall toward Gray's room. From inside, the big brother called out: "One more step and I'll blast ya." Of course, the wild brother took the step and the Bond brother pulled the trigger and the .38-caliber bullet tore through door and kid. The brother survived, barely. Only a few years after, he succumbed, supposedly of unrelated causes—something to do with his craziness, but who knows.

"PARK AVE BOY SHOOTS BROTHER" enthused the papers. It was a big story. But someone—a well-connected school supporter, maybe a parent who happened to be Police Commissioner—shut it down before it got on TV. To make sure it stayed shut—and to assuage restive parents—the school, per the Lord's teachings on mercy, awarded my troubled seventh-grade friend the summary boot.

* * *

SURE, THEY KEPT THE GRAY TURNER story off *Eyewitness News*, but, among the families of his classmates, the grapevine continued broadcasting it for months. Eventually, everyone agreed that what had happened with the brother was because the father had died—Hodgkin's—a few months earlier. It's true that things were never the same and that even long after the dad was gone, the curtains were still drawn, there was still a hospital bed in the living room, and all else—sun, sound, breathable air—was banished. You didn't go back to that apartment often, until you didn't at all.

"Bringing the father home is what made that Turner boy go bad," tssked Mother, who firmly believed the wounded only weighed you down.

I liked Turner's dad. One time he took Gray and me to Mott Street, in Chinatown, to buy firecrackers. It was illegal, which is most of what made it cool. You had to keep telling yourself, no way someone's father would get you arrested. Just before we walked out of the apartment, Gray's mother freaked—I could hear her screeching to her husband in the kitchen about taking a "stranger" on such a "stupid errand." Being her son's best friend of six or seven months, the "stranger" part stung. I told myself maybe she wasn't so nice after all and, anyway, she freaked about everything—pigeons, butterflies, dogs that jump up.

Gray's mom looked a lot sicker than Gray's dad. She was skinny—bones after her husband died—with tousled gray hair and raccoon eyes, and, while we played in her son's room or watched the British Invasion on the living room TV, she slumped behind the marbleized green Formica of the kitchen table in a cloud of tar and nicotine before an overflowing crystal ashtray. Not studying the latest *Life* or *Look* or *Good Housekeeping* or reading the mail. Staring and smoking. I later heard she drank. But all parents drank. I'm pretty sure she had the craziness her younger son died of, more or less. In a few more years, she would be gone. Before the father got sick, I liked hanging there. It was looser than my house. But I guess it was a fucked-up family.

Gray Turner, who wanted to be 007, wanted to be the Fab Four, too. Being blown away by the Beatles on *Ed Sullivan* was what first brought us close. He'd even busted out his dad's fancy camera to take a picture of the TV—John Lennon smirking between the scan-bars. Before the deluge of fanzines, it was as inside as a Beatlemaniac could get. And there was no Beatle fan more maniacal than me.

* * *

After his father succumbed, before he shot his brother, my friend who pretended to be Bond and then the Beatles did something even more reckless. He strolled into Bill Rane's seventh-grade classroom wearing a new pair of Beatle boots—which, after our Beatle-booted band had caused a stir in assembly a semester earlier, were specifically proscribed by school authorities. Turner understood it was against the rules. What he didn't understand was Rane.

Bill Rane was tall and young—though we thought old—with thin lips and a long nose. When he got angry, he got loud, and a white gum accumulated in the corners of his mouth. He was a painter, with an MFA from Yale, which—to prove his grit—he assured Mother he'd attended on scholarship. Mother was unimpressed. Along with homeroom, Rane was the school's art teacher, tucking his tie between the buttons of his white shirt and rolling his sleeves above the elbows. In the context, it was positively Bohemian. In that pre-Beatles proto-flowering, when the Bohos—in the person of Maynard G. Krebs—had infiltrated even network TV, such a creature was both a source of amusement and, beneath the *Dobie Gillis* sitcom frosting, alarm. One of our first nights in New York, when a local friend detoured his car down Bleecker Street for a peek at goateed ground-zero, Mother had cried out: "Lock the doors!" The columnist Herb Caen, mashing up Beat Generation with sputnik, the Soviet satellite that had beat the US into space, had dubbed these cultural barbarians "beatniks."

More than a prick, Rane was a beatnik sadist, his artistry most potently realized in his punishments. I'd witnessed this guy scan a classroom and invent a fiendish torment on the spot. Actually, I wasn't only witness, I was victim: condemned by Mr. Rane to squat—not sit, squat—in the classroom fireplace. What CIA interrogators would euphemize as a "stress position." It quickly became gummy-lips' go-to technique, one that he would go to with undisguised glee at the slightest provocation. When the fireplace was occupied, miscreants would be made to squat under a desk or in a locker. Tip over, touch ground, he'd bellow and lather and force you back onto your burning haunches. When the school instituted sex ed, and Rane started showing fifth-grade boys schematics of vaginas, there were four or five guys squatting at all times.

And Gray Turner shows up in this sicko's class with verboten on his dogs?

Though my friend made a halfhearted effort to conceal his boots, our six-two overlord, a man whose bugging eyeballs rarely missed a transgression, didn't miss this one. Gummy-lips came ungummed. I was scared shitless. Gray stayed as cool as the sociopath we would soon discover him to be, even talked back, calmly, in a tone that no one in the class—not a one of whom knew the meaning of "ironic"—doubted was anything but.

"You know, Mr. Rane," said the 12-year-old Turner, "this doesn't seem quite fair—"

A dense, searing tension shot through every cubic centimeter of the room, electric tension that was asphyxiating and spooky-silent—except for a sinister background hissing, which could have been the HVAC, the pounding of blood in my ears, 22 seventh graders simultaneously pissing their pants or a crazed homeroom teacher breathing hard through his big nose, like a bull about to charge.

Charge he did: launching himself across our homeroom, pushing a foaming face an inch from Gray's, clearing the boy's desk, and, for good measure, the one next to it, mine, and, leaning back to put all his lanky frame into it, penalty-kicking Turner's book bag into the wall to fully expose the contraband footwear. While no one got hit—except maybe by foam—my sir was blowing so hard the entire building could hear, and the next thing we knew the assistant headmaster had descended.

"Mr. Rane," said Mr. Pavlik from the classroom door, "could I see you for a moment?"

Rane was blowing so hard it was the last we saw of Rane.

Even in seventh grade, we figured out the guy wasn't merely furious. And while we'd seen teachers and priests tipsy at parents' Christmas parties, this was first period and shitfaced, one flickering neuron from violently out-of-control. Still, if it meant I wouldn't have to endure another full year of the fuck, five minutes of terror was a small price.

* * *

BEFORE GRAY TURNER WANTED TO BE a Beatle or Bond, he wanted to be Hitler. Turner didn't hate Jews. He didn't know Jews. None of us did. We hardly knew Presbyterians. Back at St. Olaf's,

I'd been taught to stay away from all of them. Protestant, Hindu, Muslim, Jew, it didn't matter. Stick to your own kind, said the priest, speaking for the crucified Defender of the halt, lame, and blind. Meanwhile, Turner got his chance at infamy with the Mob.

Two Saturdays a month, our parents entrusted us to the good graces of "Manny's Mob," a playgroup constituted to give city boys a breath of fresh air and the kind of wholesome outdoor fun only city boys can so thoroughly pervert. To a wholesome kid from Minnesota, accustomed to getting his own fresh air, it at first seemed like a real New York thing, corrupt and decadent. Soon, like any gullible hick, I got the hang of it. Playgroup regulars included my little brother Roger, my seventh-grade best friend Gray, my regular best friend Sean, and our sometime best friend Bob, joined by whatever other random 12-year-old hellraiser was deemed by his wit's-end parents way overdue for an airing. The group was the side-business of Manny Ortiz, a rumpled Laughing Buddha out of Spanish Harlem, who was everyone's favorite school bus driver. Frequently, before we hit the park, we'd stop by his apartment on 106th Street to see if one of his kids wanted to join us. You didn't have to be good at math to know 106th Street was in Spanish Harlem, which, for us, was like the trip to the moon that NASA was frantically cooking up. Nestled against the uppermost Upper East Side, immediately across 96th Street, three blocks from Turner's Park Avenue apartment, five blocks from S.I., as close a neighbor as a neighborhood could be, Harlem—Spanish or otherwise—was a region we were taught to fear, to pity, and to most assiduously avoid. After the first time, amazed to have survived, we came to love the detour—and to learn not to tell about it when we got home. If Manny's boy wasn't quite ready, all the better. Our jolly overseer would hand out quarters and tell us to hang downstairs at the bodega. It was at 106th Street, at Manny's urging and with his quarter, that I discovered the quintessential New York delight—what I will always think of as the quintessential Spanish Harlem delight—the curdled chocolate bilge-water known as Yoo-Hoo (unrelated to the time-stopping "YOO-HOO!" my mother liked to shout in restaurants). And it was with Manny and in Harlem—at one of the handful of by-the-slice joints in all the five boroughs—that I was introduced to the elastic ecstasies of New York pizza.

I loved going to Central Park, too. Manny's kid a-hand, we'd head over to play World War II. In our version, we were the Nazis. It may have been Turner's idea, but as our Führer goose-stepped about in an Army surplus jacket, we happily followed orders. Which were barked in a German accent from the nearest protruding granite, signed off with a stiff-arm salute. We crisply hoisted our toy rifles, and when not hitting the dirt or hiding behind trees to shoot Americans, we marched through the park behind Turner to smoke them out.

Not hard to notice it wasn't how others played the game. Being city kids, no matter how insulated, and Catholic kids keenly aware who was and wasn't, not hard to notice there were other kids in the park—especially the ones scowling nearby—with a different point of view. If we had a pretty good idea it wasn't right, it was still playing war, and there was nothing in the world more fun, on a sunny Shabbos. Gray was obsessed, demanding as Shicklgruber himself. Which made it even more fun, like a real army. And when we were finally attacked by a group of older boys in yarmulkes, we thought that was fun, too—at first—running and hiding and then running for your life and shouting for a beloved brown bus driver to chase the other white boys away.

CHAPTER 7
Itch

FALL, WINTER, SPRING, WE WERE SENT to Manny. Summer, all summer, every summer, Roger and I were sent to Dick.

Math instructor and assistant head of school at S.I. (he was the one who retrieved Bill Rane), Dick Pavlik was top dog at Great Pine, where he invited campers who knew him in the city as Mr. Pavlik to call him Dick. Even when he was Mr. Pavlik trying to force numbers into my brain, I liked Dick. He was not a child molester. This isn't *that* campfire story. There was sex, but it didn't involve me. Not exactly. And I was not unhappy at camp. To the contrary, once I'd gotten over the motion sickness from six hours in an ancient, airless train—Grand Central to central Maine—and a day or two of homesickness, I was perfectly content. I missed my dog and, of course, my mother, but I especially missed my big brother. It was that summer I started to write to him, sharing the inside dope on camp ("Don't tell mom!" was my refrain). More importantly, it was that summer my brother started to write to me.

In a cursive closer to printing, in sentences that even I knew were full of misspellings, Sandy shared stories from the Navy, from the streets, and from his current adventure: getting a GED and then a college diploma, so he could qualify for flight school. On the USS

Lake Champlain, barred from becoming a Navy flier, due to his truncated educational credentials, he still rose to be chief of the ship's air traffic control crew. One of Sandy's letters recalled the day the carrier recovered the first American astronaut—in that moment, the top flier in the world—from the middle of the Atlantic. He enclosed a picture of himself in the tower with headset and NBC microphone and another of a space-suited Alan Shepard saluting him from the deck. I thought it was just like my brother to be there at the dawn of the Space Age. I'd let the other campers look at the photos, but not touch.

I think Sandy came to relish the role of big brother and started writing to buck me up, though I was actually doing fine at camp. Within the confines of uniforms, curfews, punctilious mealtimes and activities meticulously penciled into a clipboard schedule by Dick himself, I enjoyed the freedom. Compared to the Latin vocab torture of school or Mother flying off the handle or making us overdress or abandoning us to the maid she first made mad, camp felt like a two-month breather. At Great Pine, I played third base. I whittled. I shot arrows, .22 rifles and, in epic battles around cabins, tents and flagpole, all manner of plastic squirt gun. I became a Certified Junior Life Saver by pulling a big, greasy man out of the lake. I paddled, rowed, trotted, and cantered. I sang around the fire—the minstrel number "Camptown Races," the socialist anthem "This Land is Your Land," and that jaunty paean to blackout alcoholism where all the little campers would shout: "Yo-ho-ho and a bottle of rum!" Tennis I liked alright, except for the pressure from Mother, who assured me it was the key to success. I loved the field trips, the two- and three-day sorties into the wilderness via horse or canoe or the freshly purchased hiking boots that could shield you from rocks, mud, and nettles, but not hiking's greatest hazard: the blisters and sore spots from new hiking boots.

The counselors were nice, too, most of them. Some we called Jim or Bill or Rick—or, in one unfortunate case, Winky—but ours, 40 years older, we addressed as Mr. Mallon. The three other seasons of the year, Mr. Mallon was a ninth-grade teacher in suburban South Jersey. With his white hair, utilitarian glasses, and unsmiling, deliberative manner, there was something of the coiled backwoods preacher about him, a whiff of fire-and-brimstone. Mr. Mallon was strict. He was serious. Above all, he was sanitary. Since there were no showers at our camp, every evening at seven he would march down to Millinocket Lake, slide off his black trunks, carefully folding and stowing them atop his carefully folded white towel, and, washcloth in one hand, brick of Ivory in the other, wade into the alpine drink, unsmiling and deliberative—as if warm balls in freezing water was exactly what a sinner deserved. The path to 99 44⁄100% pure.

Mr. Mallon spoke in a round, nasal tenor that might have been the model for Kermit the Frog. Like the other counselors, he slept in the cabin. Unlike the others, his sleepwear was an old-fashioned, sleeveless white t-shirt, tucked into voluminous white boxers. The campers wore flannel pajamas, methodically labeled with last names. Every morning, awakened by the lucky camper picked to clang the bell that week, before peeing, pooping, or eating, no matter how damn cold the freezing Maine morning, we would strip off those PJs and line up nude. Seated in his giant undies on the edge of his cot, Mr. Mallon would gingerly retrieve his specs from the upended crate that was his nightstand and crowded bookshelf—full of pamphlet-like, church-published correctives with two-color covers—and, one by one, conduct the troops through scratch inspection.

As a new kid, I assumed scratch inspection was just the way it was at camp, any camp. And maybe, sure, another manifestation of Mr. Mallon's codgerhood, keeping up the protocols a younger, less conscientious generation of camp overseers had left behind.

Like so many of the life-saving modern hygiene techniques—handwashing or covering your cough—scratch inspection couldn't have been simpler. You'd stand facing Mr. Mallon, his eyes level with your privates, and first lift your penis, so he could see there were no hidden scratches. Then you'd slowly rotate, so he could scan your whole body. Once your butt was to him, you'd pause to spread your cheeks, in case of problems back there.

"Next!" he'd call in Kermit tones.

Simple as that. No touching. No poking. No nothing, ever. Except scratch inspection. After which you'd dash off, in a towel, to the outhouse, confident you were safe—at least from out-of-the-way infections.

* * *

MY SENTIMENTAL EDUCATION WAS TO GAIN another kink, in the person of young Wally Taggart. Taggart arrived from Boston my third summer at Great Pine, joining me, Sean, and another Upper East Sider named Danny Sutton in one of the big army surplus tents reserved for the older campers. Having graduated from the cabins, I had assumed a distinct upperclassman swagger and greeted my new tentmate coolly. From scratch inspection to smuggled hero sandwiches (or grinders, as I now knew to call them), I was the wizened veteran who had seen it all. Wally would prove otherwise.

Not enough that he had once died, Wally Taggart held the world record for it. For being dead. It had happened when he was a newborn, but there were residual problems: cleft palate, deaf ear, dim vision—corrected by Coke-bottle glasses—and a hole in his heart. His brain was fine—in fact, he was smart, especially in math. But the halves of his body, he'd happily explain, with a lisp and a snort, had imperfectly fused. To add to the picture, his teeth were caged in complicated braces that collected a ton of nasty food, and from time to time in the mess hall Wallace would reach a finger in his mouth to shoot a fellow camper with the most horrifically encrusted rubber band, accompanied by a great, wet guffaw. That was Wally Taggart. None of his afflictions, congenital or orthodontial, seemed to trouble him. To the contrary. He was outgoing. An accomplished athlete. An enthusiastic singer—if tone-deaf—the loudest, and flattest, at every campfire. He could spit milk out his nose. And he was double-jointed. Not just in his fingers. Turns out the record-holding dead baby could bend everything backwards and, more importantly, in ways other boys could only dream, forward.

Because, as he now demonstrated for an astonished trio of tentmates, Wally Taggart could blow himself.

I'm not saying it was the best blow job ever—visually speaking. I'm not saying it was much more than tongue on tip. It was enough to call it a blow job. That was enough for Danny, who dangled visions of untold treasure—for all of us—if Taggart were only willing to share his gift on a slightly larger scale. And it came to pass we entered the blow-job business. Which seemed easy, under the circs. It turned out happy-go-lucky Wally could be a prima donna himself. Sometimes, with curtain imminent and crowd queuing, he would curl up on his cot facing the corner and, no matter how Danny scolded and cajoled, silently withdraw into his super-flexible self. When our star attraction was up for it, a steady stream of snickering campers would step in, five at a time, and soon all snickering would cease. With the grace of a mountaintop yogi, Wally Taggart would fold himself in half and insert his 12-year-old boner in his yap for a fraction of a second and an inch.

And a quarter, please. Thank you.

This went on, intermittently, for several weeks until an older camper, a kid who happened to be the biggest hustler in the whole place—charging an unconscionable 100% markup on grinders smuggled from Lewiston—decided to fink. Out of knee-jerk Catholic disgust or capitalist anxiety that the shenanigans in Tent 7 might bring on a camp-wide crackdown and squelch the black market in foot-long sandwiches.

Whereupon Mr. Pavlik, head of camp, summoned Sean and me to the office on the hill.

While I liked Dick, I couldn't help but find the invitation worrisome. Leaning back in his wooden swivel chair, in short-sleeves and tan, so much more slack than at school, he motioned us to the seats facing the desk and started with generic chit-chat.

Having fun? How're the folks? What are you enjoying most this year? That sort of thing—before casually, but authoritatively, steering the conversation to Taggart. As cheerfully as you could contemplate asking such a thing, Pavlik now asked two soon-to-be eighth graders:

"Did Wallace Taggert masturbate for money in front of other campers?"

I didn't respond. I couldn't. I mean, I wasn't equipped. I looked at Sean. Who didn't look back. Didn't flinch. And didn't miss a beat, fielding this most esoteric inquiry with an only-child maturity and Manhattan-bred sophistication well beyond his tender years or, for that matter, mine.

"Yes," he said.

Sean Kelly's balls, his savvy, even the nonchalance of his treason—after all, he was betraying a tent brother, no matter how much the freak—filled me with both admiration and chills. The camp head was satisfied, and we were free to go. As soon as we got down the steps, I turned to my coolest-cuke of an all-time best pal and fired the red-hot question:

"What's masturbate? Is that like giving yourself a blow job?"

CHAPTER 8
Krypton

BETWEEN SCHOOL, CAMP, PLAYGROUP, MAIDS, PARENTAL vacations, Father's business trips, and summers in Memphis trailing grandpa's servants, I didn't actually spend much time as a kid with the family. That changed when I was 13. Because that's when, with house-coated Mother venturing a wan salute from the front window, a liveried chauffeur in a long, black car arrived to spirit me away from the family entirely, from home, dog, bro, maid, friends, New York City, and the 1960s. I was to be gone four years—forever, by a 13-year-old's calculus—flung like Kal-El from an exploding planet, bound for a distant orb yet predicated on the traditional verities: short hair, high class, wide lawns, deep pockets. An orb of rare privilege and special pain, where, by the way, no one would be caught dead pulling up in a rented limo with a rented man. The truly rich—the multi-generationally, unsquanderably well-off—delivered the heir in a dinged-up Country Squire, the lake-house car, piloted by a healthful mom in man-tailored shirt, with a cultivated mess of dirty blonde, accompanied by baby bro and the golden. The scholarship boys arrived in ten-year-old sedans of scuffed maroon or blue. The Black kids—there were three or four—came via the Peter Pan Bus Line, dropped two miles away, just across the New York line, in Amenia, to try and hail a cab. When Mother had invited me to make my big-boy choice about where to go to boarding school—not *whether* to go, she stressed again—I had decided, if nowhere was out of the question, it would be Preston. Then she reprised the family chestnut about how, at the University of Virginia, Papa had discovered that the smartest boy he'd ever met had gone to a school called Harkness. At which point, I understood the decision was really about youth, beauty, power, and her beloved Papa, and maybe getting the old skinflint to pony up.

"Harkness it is," Mother assured me, with a dismissive exhalation of Viceroy.

Now here I was in the tufted-leather escape pod, afraid, ashamed, and far as possible from the mute Android at the wheel, applying frantic, safecracker-fine fiddles to the radio dial, as the buffed black hearse moved inexorably in the direction of far away, mirroring limestone skyscrapers, dirty brick tenements, soot-black fire escapes, chop shops, chop suey shops, red neon BAR signs, billboards en Español, wooden rooftop water towers, elevated trains, second-floor synagogues, butcher store windows, strutting jaywalkers, lounging cops, cart-dragging babushkas, moonscapes of crumbled masonry, columns of white steam, blankets of greasy smoke, gathering momentum as it shed the gravity of metro traffic, into nausea, suffocation, oblivion, and the terra incognita north of White Plains. In pulsing blooms of static, the powerhouse station began to dim. Soon, we'd be completely out of reach, beyond the ministrations of Cousin Brucie, Murray the K, Dandy Dan, all the cheeky New York DJs, beyond John, Paul, Mick, and Dusty Springfield, out of range of the Wicked Pickett and Sam the Sham, present accelerating into past, Positively Fourth Street screaming off a granite bluff into the maw of an infinite dragon of trees, trees, and more trees. But as the soaring red brick smokestack of New England's longest continually operating psych hospital emerged from the forest to wrap itself momentarily around the exterior, one last ragged voice slipped through:

I know you deceived me
Now here's a surprise . . .

* * *

WELCOME TO THE HARKNESS SCHOOL FOR BOYS—founded AD 1884 and instantly sealed in amber—where the syllabus was Latin, Greek, French, Math, European history, Western lit, and the Windsor knot, and imagination a vestigial organ. In a time of upheaval, with a world on fire just a few hours south, the school and its lantern-jawed headmaster were dedicated to the proposition: don't rock the boat. A not unreasonable tack for the financiers, manufacturers, lawyers, builders, and museum board members whose families had consigned their progeny to Harkness for more than a century and which progeny, after a pitstop in the Ivys, went on to populate the financial, commercial, cultural, and political institutions up and down the Atlantic seaboard, preserving and propagating their overlapping fortunes, before dispatching their own progeny to the tree-infested campus for proper induction into the cycle. It wasn't a nefarious conspiracy. A few generations in from the founding go-getters, it wasn't even a conscious choice. It was just the way it was.

I didn't meet the smartest boy ever at Harkness. I met some good guys, some smart guys, some dummies, assholes, and a lot of squares—roughly in proportion to the general population I'd finally meet when I got out—and suffered about as much as I'd feared, which (with the world on fire a few hours south) was plenty. Though not as much as all the people who got burned.

* * *

News of the inferno was transmitted to our brass mailboxes, located in a wall of 400, basement of Main. The news came on paper. No real radio station reached us in the woods. Network TV, only in the common room and only between certain hours (though if the Beatles or Stones were on, you bet I'd find a way). The sole computer was an industrial gray terminal in the science building, hooked up to a scientific database at University of Illinois and operated by punch cards. There were students with subscriptions to the *New York Times* and *Boston Globe,* to *Life, Harper's,* and *National Geographic.* There were "dorks" who went to the library—their second favorite place after the lab—to read *Popular Mechanics* and *Popular Electronics.* As to music, it would be a couple years before there was a *Rolling Stone* or *Creem.* If you really wanted music coverage, you'd have to resort to *Hit Parader,* which was aimed at pre-teen girls. You never would in a boys' school. I had a subscription to *Time,* discounted for Harkness students because the founder was an alum, and my roommate, whose father was an ambassador, got the daily *New York Times* (which actually came a day late). And for a while, I wrote Sandy, who always wrote back.

After freshman year, they let us have portable record players. If you couldn't get someone outside to mail you a new record, there was a limited selection in the school bookstore—a random one: that's where I spotted Alice Cooper's first LP, alongside Herb Alpert and the Tijuana Brass. Much of the news I got was smuggled in on those records. But it could be hard to listen, painful to realize all you were missing—from Kent State to Dylan's motorcycle accident to full frontal in the movies. The ambassador's son had lived in Israel as a boy, and, in 1967, poring over his *Times,* desperate for discussion, he tried to make me understand the earthquake that was the Six-Day War—which only had five days to go by the time we got the news. I tried to make him understand the earthquake that was *Are You Experienced?* Pretty sure neither of us succeeded. Still, the news of the day got through.

Oh, and drugs. One way or another, drugs got through. Acid, pot, speed. Booze got through. And you could always do a little acting at the school clinic for a bottle of codeine cough syrup. Nothing was going to block the highway to altered consciousness, not the locked green arms of New England trees, nor the Connecticut State Police, who came, in force, in the middle of the night, to haul off one friend on a bad trip—which, combined with the trip itself, immediately followed by early-morning expulsion proceedings, opened up a terrifying new frontier in bummers.

There were Thanksgiving and Christmas and spring vacations, when you could bulk up on teenage news—along with drugs—even grow your hair out a little, if your parents were cool, which mine were not. Of course, there was that most devastating vacation of all: Summer. Which, between its irrefutably bad parts—a slog of a summer job (messenger) and proximity to cruel and capricious parental authority—and its indescribably amazing parts—the scary, funny, ecstatic nights and weekends—only ever seemed to last a week. Then: back to Harkness. The thought would knock the wind out of me.

* * *

BETWEEN REPUBLICAN OVERLORDS, SUFFOCATING SCENERY, AND an abiding ache for a real world of social upheaval and keening Marshall stacks, the oppression at Harkness weighed heavy. I awaited a rupture in the space-time continuum. One day, to my surprise, it came.

The campus went silent, its inhabitants still, and, before the light went fully dark, it went eerie. Trippy. A total solar eclipse. But the black and eerie soon dispersed, the silence refilled, and next day, sacked out on the library grass, I could remember it only dimly, as through polarized glass. Three years into a four-year hitch, I had adjusted: I was alone, alienated, and fully looking the part. My mandatory jacket—from Goodwill, not Brooks—was of an antiquated style, pinstriped black-and-red on cream, a boating jacket (whatever that is), and two sizes too big. My mandatory neckwear was parody: a purple clip-on bowtie meant for a child. I wore a straw space helmet, painted silver, with "NASSA" [*sic*] red-stenciled on the front—made-in-Japan costuming, back when that meant cheap and flimsy, even in the copy editing. For the finishing touch, I stretched a baby's white-framed, rubber sunglasses across my face. Special occasions I wore my girlfriend's Catholic school jumper. If I was making it up as I went, I was also stealing from album covers—especially, with the weird glasses and cross-dressing, album covers from Bizarre, Frank Zappa's label, home also to Captain Beefheart, Wild Man Fischer, and the aforementioned Alice. My prep comrades were unlikely to spot the larceny, but I knew. In any case, no quiet desperation for this guy. I was nothing if not easy to find.

* * *

HE CAME OUT OF THE BUSHES, or that's how it seemed, sidling up, with nervous salutations, and launching into what I came to understand, after several minutes, was a grand theorem that, after many more minutes, I came to understand had something to do with the eclipse. He was a Black kitchen worker, maybe a decade older, still in splattered work shirt and pants. At first, I was embarrassed by his nervousness, which I took to be deference. Soon, with all the prattle about math and science, I was bored.

All he wanted was for me to come to Bissell.

His mission was to get his treatise into the hands of George Norman Hardy, the august head of Harkness mathematics. He wanted me to review, endorse, and deliver it to the big guy, ultimately for dissemination to the world—a world that would pluck him from the underclass and bear him on its shoulders to immortality, if not a better paying cafeteria gig. The folly of conscripting me into pursuits mathematical should've been plain from a cursory scan of my appearance, much less my report card. He didn't care. I was odd enough and handy. "Come! See!" he implored, stepping into the fraught proximity that social psychology had only recently identified as an individual's "Personal Space," leavening both his desperation and aggression with periodic chortles. Probably stoned, come to think of it. Probably, with my boating jacket, rubber glasses, and purple kiddie tie, thought I was.

Moment of truth.

Justice, democracy, revolution, Sly, Otis, Jimi. The triumph of the underdog. Divinity of madness. To not give this man the benefit of the doubt would have been to give the lie to all I claimed to stand for. As my Arizona pops used to say: big hat, no ranch.

* * *

NOT MEASURABLY REMOTE, THE HULKING YELLOW castle known as Bissell Hall still felt like an orb beyond, its crenelated parapet looming six stories above the low campus of red brick, white clapboard and green old-growth. It was built in 1890, half-a-dozen years after the school's founding, amidst the first flowering of the American industrial plutocracy, and named—perhaps presciently—for the lavishly mustachioed blowhard who bankrolled it: the robber baron of carpet cleaning. At some point, the edifice had been demoted from a dorm for rich, white students to a warehouse for the brown, Black, lightly educated, poorly paid seasonal workers who served their needs: the "wombats" ("bats," for short), which is what, for reasons not explained, but well-understood, budding plutos had called them for more than a century. No student I knew ever went inside. If it wasn't officially off-limits—which I'll bet it was—I'm not sure any would have cared to. In the prep imagination (such as it was), Bissell resided somewhere between socially out-of-bounds—even if you told yourself those things didn't matter anymore—and haunted, by living and dead.

Though I suspect it never entered the prep imagination.

It was dark, damp, and musty, and, as the door swung shut with a moan, we entered from the back. Where the other dozen Harkness dorms had long ago been modernized, the interior of Bissell retained all its charming original details, without the charm. Mahogany wainscoting slapdashed with drippy brown gloss, a brass chandelier that had oxidized to pink, deeply rutted floorboards that hadn't seen varnish since Grover Cleveland, wooden handrails that finished in nineteenth-century curlicues, but had been carved up and down with twentieth-century initials, the walls painted the pale green that once proclaimed hospital or jail, but would soon find favor among elite home-furnishings consumers.

We ascended three squeaking flights, him repeatedly apologizing for the climb, and opened a pale green door. The room was inescapably cell-like, crammed, vertically and horizontally, with books and papers, and watched over by Kennedy and King, neither long in the grave, both already cliché. If I felt uneasy, I admonished myself for being such an irredeemable white boy. Why couldn't this salt-of-the-Earth be the new avatar of the cosmos, Black Copernicus in a work shirt? Clamped in a clear plastic report binder, his treatise spanned eight leaves of onionskin typescript, with black-and-white Polaroids pasted in. In addition to his byline and yesterday's date, the title page, in title case, announced: "Theory of the Total Eclipse of the Sun." It didn't look crazy. As part of my self-defense strategy, I never sat down. As another part, more transparent, I told him that I didn't have a lot of time, due to a pressing engagement. I stood in the crowded garret for six or seven minutes and tried to read, as he crowded next to me, pointing and clarifying. Since he happened to have been a "few minutes late" for the eclipse, he explained when we got to the Polaroids, the pictures were taken right after the event.

"*Right* after," he emphasized, smugly tapping a finger on the page.

The immaculately-typed words were mostly incomplete sentences that were mostly complete gobbledy-gook. The pictures, nine snapshots of a blazing, white sun, were indistinguishable. As I turned the pages at a solemn pace meant to signify dawning awe, he was shooting me the grin with raised eyebrows to signify: Now do you believe?

When I thought I'd done enough nodding, chin-stroking, and slow-turning, I checked the Timex I wasn't wearing, tucked the magnum opus under my arm and assured him his astrophysical bombshell would find its way to the tippy-top.

I hurried down the stairs—not so fast as to give myself away—and back to the charted regions of campus, where I put his proof in a dresser drawer. In the secret tunnel under the library, I told a couple of other smokers and fellow freaks about my adventure, played it off as a goof, trying to gauge by their reactions if it really was funny or I was in too deep. But I knew. Every once in a while, the guy would pop up around the cafeteria and remind me, asking did I give it to Mr. Hardy and what did he say. Eventually I told him I did, and that Mr. Hardy was considering it, or something noncommittal. I didn't, because even a science doofus like me could tell it was nonsense. Wonderful, stoney, audacious nonsense, effective as parody maybe, but, as astrophysics, nonsense, pure and simple. To the humorless Mr. Hardy, it would just be one more piece of evidence I was hopelessly high, another opportunity to stir up the folks. I should never have gone along in the first place. Then one day, across the cafeteria line, I got the slitty stare that said the kitchen worker had stopped believing. At some point, like all bats, Copernicus flew the coop.

* * *

BIG HAT, NO RANCH. I WAS ashamed. Of myself, the school, the rich, the white, the whole grinding gizmo—"the system," the counterculture had termed it, with irresolute vagueness—that seemed to ensure a guy like me would someday be able to write his adventures and a guy like him would be able to get crazy, get high, get ten years for possession and die before his time. Total eclipse of the sun.

I kept his theory through high school, college, and into the band. To discard it would have been the crowning insult. Besides, I told myself, this is how I'll remember. When I lost my apartment, and, accompanied by a Great Pine duffel of clothes, took up wandering, I mailed a big box of Harkness stuff to my big brother for safekeeping in his garage. When he got sick, and had to move to a smaller condo, before moving full-time to the hospital, his bride put it in a storage locker and, angry at the cosmos, and especially at Mother, whose mercy had strict limits, sent me the tab. I couldn't pay. After a countdown of progressively ominous Final Bills from Jupiter Stor-U-Self, the inevitable happened. Jupiter Stor-U-Self auctioned my stuff, or junked it—typescript treatise, rubber glasses, straw helmet, and all—and it shook me in unexpected ways for unexpected miles.

And miles and miles and miles.

CHAPTER 9

Otis

FROM THE TOMBOY IN A MINNESOTA sprinkler to a curly-topped Boho on Positively Fourth Street, I cannot remember a moment before desire. I've wanted sex since before I knew what it was. Wanted it like crazy. Chased it—ignorantly, shamefully—at school dances, basement dances, at underage bars—Mike Malkan's on East 79th Street—and just about anywhere and everywhere else. Sometimes I had to stay on the city bus a stop extra with a bookbag on my lap, so besieged was I by hormones. And a few months after Wally Taggart had demonstrated his extraordinary skill in the field, I was finally recruited into the sin of masturbation by a small, smudged ad for the Folies Bergère, a touring French burlesque show, whose spangled, bare-midriffed star leapt from the theater pages of the *Journal-American* and seized me by the brimming libido. It would be the end of confession for me—who could confess that?—and ultimately the demise of my Catholicism. But real sex didn't start until ninth grade summer, with Maria.

Actually, sex started with Johnny Shannon.

Last-born of a brutish Irish surgeon and shell-shocked Paddy housewife, runt of five Catholic boys, Johnny was a best friend you later wonder how. The main attraction was comedy—Johnny

Shannon would do anything, sometimes cruel, always unforeseen, for a laugh, and—a few years before the death of the punchline—in a way that came to seem prophetic.

Not everybody found Johnny hilarious. His routines were never a hit with the girls—admittedly, it could be tough to defend loosing a live lobster on the Madison Avenue bus or shouting "Uterus!" on a crowded beach in Montauk. But it was never about the text—the joke-like thing was merely a pretext to point up the emptiness of jokes. The funny part, the core of the tickle, was how, as embodied in Johnny's abnormal psychology and his performance—always generated on the fly—the event would come hurtling out of the blue, random as a meteorite, another rupture of space-time.

Important to note that, for all his stupid, crazy, dangerous antics, Johnny was also the most nervous guy I've met. Shrieking like a 10-year-old girl—both his honest reaction and part of the show—Johnny would sprint away from whatever misdemeanor he had pulled the minute you let your guard down, sometimes running straight into traffic, where, to compound both the tension and the gag, he would berate the bus, truck or cab that had almost run him over, standing in the street in front of the vehicle, glaring, finally lighting a truculent cigarette and flicking the match at the driver. Not only did you never know when a bit was coming, you never knew how far Johnny would go. Or if, this time, it would be too far. Or how it might get you killed.

Johnny Shannon wasn't just the funniest, most nervous, and most nervous-making among us, he was also the horniest (which is saying something), his holiest grail of a prank, to figure out how to get his freckly ass laid. But he had a plan. Actually, it was Ryan's plan, the brother just above him, who was given to bold claims about erotic expertise. At the end of every wasted night—of which there were more than you might imagine for 14-year-olds—Johnny would harangue us to translate his big brother's hard-earned *savoir* into our own manly *faire*, to once and for all carry out The Plan. Or as he would say, with his sporadic, stress-related stammer:

"Let's g-g-g-get whores!"

We'd laugh. And eventually carry home whomever was too trashed to walk—Johnny—and forget about it, until next time. Because, when you thought about it, a New York prostitute was probably an excellent way to get robbed or killed. Or, worse, busted, and—like Gray Turner when he shot his brother—plastered all over the New York papers:

"PREP BOYS IN BROTHEL BUST."

Not to mention a direct route to certain infections and infestations that might necessitate a visit (or two or three) to the doctor, and a pricey prescription, and would be tough to keep from your mother. Johnny was unrelenting. Sometimes we'd even pretend that, this time, we were going through with it. Until early on a stone-sober Saturday, the phone rang, and Mother belted out from the bottom of the stairs:

"Thomas! It's Bob."

Even after five years in school together, Bob remained a mystery. That may have been the attraction. The idea of a 14-year-old who kept his counsel, who was tightlipped—visibly—and who, when he did speak, did so in a staccato monotone, with not a single surplus syllable, like a gangster from a black-and-white *Million Dollar Movie*—was a marvel to a jibber-jabbering 14-year-old like me.

"We're doing it," said Bob. "You coming?"

"Wait, what are we doing?"

"The Plan."

Bob had made his decision and wasn't interested in discussion, not with me, not even with Johnny. If it was a little early to be thinking of prostitutes and a little early (if, at 14, not a little young) to be thinking of drinking, the agenda was set. Meet at Tiger's—an S.I. scholarship boy whose parents worked Saturdays—and Johnny'll bring the bourbon his raging dad thinks is safely locked up. Tiger wasn't sure if he was joining in, wasn't sure about the entire enterprise. But Bob had strong-armed him into letting us use the apartment anyway.

"You coming?" Bob repeated.

That, I knew, would be the last of his arguments. What could I say?

I wasn't stupid or unaware. In the freak-flag days of love, peace and mind-expansion, of upending norms and suspending judgment, of sexual liberation and ERA, I knew the whole thing was hopelessly old-fashioned. Maybe even wrong. And I told myself it wasn't me. I wasn't Bob and certainly wasn't Johnny—part of why I liked them. No, I was a singer, poet, writer—sensitive and special. Then again, here in my overheated little hands was a rip-roaring adventure, a future movie, song or story—and, coincidentally, one with a deliriously happy ending, after a thousand pent-up years. Wouldn't it also signify my breakthrough into romantic maturity? My certification as a man? My great leap forward from slipping a knee between the thighs of a St. Cecilia's girl while slow dancing to "Groovy Kind of Love" to slipping something else?

Still, I'd need that bourbon to get brave.

Sure enough, by the time Tiger's mother surprised us by coming home early, unleashing a torrent of Neapolitan despair about the Kids Today, hounding Tiger to his room as the rest of us scrambled out the door, I was so brave I could barely hang on to the bannister.

* * *

JOHNNY HAD THE MOST MONEY BECAUSE, when he wasn't stealing jelly jars of booze from his dad's well-stocked bar, he was lifting cash from his well-stocked wallet. While he knew he'd get a beating if his father found out, he knew he'd get a beating no matter what.

Johnny sprang for the taxi to Times Square, and fifteen minutes later, having abandoned Tiger to his mother's rough justice, the three of us tumbled out in front of a vintage movie palace, now on its last spread-legs pimping porn.

It was summer in the city, just like the Lovin' Spoonful had played it: "cool cat looking for a kitty." The brutality of the actuality, for me, was that, here in Times Square, it was too hot, too crowded and, behind most of a jelly jar of Canadian Club, too fucking spinning. Not a minute after we got out of the cab, I looked around and the guys were gone. It always amazed me we survived, young, high, out of control, on the streets of New York, that we didn't get run over or knifed or fall off a roof. We seemed to have incredible luck (didn't yet know about the "incredible luck" of being born white), but doesn't mean we weren't scared. Now I was mostly scared I was missing the story. Slapping a hand over one eye and drawing a deep breath, bracketed by hiccups, I eventually caught a glimpse of Johnny. As I moved unsteadily in his direction, I could hear him stammering up at a six-foot Black woman in a blonde wig.

Even without double-vision, it wasn't hard to see The Plan wasn't working. It didn't help that our front man was not just young, but petite. Or that, as the culture had gone flower-power, Johnny had remained resolutely prep, sockless in penny loafers, button-downs, creased chinos. Most of the prostitutes didn't even want to talk to the little jailbait, much less risk the wrath of cops or well-connected Upper East Side parents by fucking him. As a further complication, his big brother had instructed Johnny that the savvy approach was to ask:

"Are you free?"

"Am I *what*?!?"

The big, Black blonde had to think a minute about whether to punch the pipsqueak.

"Am I *free*?!?" she muttered to herself, clomping off in vast red heels. "I'll show you what's free . . . "

After a minute or an hour, I found myself side by side with Bob.

"Hey!" I called out. But he had his eyes on Johnny—and the prize.

As the bourbon started to settle, I found myself secretly relieved the adventure was turning into the usual Johnny jerkoff. Which at least meant nothing more to fear. Bob wasn't giving up.

"Don't think *free* is working," he deadpanned.

Not sure how Johnny became our front man. Just as he was the nervous nelly who lived for nerve-rattling pranks, he seemed to simultaneously recoil from and embrace his role as procurer. Eventually he attracted the interest—in a twitchy, sniffly, disinterested way—of a skinny white woman with pimples.

"All three?" we could hear her say. "Sixty bucks, plus the room."

Like many of the extralegal entrepreneurs of Broadway, her closing technique lacked finesse:

"You want it or not?"

We tried to hide our wallets as we double-checked our funds. She probably wouldn't rob us here—though there were plenty of ratty vestibules and dim stairs on the side streets. More likely, in the room, door shut, shades drawn, screams muffled.

"All we've got is 35," Johnny told her.

"You little faggot!"

Whereupon she launched into a tirade that, subtract the faggots and motherfuckers, could have been a stock Chamber of Commerce sermon on civic responsibility. As she continued to rant, another woman, older and better-fed, drifted over.

"What do they want?" she drawled.

If the ranting woman answered, as she eddied back into Broadway's human rapids, we didn't hear. The new lady—dark, tiny, in-control—took control. Turning to Johnny, she said:

"Thirty-five. And you pay for the cab."

Without a nanosecond of contemplation, the horniest boy in New York City—not only a thief, a bald-faced liar, holding back more than enough for the whole deal—blurted:

"D-d-d-deal."

* * *

CRISP, QUIET, BUT NOT UNFRIENDLY, SHE gave the driver an address on First Avenue in the 30s, Kip's Bay, between Bellevue and the Tunnel. While it might not have been my worst white nightmare, I'd still never known anyone who lived there. I memorized every detail.

Her name was Maria and, by the standards of the time, no less than the profession, her waist-low neckline and pubis-high hem were barely outrageous. And there was a serenity about her that suggested, if she was on drugs, it was precisely the right dose.

Unless it was a setup.

For 35 bucks? No, as an economic crime, the numbers would never pencil out—she'd have to want to rob us out of spite, out of race-hate and class-war. But that's something you think of when you're calmer. Not when you're standing in the elevator—a 14-year-old preppie virgin—with a veteran New York hooker.

An undogmatically modern complex with generous windows and intermittent style, the building had a well-lit elevator—instead of steep stairs leading into darkness. The block was tidy—no nodding junkies or, for that matter, prostitutes—if a bit noisy, from trucks banging through the potholes as they raced the synchronized lights. When the elevator doors slid apart on five, no pistol-packing pimp leapt from the shadows. Nor did Maria's apartment have any of the Black-hooker kitsch a sheltered paleface had expected. No pointy-breasted velvet ladies. No wicker thrones. And no glass pipes, dripping needles or charred spoons. Just some watercolors of sailboats and a big, wide fireplace of white-painted brick, above which was propped a framed photo of her grinning eight-year-old son.

About whom, to my horror, Johnny promptly inquired.

"Who's that?"

Johnny was casting about for comedy.

"Your boyfriend? Your Pops?"

Maria smiled politely to acknowledge a jumpy teenager's lame joke.

"My son."

Johnny grabbed the photo. For a guy who'd never be top of the class in anything a normal report card could measure, he had a genius for knowing at any one moment how and where the transgression was.

"Handsome lad . . . " he said.

Maria was clearing the throw-pillows from the couch, making room for us, and gave no indication she was listening. Mostly she seemed relieved to be home.

On an end-table by the fireplace, next to the couch, was a record player, and, displayed above it, a sweaty, shiny-faced Otis Redding—cover of a live album—proudly surveying all. To me, the one Black touch. If this was a den of iniquity, Maria could not have been a more amenable den mother. It made it better. It made it worse. She gestured at the sofa and told us to get comfortable and, indicating a few dozen more records nearby, invited us to put on whatever we wanted. As Johnny and Bob exchanged nervous noogies, I knelt in front of the record rack and started to flip through. Aretha, Sam and Dave, Dionne Warwick, Lou Rawls, a fat guy I'd never heard of—Solomon Burke—in cape and crown, and then, to a white youth of limited sociocultural ken (and unlimited whiteness), what seemed to be a joker: Glen Campbell.

The browsing was interrupted by Maria offering drinks from the kitchen. We looked at each other. "Grownup drinks," she clarified, with a friendly smirk, pouring us three of the same—Old Grand Dad, water, rocks. Then and only then, three pale preps on the couch wide-eyed as baby birds, did Maria's hospitality turn—briefly, genteelly—to business, as she collected my ten, Johnny's ten and Bob's 15.

"Gonna give you something extra," she said to Bob. "OK, who's first?"

* * *

BEFORE SHE TOOK OUR STAMMERING FRONT man to the bedroom, she took him to the bathroom. We could hear the faucet, but, until Johnny returned, clutching his chinos, clad only in the old-fashioned boxers his brother had prescribed for manly boudoir wear, we had no idea why. With hands expert as a veteran RN—or master butcher—she turned our penises, kneaded our scrotums, scrutinized our virginal manflesh and scrubbed the whole apparatus with hospital-style antiseptic soap, rinsed with water so hot you could hardly stand it. (Later, pursuing my own hygiene protocol, I'd write my big brother, who'd had the clap, asking how you could tell.)

Patients prepped and certified and returned, in undies, to the waiting room, the scrub nurse transformed into the seductress and, with one smoky finger, summoned Joking Johnny to the promised land.

The door to the bedroom closed. The door to the bedroom opened. Not ten seconds had elapsed. And here comes Johnny, backwards, stammering up a storm.

"G-g-g-gimme another chance."

"It's OK, baby," we could hear Maria soothing. "Just wait out there."

For the record then, it was actually Bob who went first, because it was Bob who went next, performing—even after the addition of "something extra"—without incident. And it was Johnny who, after recovering on the couch, finally went again, last.

I don't remember when I finished going through Maria's albums and decided to stick with what was already queued. By the time it was my turn to be deflowered—drunkenly, foolishly, mechanically, and almost incapably (ironically), after all that mad yearning—Otis was singing his heart out.

CHAPTER 10
Suzanne

NOT THAT MURDER WASN'T FROWNED UPON, but it was New Year's. And, by law and custom, a parent was well within his or her rights. Mothers and fathers could hit their children. Imprison them. Neglect them. Belittle them. Bruise their bodies and minds. As a society, we didn't seem to know kids had feelings. A parent of mine didn't seem to know they had memories.

Granted, it's not the kind of thing you bring up—casually or ever—but my mother never said anything about that night. Once, later, she alluded to certain "failings" as a parent, but that was intended to contrast her measured maternal technique with the overindulgences of contemporary parents. *Mea culpa* qua dig. The nearest she came to discussing filicide was one barrel-aged late-evening when she sighed that she was sorry my little brother was there to witness "it"—but the antecedent was left unspecified. Of course, that was both a mea culpa and a dig at Roger—because, in her analysis, he was weak-minded, and that night was why—and a dig at me—because, weak-minded in my own way, I had brought it down on all of us.

I think she did remember. But what did I want? An apology? For caring about your kid? Compared to Sandy's and Connie's childhood, it was child's play. Maybe even compared to Mother's, at the hands of Mama—who, long before the circulation problems that stiffened her legs, used a walker to get around when stiffened by potation.

* * *

IT WAS JUST BEFORE HARKNESS LET out for Christmas that George Norman Hardy—head of math and Great White Hope of the wombat astrophysicist—inscribed F on my fall report card. Then, without so much as a Miranda warning, summoned my folks from New York.

"Because, frankly, Mr. and Mrs. Ransom, there's a Big Problem."

When they arrived, in another rented limo with a rented driver, after two-and-a-half hours of nothing to do but boil, Mr. Hardy delivered the coup de grace: the boy's not just flunking, he's on drugs.

Speed.

Mr. Hardy would've said *thpeed,* because he had a lisp. His incontrovertible proof of meth was my inept proof of math. The blue book from my final. Making his case with scientific rigor, he walked my parents through the highlights of my amphetamine scribbles as they careened outside the lines and into the margins and through pages upon extra pages before circling back across the inside cover, in diminishing script, on a ceaseless quest for QED. No question it was a ludicrous tangle—or, less judgmentally, in computer terms, an Infinite Loop—but wasn't it also a picture of determination, perseverance and New England grit? Stuck in his own loop, Mr. Hardy could see only tweaking.

QED.

George Norman Hardy was a towering figure of fierce demeanor, with a voice as authoritative as his tripartite name—compensating, no doubt, for his speech impediment, but magnificently. August barely begins to describe him. Mr. Hardy was so far beyond merely credible that my proud progenitors were buying none of what their sniveling tweaker offered in defense. Which was, alas, the truth:

I'm so bad at math it only seems like I'm high.

Farfetched perhaps, but, save for smoking under the library and an occasional chugalug of syrup, I had stayed clean on campus, assuming that being any kind of buzzed would only be that much more of a bummer. Anyway, I was already under suspicion for being the clown in the kiddie bowtie and straw helmet who seemed high, even to the bats.

* * *

IF MY FOLKS WOULDN'T LET ME exit gracefully, voluntarily (they wouldn't), why not provoke the school into the old heave-ho?

It was a question I asked myself repeatedly, and it repeatedly led to the same answer, the obvious one: if I'd gotten tossed from Harkness, Mother would've killed me. For keeps. Or packed me off to the longest continually operating psych hospital. Or called the cops and had me hauled off to jail. Since a speedfreak no longer qualified as human, any and all of it would have been frightfully justified.

It wasn't death I worried about, so much as the days in Mother's custody awaiting death. Or just the days in Mother's custody. Going home had become so odious that the last two years I'd volunteered to spend spring vacation at school getting tutored in math—by Mr. Hardy. Death, prison, or the booby hatch would be a mercy.

To be fair, it wasn't all Mother. While I was never completely sure what to make of Father's role in all this—home, school, murder—I resented that the cowpoke was cowed. I resented that his dedication to being "a leader, not a follower"—as he liked to style it—to questioning everything, went out the window when it came to Mother and the family. I resented that a genius could be so dumb, a badass such a pussy. Still I had the feeling that, for all his flaws, he might fundamentally be nicer.

So sometimes I resented him more.

Now, summoned to judgment by an authority more commanding than any mere god, my parents had circle-jerked themselves into a state beyond despair. Their ungrateful Sonny Boy, upon whom they'd slathered a lifetime of cash and prizes, was ruined. Until they could decide where to dump the body, he was also grounded.

But, back in New York on winter break, on New Year's, the holiest troublemaking date of the calendar, I had a date. With the folks preoccupied with bubbly and best friends, I took the opportunity to unground myself via the back stairs.

* * *

THE DATE'S NAME WAS SUZANNE, AND, before we left her parents', she pointedly put on the Leonard Cohen song. It seemed a tad immodest, if not—I fantasized—a tad forward. But Suzanne, who used to be a dancer, was a poet now. And Leonard Cohen was her favorite writer. Her brother, a faux artiste in the faux-friendly field of photography, who happened to be two years ahead of me at Harkness, was her favorite artist, she confided, reverently lifting from the wall a framed picture of footprints in prep school snow. It didn't take long for me to figure out that, between cueing up "Suzanne," when it's your name, by the Canadian laureate of the lugubrious, when it's America's most raucous night, this thing was not predestined to fly. Still, lust springs eternal. And poetry and art having had their hour, we set out for coarser pleasures.

I would soon discover that this particular poet was not just sensitive, but sensible, and by two of New Year's Eve, many gallons of mischief too soon, she had steered us back to her place, her parents'. I held out hope that the premature retreat presaged a "Touch her perfect body" session, but when we walked in her place, the phone was ringing, and all hope—more than I could imagine—was lost.

* * *

How she got the number, I will never know.

When we were little and Mother admonished us through the wall about jumping on the bed, she explained she had x-ray eyes. I believed it then, but maybe I should've believed it later. How else to explain her powers of surveillance? A pair of penetrating eyes wasn't even the half of it. My sainted mother also packed a pair of balls. And that meant, whether it was calling my date's house at two in the morning or insulting her friends' kids over lunch at the club, there were no boundaries. Boundaries were for lessers, for losers, and for her alone to enforce, and to enforce without any boundaries. Beaten before I was beaten, panicked Mother might call again—knowing she would, this time rousing Suzanne's sweetly progressive parents—terrified the whole pathetic story would blaze through Harkness via Suzanne's faux-bro and too humiliated to grab even a promissory peck goodnight, I scooped my coat from the floor where I'd overenthusiastically dropped it and sprinted the twenty blocks home.

Clumsily unlocking the front door, I leaned on the doorjamb, coat over shoulder, Sinatra-style, in what I imagined, in my stinkoness, was the picture of trans-generational cool. Father and Mother, lying in wait in the dark, woozily worrying the words of George Norman Hardy, imagined different. Father liked to tell how as a kid in Tucson he'd seen the Mexicans hooked on marijuana, the lazy, dusty, addicted Mexicans, nodding in the backstreets, forever useless and left behind. Now, here, drooping in an Upper East Side doorway—not perhaps as Frankie as he felt—was Father's addict son: no better than a "wetback." Worse—with all that Confederate breeding and expensive Norteño spoiling.

Father snatched me by the wrist into a pool of lamplight, probing a thumb into each eye socket, looking deep for the proof that had to be there, because Mr. Hardy had said so. As he rummaged through my eyeballs and studied my skin, he panted through his thick, broken nose and cursed me like I was a stranger—"You fucking asshole!" With a single bear-swipe, he now ripped off my shirtsleeve, locking my bare arm under his—a wrestler's maneuver—dragging it closer to the light, the better to see the marijuana tracks. Hovering in the black, beyond boundaries, at the nexus of rage and joy, Mother answered Father's every snort, grunt and curse with shrieking, spitting and raising up of hands—a Memphis choir on PCP. Then gargling her vowels at the ceiling, in a tantric shudder of Dixie-speak, she called out to the universe:

"*What's he on, Daddy!!!??? What's he onnnnnnnnnn!!!???*"

It was loud in there. It was freaky. And it wasn't long before the rest of the house had awakened. The sixty-something maid, a Jesus-lover with a fluting soprano voice and hell-orange hair, an import of almost six months tenure from either Belgium or Brazil, descended to bear mute witness (and a few hours later, pass mute judgment by bumping her old stickered suitcase down the stairs and out the door forever). Seated on the step above her, half-hidden behind the housekeeper's housecoat, clutching his knees, was Roger.

But within that vortex of an arena, I was only dimly aware of spectators, alone as you can be, throbbing with the hormone that helps animals escape and genes survive. I wasn't scared. Being scared wasn't safe, the hormone insisted. Being scared took juice a threatened animal could not spare. The hormone said to look for an opening, a microsecond of distraction when a less brave lad of limited physical abilities might rip himself from the grip of the stronger, more agile animal. Then, even as Father continued to parse the freckles and moles of my forearm, I got it.

A hellhound howl. A long, keening, non-human *rrrraaaaaaa-oooooowwwww!*

I hadn't noticed her slipping away. Here she came back. Bursting through kitchen door, dining room, living room, flying from the dark into the pool of bright, arm high like a movie maniac to drive a carving knife into my heart. Inches from homicide, her athletic husband released my arm, seized Mother's wrist, pushed it back, with a twist, to make her release the blade and kicked the knife aside. And within that do-or-die bracket, I bolted. Or my *body* bolted—no "I" about it. No ego, cognition, control.

But faster than an unathletic son could even process, my father, the high school wrestling captain, pivoted from disarming Mother, planted his feet wide, and sprung across the room to recapture me at the door. Taking me hard to the welcome mat, he shouted for Mother to get up to the bedroom—"Now!" And for everybody else to get back to theirs. Twisting my arm behind my back, he wrestled me up the stairs.

Not so much despairing as detached, an animal at the end of his adrenaline, I could no longer resist. Father locked the door of the master bedroom, shoved me into a chair and slid his over directly in front to ensure I could not escape. Though probability was another of Mr. Hardy's math modules I'd failed, I calculated Father wasn't likely to kill, not here, not yet. I wasn't so sure about the banshee on the bed opposite: rocking and glaring and glorying in the afterglow, punching a monogrammed pillow to every beat of a dubious heart.

Father pressed a charcoal-stubbled face into mine and rapid-fired questions—What drugs? And who? And when? And who else?—and finally browbeat me into confessing something. Anything.

OK, yes, I told him, I had smoked marijuana, once or twice.

I didn't tell him about the thousand more times. Or the opiated hash or DMT, the LSD, codeine or the speed. It was all the same to him anyway: pot or acid, one hit or a million. Once I'd confessed to the weed, he browbeat me into telling him it had been supplied by Adam Stern—the friend I thought easiest to sell out, because my parents didn't know his, as opposed to Sean, who had supplied everything, but whose folks were their drinking buddies.

If I thought before that I was drowning, selling out Stern sunk me deeper. I was exactly the coward Father thought I was.

An hour or two later, Mother let up on the pillow-punishing long enough to enact an even more disturbing theater of calm, explaining, with exaggerated patience, that she and Father would soon be sending me off to a mental institution—not so much to save me, who was clearly beyond saving, but to protect the other boys. And with a labyrinthine, implacable, thoroughly menacing illogic, not at all unlike a bad acid trip, the terror plowed on, until, beyond the hulking shoulders of my paternal dungeon master, I glimpsed a new year rising, shades of gunmetal, behind Simon and Garfunkel's Feelin' Groovy bridge.

CHAPTER 11

Providence

FATHER SAID I LOOKED LIKE THAT "fag" in *Life.* Who he meant was Sam Andrew, the longhaired guitarist for Janis Joplin's band, Big Brother and the Holding Company. One thing Father didn't understand—along with the difference between hippies and homosexuals—is that Sam was a rock star and, to me, a hero. Rolling into New York City from four years in capital-F faraway—prep school in the New England forest—my vow, to my father and myself, was immutable: no way would I cut my fucking hair.

"Destiny," I replied with an ambiguous grin, before scooting out the door, one step ahead of his unambiguous death-stare.

Generally, there was no destiny—musical, sexual or sundry—that wasn't available in the back pages of the *Village Voice.* Destiny being destiny, however, a truly determined aspirant would also want to sift the overstuffed bulletin boards at record shops, music equipment stores, coffee houses, clothing boutiques and anywhere random else he might imagine a cool cat would pass.

As I chased my fate, sifting, scheming, posing, drinking, tripping and waiting for my hair to get good, I took a tilt at higher ed, mainly to get my parents off my case. Father had never made it to college. At 18, he'd been too busy supporting his widowed mother and younger brother with a gig loading freight trains in the Arizona desert. His father, a terse, freakishly tall man who'd eventually be elected sheriff of Tucson and died at 39 in a B-movie poker-game shootout, had come to Arizona from Alabama when it was still a territory. No college or high school for him. Nor, through all their family turmoil, for my older half-sister or half-brother. Though Mother had earned a BA in literature from St. Agnes College for Women, she believed, with a typically unstable compound of slavish admiration and bilious resentment, that in a man's world it didn't really count. They wanted me to be the family's first real college grad—first male—after being, by the skin of my buck teeth, its second high school grad. Which was when Mother, per usual, took it four or five steps too far and wanted Harvard. But by nature and by inclination—abysmal at math and, anyway, destined to be a rock star, with zero need for bourgeois certification—I was not equipped to cooperate. The college counselor ventured: "NYU?"

In the prep school scheme of the day, New York University was a safety school, strictly second-rate. Which an insulated Catholic boy would find surprising, in that the student body was so dominated by Jews—brilliant and hard-working, by my reverse-discrimination—that even they called it, with defiant pride, "N-Y-Jew." While I'm sure it was not what Mother had envisaged, my F's in math left Ivy admissions departments less than overwhelmed. Anyway, downtown New York was right where I wanted to be.

By a further twist—snotty interview? too much New York in the incoming class? too much shanty Irish in the applicant?—my best friend Sean, a straight-A, advanced placement, snotty-till-you-get-to-know-him candidate from Exeter, had also been shot down by Harvard. While it must have been some bitter blotter-acid to end up on the second tier alongside a guy who got in with F's, one hopes there was a measure of consolation that the guy was his onetime grade-school classmate, longtime neighbor, former fellow school bus passenger, playgrouper, camp tentmate, coeval, and boon buddy. Also, critically, his bandmate. Because it was my dear Sean who, with a roll of eyes and throwing up of hands, had finally acquiesced to me joining the Lamps, our elementary school's one and only rock 'n' roll group. When mine was first of the Lamps voices to change, even as our instrumentals-only repertoire precipitously turned passé, it was Sean—more mortified to be out of fashion than to share the spotlight—who insisted the rhythm guitar bungler be redeployed to microphone and the band learn some Stones, Kinks, and Paul Revere and the Raiders, pronto.

My musical enthrallment started well before I knew Sean, in Minnesota, when a few days after Elvis scared me in Sandy's hot rod I was imitating him in music class. As Sister Unmerciful conducted the second grade through the greatest hits of Catholic hymns, I sang along "All Shook Up"-style, chin to chest to help me hit the uh-huh-huh parts. That was the day Sister called home to tell Mother I had perfect pitch. Which may or may not have been perfectly true but was better than any other call from St. Olaf's.

While I didn't need Sean to demonstrate the appeal of music, he did, with his straight-A, advanced-placement approach, help me love it to a new depth. More critically, when my parents tried to shield me from the music-driven mischief afoot in the world by shielding me from getting an allowance, one that I was increasingly likely to squander at the five-and-dime on 45s, I got to hear all the nasty records I wanted around the corner at Sean's, whose mother was more indulgent and much older father mostly uninterested in kids (unless they were the coat check girls at the 21 Club). Sean taught me about these sneering scruffs called the Rolling Stones and their scruffy purloined sound. And instructed me in the profundities of *Buffalo Springfield Again*—the second album, the masterpiece. And Sean was all over the Mothers. He said they weren't the big joke *Freak Out!* made them seem. And he got his father's driver to take us downtown, 12-year-old hearts a-thumping, to the Electric Circus to check out this new group from the Coast. They had horns and girls and a lot of them were Black—and there were a *lot* of them. Called themselves Sly and the Family Stone. And under a light show that flowed colonies of amoebae over musicians, audience and mobius-strip walls, the joint went nuts. Sean, too. And soon, as my young friend had predicted, Sly had changed music. Then, on August 23, 1966, a Tuesday, Sean got his father's driver to take us, along with our first-ever dates, to the outer borough of Queens, to Shea Stadium—a few weeks after he'd gotten his father to cadge us seats in the press box—and, for 49 indelible minutes, amid gales of insect screams, we stood in the presence of the godhead, Liverpool's own.

More than wealthy and connected, my new best friend was sophisticated—when rock 'n' roll, in transit from 45 to LP, AM to FM, *Hit Parader* to *Rolling Stone*, was reaching for just that. And in the manner of unathletic cognoscenti everywhere, he enjoyed nothing more than knowing what other boys didn't—other boys, for the most part, being the hick next door, just in from the upper Midwest. But gathered around the record player in his room, gripping album covers like hymnals, I imagined I was getting sophisticated, too.

It turned out Sean was more than just talk. When the Beatles struck, Gray Turner and I responded by scratching tennis rackets at the TV. When the Beatles struck Sean, he started guitar lessons. Since there were no rock 'n' roll teachers, Sean took classical from a squat, elderly Russian—Golem with a three-strand combover—Theo Zeldovich. When I saw how good he'd gotten, and how quickly, I signed up, too. But Sean would pay attention in the lesson and do his homework afterward. He learned to read the confusing notes, even when piled into impenetrable chords, and, through a couple hours of daily practice, to deftly pluck a complicated-sounding Russian waltz, as demonstrated at his rapturously received recital. The gleaming Mr. Z wanted to mold a new Segovia. I wanted to be any old Beatle—instantaneously. The only time the maestro lost his temper with me—after a million opportunities where I showed up late, contemptuously unprepared—was when he glimpsed the John Lennon picture scotchtaped inside my guitar case.

"You like that?" asked Mr. Z, in his thick, flat accent.

Ordinarily, I took care to sanitize the case of the pictures and fanzines that lived there, but, apparently, I'd even gotten lazy about that.

"This is what you like???" he reiterated with guttural agitation.

My face flared. I felt guilty. Mostly, after all his patience, I felt bad for Mr. Z. I tried to do better for a few weeks, to be more like my best friend. But I was impatient, overamped, incorrigible, and eventually Mr. Z encouraged me to quit.

"Study drums," he said, with a snorting chuckle that seemed to lower the mask on something.

In the meantime, there was the golden Sean—who, away from the maestro's satisfied beam, was working hard on a betrayal, transposing his classical chops into Stones, Kinks, Animals, Yardbirds, Sam and Dave, Rascals, Wilson Pickett, "Hang on Sloopy," "Game of Love," "Woolly Bully." We even tried "Ticket to Ride." And that pout-pussed cherub, my best friend, was so natural, so inventive, so astonishingly good—not just a straight-A technician, but a fount of variegated feeling—it seemed possible he'd change music himself.

* * *

AND HERE WE WERE. TOGETHER AGAIN, against all odds. Overeager singer and wunderkind guitarist. Beelzebub himself could not have planned it better. As we lounged in the student union, before, during and after classes, my natural gush gushed.

I would be Mick. He would be Keith. And if it was a dream, mostly mine, I pursued it as if it were a plan. First of all, I was a not-bad Mick. I could carry a tune, in the rock 'n' roll way. Which, a few years before CBGBs, was lowercase-p punk with a heaping helping of wanna-be-Black. Wanna-be Howlin' Wolf or Little Richard or—more to the point—one of their pasty-faced young epigones. Peter Wolf. Or Mick. And while I might have been gifted with decent pipes, a soupcon of style and pique deeper than hormones, Sean was gifted. Pity he didn't let it happen. I tried, for both of us.

I dragged my boy-genius along in search of a rhythm section—our Bill and Charlie—and together over the months, at stinky studios in moldy basements rented by the hour, we entertained a parade of weirdos, incompetents and, worse, competents—serious, ponytailed adult men, five to ten years older, a hundred-times more accomplished, and a thousand-times more bitter—where, if the weirdo even showed, we'd struggle to find tunes that might bridge the chasms of age, skill, and mental health and allow us to jam.

Then one otherwise unremarkable day, on the crazy-quilt cork-board outside the NYU cafeteria, I somehow spotted this:

"Bass & drums seek guitar & singer. Fred & Steve."

Fred told me later that the flyer, with its pluckable phone number fringe, had been there for a year and he'd completely forgot. I could hear him scrambling when I called—probably because he was also stoned. Nominally, he was attending second year of law school. Mostly he stayed baked in the apartment he nominally shared with Steve, his old friend and fellow law student. Nominally, because most of the time, the apartment was occupied only by Fred and his two cats, who were either vague on the concept of litter or as disgusted as Steve that the box was never emptied. To make matters worse, Fred liked to pamper the beasts with orgies of offal, lovingly prepared in the kitchenette that Fred did not lovingly clean and which with its bloody splashes and rancid streaks was not just viscerally uninviting, but Mansonesque. Most nights—not yet equipped after only a year of legal instruction to extricate himself from the colossal error of co-signing this lease—Steve the roommate beat a retreat uptown to his girlfriend. Until Fred called him about our thing, he hadn't been back in three weeks.

Pausing across the intersection, I sorted through the shirt-pocket full of scraps that served as my notebook. On the northern border of artsy Greenwich Village and southern of working-class Chelsea, 14th Street was not quite either. By day, crowded with bargain-hunting Puerto Ricans from the adjacent Lower East Side—the "Loisaida." By night, a hollowed-out no-man's-land of the city's most undistinguished architecture, with pink bags and pissed-on tabloids surfing the sooty thermals above where five converging subways generated a never-ending 5.5 temblor. It wasn't 14th Street that was throwing me. It was the 14-story tower of glazed white brick with a French name and uniformed doorman. Fancy, in a cheap way. Not what you thought of as 14th Street certainly, but not what you thought of as rock 'n' roll. Eventually I turned up a scribble that offered shaky confirmation: Le Parasol.

Ah, oui.

* * *

THE TALLER ONE, FRED, WAS A little snide (and not, that day, obviously stoned), and his roommate Steve was a little square. Within tolerances. If Fred proved to be an unspectacular bassist, his instincts were good. Mostly liked what I liked—Stones, Beatles,

Creedence. And, more importantly, disliked Jethro Tull. Though at first I didn't notice, he was handsome, in a hard-to-pin Mediterranean way—long, black, wavy hair, olive skin and an Elvis smolder that, while cultivated, still came naturally. Girls noticed right away. Steve was somewhat less than unspectacular as a drummer, but he was game. If his hair was a bit tidy for the marauding outfit I'd imagined, he owned a full kit. Besides, Fred and Steve had something that, in New York City, was worth its weight in mediocre rhythm sections: a place to practice. Even if it was next to the boiler, under the asbestos, in Le Parasol's stifling basement.

It was a start, only a start. But I got pretty jazzed about our baby rock band. Soon my hair was untidy enough to make my exasperated pops run me out of the house for being a hippie pervert junkie and cut off funding for college. Meanwhile, Fred and Steve's apartment had gotten disgusting enough that Steve had pretty much moved in with his girlfriend permanently—but not yet left the band. Whereupon the bassist offered me the drummer's room, which, technically, wasn't his to offer (with the ever-principled Steve still paying half the rent). And since it was a damn sight better than whatever couch, floor, or park, I took it. And for long hours every day, months on end, the four of us—me, Sean, Fred and Steve—rehearsed in the carcinogenic catacomb.

We called ourselves Romper Room, after the kiddie TV show. And we got better. Especially after we traded sweet, hapless Steve for a drummer who'd once played on *American Bandstand* and added a rhythm guitar in the person of my prep school pal Adam Stern, whose arty Village parents had encouraged him to pick up the guitar in the folk era, before the Beatles, giving him a head start in fingerpicking and harmony singing. The band got better still—tighter *and* looser—but not yet terrific. Although one day a stubby old man chewing a stubby old stogie peeked into the boiler room, en route to the laundry, to tell us we were. He also said he should know—he was the father of J. Geils, lead guitar for that much-admired white R&B band featuring Peter Wolf at the mic.

Anyway, I believed his claim to be J's dad. Fred believed it all.

While my old friend Sean harbored not-so-secret notions that, as fun as it might be, the band was another of my overexuberant fantasias, defying actuarial reality, and my other old friend Stern, less cynical, more practical, saw it simply as a long shot, something his arty parents would countenance for a year or two before he'd have to head back to college, my new friend Fred—who'd made the mistake of giving up once before—was ready for the cross.

Sometimes Fred's belief scared me. If you really thought about it, it *was* ridiculous to suppose we'd become rock stars—exactly the improbability Sean and Adam estimated. Which is why I never did—estimate, that is. Not thinking, and definitely not thinking ahead, has always been my trick for cheating fate. That Fred was filled with fierce belief based on what he deemed a rational assessment—I mean, that was just nuts.

It was. But it was also a shot at transcendence, at becoming, in Nick Lowe's coinage, the Jesus of Cool. That wasn't nuts because we'd seen it with our mortal eyes. On Sullivan, in *Hard Day's Night*, from the press box at Shea and over and over at the Electric Circus and Fillmore and Garden. Rock stardom was the true panacea. It solved every personality crisis. Even offered a constructive outlet for a guy with a busted vocal knob. It solved money problems—so when friends and lovers were doling out cash, I could wave off guilt, knowing I'd be paying it back soon with interest. It solved being lonely and funny-looking and getting laid and was so much more appealing than tightening a conservatively patterned noose around your neck and marching off to FarGo Auto Parts every day, like the *pater* most *familias* to me.

What about the future? parents wanted to know. "Hope I die before I get old" was my reply. To a music fiend in a music epoch, a moment when the center of everything pierced the middle of a record, no way to account for the pursuit of song any more than the pursuit of sex—especially when, for a brief, shining moment, they were one and the same.

* * *

WE'D JUST PICKED UP THE CATS' kidneys from the butcher when Fred said: "Look at that ass . . . " It was a damply intense note I had not previously registered from my friend.

"You want to . . . touch it?" I asked. Turned out the only thing Fred liked more than rock 'n' roll was ass—touching it and much more—and Lennie's was ready. Lennie Katz, the girl with the cab driver name.

"Funny thing," Fred would tell me after, "she plays piano."

I could see it coming, even though girls in bands weren't a thing, even though girls in bands—to some boys in bands—seemed an undue complication, even though a petite pretty girl—to some fey, skinny boys—didn't exactly scream marauder. Even though it was clear—to Fred, more than anyone—that this particular girl was crazy. Not just dizzy or kooky or other girl-hater knocks—certifiable.

Neither that, nor any other variety of unabashed prejudice, could deter Fred, who helped Lennie pick out a new Fender Rhodes and invited her down to the boiler room. How are you going to say fuck that, when he's your friend and benefactor and the girl is sitting right there?

We counted off, and she had the thing turned up way too loud, not having a clue about amps or electric pianos or, for that matter, bands. Sure, she could play the notes—unlike the rest of us, she could even read music. But that's not what it was about.

Besides, she was crazy.

Of course, in rock 'n' roll, in a band of would-be Visigoths and a time of tearing down, crazy was not generally a term of opprobrium. Anyway, this crazy keyboardist was the one with the rock 'n' roll pedigree. Her older sister, to Lennie's chagrin, had written a bestseller about the two of them as high-end groupies—McCartney's name was bandied about—and Lennie had also worked as a publicist for the Carpenters. I wasn't quite sure what to make of those accomplishments. Groupie, well, OK. But the Carpenters? Later, when the gorilla who owned the biggest club in Rhode Island strongly suggested we put the hot chick up front, I wanted to say to Fred I told you so.

Yes, I thought Lennie Katz was a drag. But for all the wrong reasons.

* * *

It wasn't long before she'd moved down from her apartment in Le Parasol to Fred's. Ours. Well, Fred's and Steve's. And I got to know her too well.

When I say Lennie was crazy—clinically—I should specify that she suffered from what was called manic-depression and, from time to time, had breakdowns. Little breakdowns, where she'd burst from Fred's room in t-shirt and panties, black hair electric-socketed like Frankenstein's bride, trying with trembly, translucent fingers to light a Virginia Slim. Ask her what's wrong, and she'd shake her hands like they were pom-poms or covered in bugs, before scrambling to a neutral corner. And big breakdowns, like hanging out the window topless, hollering for the Puerto Ricans to come up and fuck, disrupting crosstown traffic the breadth of Lower Manhattan. I got home just in time to see the cops throw on a blanket and spirit her off to Bellevue.

Fred told me it was because she'd stopped her meds.

"Decided she was all better," said Fred.

Thought the meds were doing weird things. Didn't want to take them anymore. Always made sure to hide it—until Fred would get the call from the super or the cops, or come home and find strange men in the house.

I found the meds issue confounding. I decided it was another instance of Lennie being a demanding, self-absorbed asshole. Later, I got my own meds. Sometimes I decided I was better (usually when I was worse). Sometimes I just didn't want to, fucking didn't.

* * *

LENNIE LEARNED ABOUT ELECTRIC PIANOS AND amps and bands, and ours got good enough to get an agent—which was a big deal—and to seal it, the agent passed around a sickly-sweet pint of Southern Comfort, trying too hard to be Janis Joplin, and then took the new drummer to bed—trying too hard to be Janis. And she booked us a tour—a short jaunt through New England, but a tour nonetheless. And one achingly sunny day found our fresh-faced gang of desperados—including Jerry, our 9E neighbor, number one fan and now chief roadie—stuffed into Stern's prehistoric station wagon, alongside the guitars, bass and keyboard, wobbling down the freeway into Providence, as Fred and Lennie, with the drums and amps, struggled behind in his laughably under-powered microbus.

The gig was for a rock 'n' roll week. Not just a couple sets, or 20 minutes before a headliner. The stage would be ours, all night, five nights, at the biggest club in Rhode Island. The agent had sent a contract for eighteen-hundred heretofore unimaginable dollars and secured us digs among the hippies and design students of Benefit Street. I had really good hair—"caveman hair," my tight-lipped friend Bob called it—faded black jeans and a BSA motorcycle shirt, if not yet a motorcycle. After all that work in the boiler room, after toiling in bands since my ankle-boots had scandalized my grade school, after the proto version of Romper Room (with me and Adam) had scandalized a Harkness talent show ("Something's wrong with that boy!" the headmaster's wife exclaimed, when the singer in the silver pith helmet dropped his pants), after the ire of Zeldovich, wrath of parents and puzzlement and ridicule of sensible friends, I was primed.

Silent, but grinning loudly, I watched Rhode Island roll up in reverse from the wayback seat and had the discrete thought—even thinking I should mark it, *nota bene,* for posterity—that this camaraderie, youth, freedom, anticipation, sex, money, highway, sunshine and blue sky, this whole world and ridiculous idea, this impossible holy-shit, had just busted wide. Then a commercial came on the radio, and over a raucous bed of rock 'n' roll that sounded strangely familiar—wait, is that . . . ?—a big, corny DJ, like the AM wise guys of childhood, reverberated from the dash:

"If you like the Stones, you'll loooooove Romper Room (-oom-oom-oom-oom . . .)!"

And, just like that, there was nowhere to go but down.

Part II

CHAPTER 12
211

I TURNED 19 IN THE BOILER room with Fred, reclassified, as a college dropout, to 1A, the most dreaded Selective Service status: fully eligible to be plucked, sheared and dispatched, posthaste, to a shooting war in Southeast Asia—depending, that is, on lottery number. The draft lottery was an audacious new attempt at domestic pacification, a government initiative intended somehow to ease citizen anxiety by concentrating it into a single mega-anxious day.

This was that day.

In the Hollywood biopic of my life—the one I'd been filming in my head since the limo to Harkness—I could imagine the fateful newspaper page with my number wafting along on the belchings of the 14th Street subway before coming to rest, in close-up, on a pair of well-scuffed Beatle boots. Mine. Cut to: one cool customer, BSA shirt and shades, who doesn't bother to look down. Music up: "I Can See for Miles."

But in the docudrama I was living, the shot was wide and the star fetal, in a filthy, borrowed bedroom under a greasy, borrowed pillow, beset by thoughts that might have been beamed directly from his parents. Thoughts like:

OK, fake biker, now we'll see how cool.

Along with thoughts like:

Fuck.

I was rooting for storied luck, to be dead last of all the 19-year-olds in all of dick-owning America, Mister 365 (even as I worried such an attitude might spark the cosmos to irony). Then again, dead first—number one—might make for an even cooler story. If I returned to tell it. The jungle-war lotto operated by an arcane formula way beyond a math flunky, but the newspaper offered a straightforward rule of thumb: number under 100, start packing; above 100, stand down.

As if numbers weren't already scary enough.

I didn't feel like I thought I would on lottery day. I didn't feel righteous. I didn't feel rebellious or tough. I certainly didn't feel cool. I didn't even feel fatalistic. I felt stupid. Small. Film breaks, houselights on. I felt angry, too. At Mother (of course), who with endless fulminations about my war-hero grandfather, his blinded hero uncle and all the other manly mutilated of the family tree had bullied me out of becoming a conscientious objector. I wanted to write Sandy, but he was a Navy guy. More than anything, I felt stupid.

The front door of the apartment slammed. I heard Fred call out, in taunting singsong.

"Oh, Thomas . . . "

I'd long since dragged the band into the drama—even as I pretended it was about my concern for *their* futures, losing a front man. In a fog of apprehension, I cracked the bedroom door, and the band's bass player, my friend, flashed the *Daily News.*

I knew what this meant. I did not know if the towering arch of Fred's eyebrow signified I'd lost the lottery or won. Either way, it was no time for comedy. Breathless, simultaneously unmoving and shaking like crazy, I managed to open the paper to where his thumb had bookmarked it and scan down to my birthdate: November 1.

Day of the Dead. I know.

As I traced an unsteady line from date to numerical fate, Fred put a fist to his mouth and giggled, a girlish squeak. I tried to remind myself what the experts had said. Tried a few calculations of my own. Checked two or three times more, before slapping the paper back in his hand, now only fake-mad.

As a story, my number was entirely unsatisfying, exemplifying neither amazing good luck, nor amazing bad. This was never going to be a tabloid morality tale, with humiliating before-and-after shots, about a local rocker getting his sissy hair buzzed just before getting his just desserts Over There. Not this number: an ordinary ordinal from the upper-middle range. And completely safe.

Like me, I feared.

* * *

We counted off on the stage of the littlest state's biggest club just past sunset of the rock 'n' roll sabbath. With the rhythm section under the lash of our new non-Steve drummer—an unlikely music-biz vet named Pete—I went maniac, scrambling atop the PA, leaping into the crowd, dousing myself with beer, growling, yowling, prancing, pouting, crawling across the dance-floor and then, as the band continued behind me, bounding upright to conduct nonsensical *Bandstand*-like interviews with the dancers, making fun of Dick Clark schmaltz—and a perfecly innocent audience.

"What's your favorite smell?" I'd shout over the noise, bouncing around the room to sniff at necks and feet and butts, boys and girls alike.

"Where do you go to school?" I'd ask and then lead the crowd in an improvised varsity chant of "Go, Shitballs! We are the Shitballs!"

I'd ask someone for a match and, while they were looking, produce my own and light the cigarette myself. Or grasp a length of my own caveman hair and light that.

Sometimes I'd ask for money: "Hey, you! Gimme a buck." Sometimcs I'd give them a buck.

Or a sock. A sweaty, stinky sock that, dropping to a seated position on the dancefloor, making every effort to accentuate the awkwardness, I would peel from my foot and arc over the audience.

Once or twice, showing off a life-saving skill I'd acquired at summer camp, I found the biggest guy in the house, swung him onto my back in a fireman's carry and charged into the crowd. Other times, I'd close my eyes and pretend I was a monster. "Blind Frankenstein!" I'd cry, staggering about with stiffened legs, bouncing off walls, posts, and customers. Sometimes I'd steal a guy's drink at the bar and—shades of Johnny Shannon—run outside into traffic and down the hatch. It was juvenile, goofy—more Jerry Lewis than Dino—but, in a drunk, impulsive way, not entirely devoid of craft. A meta-commentary on singers trying so hard *not* to be goofy, clinging to their barroom pedestals, 24 symbolic inches above the audience. A meta-commentary, I might comment now, that went utterly unnoticed by a Saturday night bar crowd. It also went unnoticed that the first night in Providence—inadvertently solving a long festering personal problem—I stomped on the base of a falling microphone stand and slammed the SM58 into my mouth, only to spit out a tongueful of fragments that, I'd discover later, comprised a large, triangular chunk of my formerly buck teeth.

Some nights the audience would go all the way. A girl might actually give me the dollar or somehow answer the question or otherwise get in the spirit. And her greaser boyfriend would get pissed. And things would devolve. Like an Andy Kaufman bit, where getting the audience mad was part of the fun, I'd succeeded in getting a rise. Just as the encounter would begin to boil over—here's where the craft came in, arguably—I'd dash back to the stage, clamber atop the amps and rendezvous with the ongoing song at the chorus, delivering a hellhound scream of my own. Which, on top of the booze and cigarettes, would leave me near-voiceless the next night, forced to hoot and holler even louder, on an endless cycle of vocal-cord suicide. Somehow I never missed a step of the dashing or climbing, only once in a while missed a chorus. Though back at the band house, at four in the morning, one of the more sensible members might ask if I could maybe do the show sober one night? Still, even they had to admit, whether craft or substance, it was some kind of show. When a few years later rock 'n' roll turned into capital-p Punk, Adam Stern called me out of the blue and said, "See what you started."

But at the end of this gig, pressing the beer-belly of his most sincere affection against the girl keyboardist he had pressed us to put center-stage, the biggest club's big, hairy owner—not, I gathered, a connoisseur of meta-commentary—confided to Lennie:

"You guys are OK, but that singer's got to go."

At the end of the tour, the agent had no more shows.

* * *

NOTHING'S TOO TRIVIAL TO ESCAPE DETECTION in the confines of a full-time band. One thing that didn't escape mine was that the otherwise magnanimous Adam Stern had consolidated all his neuroses into the annoying habit of always bumming sips and drags. One day in the boiler room, exhaling a long stream of burning Marlboro—before handing me back the overheated cig and gesturing for a chaser of Yoo-Hoo—Stern, addressing whichever Fred fixation was then under band scrutiny, blurted, with a smoky snort-laugh:

"Fred, you're crazy!"

Fred was. Not like Lennie, not clinically. Not at first. Since Fred was also quiet—mute, compared to some of us—when his crazy spilled over, his obsessions with asses or Elvis or Puerto Ricans, it was all the more surprising. And I'm not looking to excuse him.

Or maybe I am.

Because Fred had once been generous and kind to me without limit—never hesitated, never lorded over, steadfastly waved off gratitude—and that deserves honor. At least, mine.

Between Fred's craziness and Lennie's, between niggling Adam, pussywhipped Sean and that no-good drunken loudmouth of a singer, the band's unraveling was—like, I guess, every other noble human enterprise—fated.

Sean was first to bail—his girlfriend didn't like the long hours, the travel and him not entirely under her thumb. Stern made it a few more months, until his b-school acceptance arrived. Fred never officially quit the band—just life, later. Most affecting, Pete the New Drummer hung in there.

Pete came from Canarsie, when it was tough and far, with a father, like Bruce's, who drove a bus. He was a unique combo of super-accomplished ponytailed dude—without the greasy ponytail or rancid pessimism—and a guy who still loved to fuck shit up. He had played *Bandstand* with a one-hit-wonder vocal group at 15 and a few years later toured the country with a blue-eyed soul band before the record company renamed them Hall and Oates. Surprisingly old—at 24—when he answered our *Voice* ad, he would teach me everything I know, technically, about music, how immaculate craft can advance the most intoxicated chaos.

You get so close in a full-time band—before you get so mad—that a breakup is never really orderly. This one neither. Loony Lennie went to Bellevue again. When she did, loony Fred fucked

Alkie Abby, my once (and future) girlfriend. And I fucked snooty Trina, Sean's girl—who'd been plotting to fuck me after she found out Sean also fucked Abby. Stern didn't seem to mind I fucked Maya, his old hippie flame (but only after she forced me to endure Black Oak Arkansas, on repeat), taking exception when I tried to make out with his new preppie chick. Lennie flipped out all over again when she got out and discovered Abby with Fred. Fred had some kind of ghastly makeup sex with Lennie, and Abby promptly retaliated with Jerry the roadie.

It went on like that, a rock 'n' roll begats-in-reverse, until my friend Fred slipped further, and they put him on his own meds. My friend Abby slipped further, and they put her in rehab. And I quit the band when Pete the New Drummer—seeking frontiers beyond 4/4—rallied some replacement players to learn a Jethro Tull tune. I re-joined the next day when he assured me it was a fleeting thought. The minute the 14th Street lease was up, Steve the old drummer showed up to announce he was done paying for my fucking room and to keep the creepy mattress. Fred didn't have the money to carry the lease, and I certainly didn't. We evacuated Le Parasol, losing not only our home, no matter how foul, but our practice room, no matter how perilous. The day of the move, riding low with gear and furniture, Fred's microbus dropped its transmission on Sixth Avenue. Which was just perfect.

Romper Room, summarily cancelled.

* * *

SADNESS, ANGER, AND REGRET REVERBERATED THROUGH the post-band hollow like that DJ on the car radio: *Romper Room-oom-oom-oom* . . . Embarrassment, too—there'd be no paying back friends and lovers from a rock star's treasure. And after years stuffed together in basements, cars and underpowered vans, it had sure turned cold. Those guys weren't just my band, they were my bubble. They were also my future. Now what? A new band? How long will that take? What about the songs? I didn't write any—well, none I wanted to sing. Not only would I have to depend on new players, they'd have to be writers. Good ones—I wasn't a guy to go for any old tune. I also wasn't a guy to depend. And what about the money, until the money rolls in? Meanwhile, at the advanced age of 19: tick-fucking-tock. In five years. I'd be older than the new drummer—and he'd been on black-and-white TV!

Romper Room, summarily crushed.

* * *

But not quite done.

After a while, we even played music. Not all of us, all together, that really was done. And not often. A few weeks after I'd decided I needed a more solitary endeavor, without drummers and bassists and bands, and began scheming to start over in California, Fred, following a months-long hiatus, called to ask, "Why don't you come down to the Porch?" Having lost its liquor license for serving underaged drinkers, the Porch had turned into a juice bar where underaged opiate users could fork over five bucks for a fruit-syrup concoction and a chance to nod in safety for an hour or two. Fred said, I'm playing with this great new drummer—different great new drummer—and there might be a guest. I slipped back into black denim and BSA and headed to MacDougal.

The drummer was good in a narrower way than Pete, a white guy who turned everything he touched into funk—but good funk. We did Stones, Geils, Yardbirds—best of the white-on-Black blues—I even whipped out the mouth harp. The whole thing reminded me there was nothing more glorious than hollering over a groove. Then the drummer's friend, the guest, stepped onstage with his cherry

Gibson, unleashing a series of blasts that were slinky and slashing and soaring, and we made a joyous noise till the last clueless junkie went home.

Next day the phone rang at my new house on my old friend Tiger's cat-infested couch, and it was the drummer from the Porch with—to a guy who usually slept past noon and had never experienced a business lunch—a surprising invitation. We met in the Village at Leonardo's—the coal-oven pizza joint with the tub in the bathroom—and the drummer formally introduced me to the bashful SG-slinger:

"Tom, Sam Andrew."

Though the famous locks had been stylishly sheared, I knew. From the night before I knew his playing to be more striking than ever—although, unlike Janis's notorious manager, I never thought Big Brother—including Sam—was anything less than a pounding magnificence. Perfect for the bleeding-lung Queen of Port Arthur.

But Janis Joplin was more than a year gone. And she'd been gone from Big Brother—peeled away by manager and foolish label—for a year before that. She'd tried to hold Sam over in the new band, the "professional" one. Soon enough, he knew better. If separating from him didn't kill her directly, it killed her music: buried alive in the sheen. Now Janis's old guitarist, the drummer explained, was in New York looking for a new singer.

Which is when Sam interrupted to say, almost inaudibly, if incredibly: "I've found him."

When Father had said I looked like a "fag" from *Life*, he specifically meant the one whose flowing, chest-length mane had freaked him out the most. And here, in the leather-swaddled, rock-star flesh, asking for me—a nobody—to be lead singer, was none other. For once, overenthusiasm was inadequate.

Here's the fucked-up part. After all those teachers, parents, faithless friends and bar gangsters, after boiler rooms, brokedown vans, brokedown bands and broke and homeless, after all that sweaty work and desperate play and unreasoning faith and eventual mesothelioma, it was as if that was enough. To be asked. By Sam himself.

"Let me think about it," I said to the guitar god.

Just a few hours later I called the drummer to say I'd already signed on for a new adventure, sorry, going to San Francisco, please tell Sam:

"No."

* * *

FRED MADE A BIG POINT OF apologizing for fucking Abby. While I'm aware that apologizing can be a thing spiteful people do to rub your nose in it (I've had people apologize out of spite and one was a friend named Lester), that wasn't Fred. It had been more than a year since I'd seen him, which meant, I was acutely aware, it had been more than a year since I'd failed to make my escape west. I could've been the next Janis Joplin by now. Instead, I was driving a cab and living, rent-free, alone, in the maid's room at Adam Stern's mother's place, a handsome, rent-controlled apartment on West 96th so big I had my own entrance. Fred had tracked me down through Stern and insisted on coming over immediately. I told him I had to get some sleep before my shift.

"Could we do it tomorrow?"

Twenty minutes later, he stepped into my tiny room, and, without ceremony or delay, without sitting, without, for that matter, stopping, commenced to pace beside the bed. He told me he knew I'd been avoiding him (not, technically, true), but that, worse, he'd been avoiding me. He wanted me to know how terribly ashamed he was of everything and went on to embroider his shame with the most gruesome erotic details of the affair with my ex. Trying not to flinch, I immediately waved it all off, figuring the faster the absolution, the sooner he'd be gone.

Fred was crazy, yes. Until now, I didn't think he was also coked up. He was rat-a-tat-rapping about how this new punk shit was shit and how he was playing his own originals with a rockabilly crew—here, check it out. As I listened to a cassette with the words "14th Street" roughly Magic-Markered across its plastic case, Fred giggled into his fist, the girlish squeak. The tune was Sun Records with a pinch of Salsa, the once-voiceless bassist crooning a creditable Elvis over an unhinged cowbell. The lyrics—ironic, with an odd note of pathos—imagined a lonely Puerto Rican superintendent sneaking in to a tenant's apartment and falling in love with a photo of the tenant's daughter. The chorus was about her ass. There was a lot to process when Fred finally left.

* * *

FRED NEVER LEFT LE PARASOL. HE left it physically, but not any other way. I saw him a few more times after the midnight mea culpa. He invited me to his shows—one time I even went—but he never again asked me to play. Considered me a Judas because I told him I liked some of the new music (which to him was anything after *Exile on Main Street*). Gave up on me. But not on the creed, slipping into a death-spiral of bad to worse bands, last-gasp hustlers who hired the aging nutjob for what was left of his beauty. To sustain that beauty, Fred lifted weights, bronzed his skin and, as his thick mane began to gray, turned it back to black, all the while continuing to rail against the new barbarians who were taking over the bum bars where the true barbarians had once had the stage to themselves.

Finally, one day, Fred died.

Not literally, not yet. Fred's faith crumbled, and his soul died. With the help of his long-suffering mom, he ran the rock 'n' roll biopic in reverse, back before that call from the singer. Finished law school and landed a job at Legal Aid. But it wasn't defending the indigent, for near-indigent wages, that sucked the joy out, said my friend, it was defending the indefensible.

Still, all in a day's work and fine, just fine. Until the moment it wasn't.

Which is when Fred flew over the table at the umpteenth filthy, lying rapist, the client he was sworn to champion, and beat him unconscious and would have to death, if the gobsmacked guards hadn't wrestled him off—four, it took, with Fred's weightlifting. Legal Aid put him on psych leave, and the doc put him on new meds, and the DA offered the filthy, lying rapist a pass—if he shut up about Fred. Six months later Fred finally headed back to work and driving his old VW bus with a new transmission up the Grand Concourse was t-boned by a truck.

* * *

FRED BEGGED JERRY. COMMANDED HIM. RAISED a croaky whisper and ordered his friend, neighbor and roadie:

"Put the pills in my mouth! All the pills, Jer."

But Jerry, who'd loved Fred since first tracing an unholy racket in his apartment building to a band in the boiler room, couldn't. And Fred couldn't because the truck had severed his spinal cord.

Fred couldn't feed himself, clean himself, lift weights, play bass, make love to Abby or Lennie or jump off a roof. He couldn't be a rock star—but that was old news. So Fred had a new dream that was the sum of all the dreams he'd been denied. And it wasn't a year before his lungs filled with fluid, and they all came true.

CHAPTER 13

Flare

BEFORE SHE TOOK UP WITH FRED, after the band went kablooey—before I broke up with her for the final-final, but after I was full-time cheating, before I saved her life—Abby saved mine. Not like rock 'n' roll saved Bruce. Or Fred—who, no matter what he believed, rock 'n' roll actually killed. Saved it for real.

My first real girlfriend—that is, the first girl I wanted to hang around with more than the boys—Abby was bright. She was wild. And with her cartoon faces and inverted, little-kid hand motions, her tomboy gait and monumental bray of a voice (nearly as loud as mine), she was funny as hell. I'd had my eyes on her since she was Barry Quinn's first in eighth grade. When Barry, a six-six T-rex of a boor, clomped off to greener canopies, I quickly offered his ex consolation. She didn't need much. Beneath the hand-me-down-preppie exterior, Abby was weird, too—naturally, normally, deeply. So much so it used to make me—a guy trying his ass off with straw helmet and baby sunglasses—grit teeth in envy. Meet her family, and there was nothing put-on. Of a sincerely odd bunch, she was only the least. Best of all, when we started to drink—regularly and hard, at 13—Abby was game. Not a lot of St. Cecilia's girls were.

Her parents said we started too soon. Our friends said it was the drinking. I thought it had gone south the summer after high school when, with barely a word, Abby had gone south—away with a rich girlfriend and the friend's family for an all-expense, month-long sojourn in Mexico. I was jealous, in every way, as only an excitable boy could be. Though our affiliation persisted, through attempted college, attempted bands and a fully realized druggie mess on Bank Street, I thought Mexico was when we really died. Still, like a carelessly extinguished campfire, the thing with Abby had a way of flaring.

* * *

I WAS IN THE THROES OF my half-hearted higher education when I spotted my main chance and soon had taken up residence in storied Greenwich Village. The scheme had come together around a fortuitous bit of family woe, when I had assured our parents that, if they would help out with an apartment, I would help out with their son Roger. In the prep school manner of disgorging miscreants they can't catch red-handed, baby bro had been invited *not* to return for his senior year at Essex Academy. With our folks in the thick of their evacuation from the dusky hordes, pushy tribes and inappropriately attired of New York City, en route to a well-creased, white Christian enclave in Florida, Roger's abrupt lack of guardianship loomed as more than an inconvenience. They weren't mad at their 16-year-old for getting kicked out of prep school or imperiling the tranquility of their golden years—after all, the boy was weak-minded. But they were cognizant of the legal exposure in abandoning a minor child. At the same time, with his long hair and drugs, they couldn't have him hanging around the shuffleboard courts. Recognizing how my proposition could mitigate all of that, they agreed not to further derange the delicate one and instead let him finish high school in New York—while living under the most conscientious supervision with me, his loving brother. I tracked down a reasonably priced 2BR on Bank Street in the teeming entrails of the modern Gomorrah, and our elders beat a grateful retreat to sunscreen and segregation.

None of these machinations were lost on little bro, who pounced on another aspect of the proposition—50,000 drug-sucking college kids within a 20-block radius of our new apartment—to aggressively expand the trade in Schedule 1 narcotics that had got him tossed from Essex in the first place. One time I came home to find a strung-out NYU classmate waiting on my couch. Another time, a well-known model. Soon Roger was zipping down Bleecker Street—sometimes with the model wrapped around him—astride a purple Triumph Bonneville, and, back home, plugging in a '59 Les Paul Sunburst that Sean said must have set him back five or six grand. Lately, his loving supervisor hadn't heard from him in a week. I assumed he was down in Medellin making plans with Pablo Escobar. It wasn't long after he returned that, while I stared forlornly at the single-ply sheetrock separating our rooms, my baby brother started in with the downstairs neighbor.

It was a three-story brownstone, and she was on the first floor, top of the stoop, with Roger and I one flight above that. Top floor, above us, was a gaggle of young ballerinas from the Joffrey, who, as dedicated artist-athletes, proved to be no fun at all. When Roger and I moved in, the building, according to the landlord, was in the midst of a "comprehensive renovation."

"That's why it's a mess," he said cheerfully.

It took a month or two for us to realize that the renovation had been over for a long time—mostly before it started—and the crumbling, half-spackled mess was simply the shithole where we now lived. Periodically, Howard Held would stop by to pick up a rent check or inspect the work. (Or not really.) He was a thirty-something headshrinker by trade, and, by inclination, exactly the scumbag I thought he was. But it was the criminally slapdash construction—especially a staircase that swayed like an Andean rope bridge—that really got my goat. Hearing Howard on the steps one afternoon, I leaped into the hall to suggest, not for the first time, that he might want to reduce our rent to reflect our reduced circumstances. When he dismissed me—not for the first time—with a disgusted backhand, I reached down to the bottom step and gave a protracted yank to the rickety staircase's raggedy carpet-runner, causing tacks to pop, two-by-two, one step at a time, forcing the shrink to scramble half-a-flight up to the neighbors. As he ran from the rising rug, the Harvard-trained psychiatrist called out in panic to the other residents:

"Is this guy *crazy?!?*"

When Howard claimed to be inspecting the work, he was usually inspecting his female tenants, or trying to, and he had a particular thing for our downstairs neighbor. That's not why I was mad. Though it did occur to me that, since I was not immediately evicted, arrested or shot with the nickel-plated revolver Howard liked to flash at the building's late-night gatherings, the neighbor in question may have bribed him with a protracted yank of her own. Not entirely out of devotion to me. Sex, for Jackie Florio, was just a way to get high.

Another way, since she was also into getting high.

* * *

JACKIE WAS MARRIED TO A DIFFERENT psychiatrist, a medical school classmate of the landlord's (that's how they found the apartment). She was also my girlfriend. My other. After she was my brother's. And I loved her madly.

I don't know if it was the scent of a restless woman or scent of a rogue doc cranking out free prescriptions or just a sputtering neon sign of the times—that woozy interregnum after *Let It Bleed*, before

Kiss Alive—but word in the Village was out. Lord Dan received the transmission. A wooly-haired artist manager, weed dealer and ex-junkie, Dan lived directly across the street and, though perfectly sound of gait, affected a silver-headed cane—hence the nickname—with which he'd rap at Jackie's window each evening to herald his entrance. In the sixties, he had guided the career of the one-hit-wonder known to almost no one since as Starlight, and later the blues shouter Nappy Brown, whose indelible anti-hymn, "Thanks for Nothing," would, under His Lordship's dubious tutelage, become one of R&B's great missed hits. Half-a-block west, the carnival had engulfed my NYU friend Stuttering Jim, a sardonic, two-tour Viet vet with a speech disorder, limp and lumberjack's appetite for methaqualone, who was back in academia, on disability and the G.I. Bill, to wring sense of it all from Mailer, Vonnegut, Burroughs and *Screw* magazine. A couple hundred feet east, it swept in a towering young jewelry maker with a supercilious manner and immaculate ponytail, Brett, an acidhead, whose minimalist work was touted in *Vogue* and who only seemed gay. While Brett's idea of going too far tended toward the contemplative and discreet, he had a mousy cuz, Susan, who, confirming again the book/cover dichotomy, regularly commuted from Syosset to never get enough of the doctor's medicine, not excluding—audibly, through the vellum-thin bedroom door—his acute boudoir discipline.

All these elements quickly congealed into a perpetual-motion party that swirled the merely curious in with the hard core. There was the big, tough nurse who oversaw the methadone clinic at St. Mary's, who started by popping reds but, pursuing recreational anesthesia to its logical conclusion, ended up on methadone herself. The two Scarsdale hood ornaments (whose doctor-husbands had completed residency with Jackie's), one now divorced, both dedicated followers of fashion—including all the latest in pills and kink. Sometimes the married one brought her husband, an ex-lacrosse jock with a giant dick that his bride liked to complain about, by way of boasting. Then there was Joey Spooner, an up-and-coming post-Catskills comic who was never quite post enough for me and eventually moved from Bank Street to Beverly Hills to be not funny—for bank—on a laugh-track show. It was an odd crew, sometimes a distasteful one—and, without intoxicants, probably no kind of crew at all. Of course, I merged that mob with mine, with Sean and Abby and Bob and Roger and whoever else might of an evening turn up. Which this being then, and there, was everybody.

* * *

NOT FORGETTING JERRY.

On Bank Street, we became friends with a lot of record producers. Any madcap evening, there were always two or three—and guys with real accomplishments, not just bullshit artists (not *only*). But Jerry was the first. And to me, raised on British Invasion producers like George Martin, whose name was on the back of Beatles albums, and Andrew Loog Oldham, whose *signature* was on the back of Stones albums, a guy like Jerry Scott—who'd produced (and written) top-10 hits that had once blasted from my transistor radio—was nothing less than a star.

After meteoric early success, Jerry was coolly riding out a decade of downturn, hustling—at 300 bucks a pop—a cigarette-pack-sized device he'd helped invent that let you call long distance free. Back when long distance, as I well knew, was far from it. Petite, stick-skinny, in crushed-velvet bell-bottoms, round-the-clock yellow aviators and a barely mangy moptop, the Brooklyn-born and -accented producer had squandered all his copyrights, his dibs to future earnings, on the pharmaco-carnal pleasures of Swinging London in its heyday.

His device was called a Blue Box, and Jerry and friends were called Phone Phreaks, later to be memorialized as the harbingers of hacking. But stealing long distance then was federal. One day I came home to find my next-door neighbor at the top of his stoop, flanked by an ostentatiously un-swinging duo in dark suits and ties.

"Hey, Thomas," he cracked. "Like you to meet my friends from the FBI."

He wasn't kidding. It made me wonder whether he had the world's biggest balls, or, as a complete sociopath, no choice. Sure enough the men in black led the balding elf down the steps—in handcuffs, I could now see—to a black sedan.

I ran inside and blurted the news to Jackie, daughter of a Mafia doctor, who'd learned early to keep secrets. Steely, as if she'd drilled it, she pulled a locked box from behind the socks in a bottom bureau drawer and handed me copies of Jerry's keys, insisting I go collect his Blue Boxes for safekeeping. Me, specifically, she said, because I had the least to lose.

Beyond a natural reticence to commit federal crime, I resented that she was carving me out of the gang. And "least to lose," I wanted to say, is still not nothing. But I went. I unlocked the front door and, in Jerry's bedroom closet, behind racks and racks of high-heeled boots in black leather, brown suede, blue suede, snake-skin, ostrich and alligator, found the satchel of Blue Boxes and tried to hide it under my jacket as I scuttled down the stoop where the Feds had collared Jerry, up the stoop next door and then one more flight to our place—where Roger had just filled the freezer with mandatory-sentencing quantities of psychedelic mushrooms and the dresser in his room with who-knows-what (I certainly didn't, because he'd taken to padlocking it)—all the while imagining government motor-drives clicking a million close-ups.

I didn't want to be carved out.

Late that night, unshaken in yellow shades and red velvet, the prodigal producer returned from jail and, with barely a howdy-do, much less a thanks, retrieved his contraband, along with his privileged place in the Bank Street bacchanal.

* * *

I NEVER LIKED TO TALK ABOUT the doc. Jackie's doc, the husband. Thoughts of him brought up questions that could only be answered—even when everything was up for grabs, when up-for-grabs was the mandate—in the most antediluvian terms. Starting with: Thou shalt not commit adultery.

He was a slight, left-handed 33-year-old of elliptical gestures, fly-away hair, wire-rimmed specs and a State of New York prescription pad, who had recently ascended to Chief of Psychiatry, youngest ever, at St. Mary's. By any measure, professional achievement or IQ, he was brilliant. But for all the time we spent together and all the secret shit he shared, the doctor remained, at his core, unknowable—the secret shit said aloud merely a smokescreen for the standard, sadder shit behind it. Still, if he was afraid to tell, you were afraid to ask. To scrutinize the doc in that open sore of a moment might be to finally disclose too much of yourself. Even to scrutinize him later remained fraught, a plunge into Catholic regret and the metaphysical black. Because two years after the bash finally crashed, the doc got high one more time and, not a five-minute stroll from the old place, ten months into their trial separation, tumbled from a roof.

I never liked to talk about the doc. Jackie did.

She was an actor long before she went pro, and I fell for it every time. Vexed at her husband for too much time spanking cousin Susan, she confided, through a convincing patina of tears, that Bank Street had all been his idea. All of it—the fucking other people, the drugs, the ridiculous stereo system. In Hartsdale, she'd been the model of the doctor-in-waiting's lady-in-waiting—sober, demure, dedicated to the support of medical ladder-climbing. Then he'd told her his psyche needed to soar. Affecting the deeply attentive manner that epitomized medical solicitude and scientific deliberation—an actor of sorts himself—the young physician persuaded his wife to do the overendowed ex-jock, while he did the humble-braggart wife.

"That," Jackie sobbed, "was the beginning."

From the start, more than the liberation of one libido, the doc envisioned the liberation of all. First rays of the new rising sun of the golden road of unlimited imagination—or something. No denying it was warmed-over Haight-Ashbury—from a guy carrying too many advanced biology courses to partake the first time—but what more could a lapsed altar boy ask?

On Bank Street, thanks to the doc—his libertine vision, no less than his professional accreditation—we had every vision in the *PDR*. Every night Jerry the Producer would install himself in the living room to produce new mayhem, poring over that official omnibus of potions and spells and periodically shouting above the clamor—of *Transformer, Innervisions, All the Young Dudes* and, mostly, *A Wizard, A True Star*—"Hey, doc, how many of these to get high? What about this combo?"

We popped downs of every sort, ups of every sort, and pills with directions yet uncharted. We huffed, puffed, sniffed, slurped, chipped, and some of us mainlined. When Jerry tired for the moment of exploring the frontiers of legal pharma, he'd ask the doc for a more fungible script—for Quaaludes or Benzedrine—that he could barter on the street for coke, weed or animal tranquilizer. Jerry stayed away from smack, because he'd seen too many pathetic junkies in music. Though the nurse from St. Mary's felt no such compunction, she mostly kept her heroin to herself. Mostly. We got high, chain-smoked Marlboros—or, in Jerry's case, English Ovals—guzzled brown liquors, clear liquors, Day-Glo liqueurs, and, for 59 cents a quart at the bodega, truckloads of barely carbonated Old Bohemian beer. We fucked, sucked, and fumbled each others' flesh and, in the end, made all the doc's fantasies come true

* * *

Except for maybe Abby (who harbored more secrets than I'd ever guessed), I'm sure I was the most enthusiastic drinker in that crowd. Partly it was because of the flashbacks. For half a decade, the flashbacks were a fixture of my existence. They started near the end of senior year at Harkness. Bursting with anticipation of my impending release, my overexuberance had signed me up for a weekend excursion with my old chum Adam Stern and his friend, the flamboyantly moody August Miller III, another Harkness kid who fancied himself an artist. The pair had plans to camp in the wilds of Augie's family's estate—a private property bigger than most state parks—and drop acid. L.L. Bean meets Captain Trips. They didn't invite me, and may not, it dawned later, have wanted me—too unwoodsy and way too unquiet. That was OK, I invited myself.

Once more, my overexuberance forgot I hated the woods and camping, and compounded the error by scarfing brown blotter, which turned out to be famously bad. I thought Miller—now moved to painterly tears by the flames of sunset on the pond—was maneuvering to rape me soon as it got dark. And I damn near froze to death after throwing my new space-cowboy coat at Stern—who never gave it back—because in his own drug-induced mania, he couldn't stop fondling its fringe. When at the peak of that indescribable unpleasantness—no, it was terror—I insisted we get the fuck out of the forest and find civilization, we wound up at a hillbilly diner—who knew there were hillbillies in Connecticut?—where it took a shattering mental eternity for Stern to figure out they weren't serving us because, to a hillbilly, shaggy preppies looked like hippies. Meanwhile, they looked like that horse in *Guernica.*

It was enough to give anyone flashbacks. After mine began, I became convinced that—per the experts in *Life* magazine—I had chemically icepicked a critical chunk of my thunk. It wasn't until the doc told me about this thing called an anxiety attack that I felt better—knowing there might be an explanation other than DIY brain damage—and better still when he wrote me a script for Valium, of which I became indecently fond.

* * *

BUT BOOZE WAS MY BASE. I could trust it to get me buzzed, without taking me anywhere near those tangerine trees and marmalade skies. Though if there was one compound that, for me, symbolized that discombobulated periodic table of a period, it wasn't alcohol or Valium or acid. It wasn't speed, which I loved. It wasn't coke, which no one—except Roger—could afford. It wasn't even pot—which, for me, too often, was a shortcut to paranoia and flashbacks. No, it was poppers—the stinky stuff they use to restart old folks' tickers—which were not only new and exciting to me, but convenient: no hours-long commitments, no hillbillies, just a sweet three-minute rocket to the edge of passing out. Soon my stash of prescription amyl nitrate had edged out Roger's psychedelic mushroom business in our kitchen freezer. I was doing poppers like people do coffee—blowing a gasket as pick-me-up. Doing them everywhere, and that included at my new job.

By one of those twists you eventually come to expect from life, I had been hired as an usher for a comedy revue at the Village Gate, that Bleecker Street landmark where Coltrane, Monk and Bill Evans recorded albums and where I was ejected from the dressing room by the lead singer of NRBQ. The new show was a spoof of rock festivals called *Lemmings*. While my rock-snob expectations started low, the cast was rife with uncanny mimics, plausible musicians, kamikaze comics. Funniest, the ushers all agreed, was the short, chubby one who always arrived early, working man's lunchbox in hand, distributed greetings all around and every night executed a note-perfect take on the spasmodic Joe Cocker, collapsing to the stage in the finale to tie off with a mic cord. Many nights, I was in tears laughing. John Belushi was the first actor I'd seen fully possessed of the rocker thing, and I was wistfully certain that, with his chunky frame and catcher's mitt of a mug, the lords of show biz would never let him near any screen.

Every night, after we'd seated the house, before the flashpowder explosion that startled the audience and started the show, I'd snap an ampule under my nose and have a little boom of my own. You didn't have to be an MD to know amys weren't health food, especially not at this frequency. What the hell, it was Belushi and the Village and the end of the world as we knew it. There were brain cells to burn and years before the cancer could kick in. I mention it because poppers have a strong paint-thinner smell—that's the point—and there were plenty the night Abby saved my life.

It was late when I got home from the Gate, later still when I extricated myself from the revels downstairs to rendezvous with Abby, already asleep in my bed upstairs. Underneath the resentments, I sometimes still felt surprising pangs of affection toward her. More surprising, I didn't feel more. As I slipped naked between bare mattress and dirty sheet, I was overcome by a vision of drifting away, drenched in the sweet solvent scent of those yellow ampules. Which is when Abby awakened and said, "Do you smell something?"

"No, no, no, go back to sleep," I murmured and rolled over to blot her out.

* * *

THE FLAMES—REAL FLAMES, NOT BRAIN-DAMAGE HALLUCINATIONS—FILLED the doorframe, floor to ceiling, by the time Abby just wouldn't let it go: first, that she smelled something and then that it must be smoke. You couldn't even see the smoke for the flames by the time I looked. I closed the door, scared, but not panicked—the way you aren't when it's truly life and death—and ran to fill a bucket.

No bucket.

But I did have a wastebasket. One. In the bathroom. I dumped the contents—tissues, wrappers, junk mail, dirty Stridex—onto the bathroom floor and tried to fill it under the slow-pissing shower. Halfway, I got impatient and ran to toss what I had on the growing inferno. Abby rooted around in the kitchen and found a mixing bowl, which she filled and tossed and filled and tossed. The flames were still getting bigger, more ferocious. Every time we opened the door—unwittingly feeding oxygen to the fire—the flames leapt. I shouted for help over Todd Rundgren shouting the perfect soundtrack—"When the Shit Hits the Fan"—through the floorboards. Eventually, Lord Dan heard the cry for help, climbed halfway up the stairs and reached out to beat the fire with his cane. And between my wastebasket, Abby's bowl and Dan's walking stick, we eventually succeeded in extinguishing the blaze. All that remained, atop a charcoaled swatch of carpet-runner, were the soggy, smoldering remnants of a grocery box stuffed with paper towels—the brown institutional kind you might find in a hospital.

While Dan, the doc and Jackie watched silently from the bottom of the stairs, one cop took a report out on the landing from me and Abby together. Then the other cop asked me, friendly-like: "Can I talk to you alone?"

In the living room, close-up, man-to-man, he started telling a story: "So, you've been having trouble with your girlfriend. Things not going so good . . . "

I wondered how he knew.

"And you decide," he went on, "to, you know, *do* something . . . "

Though I was no longer high on anything except adrenaline, it still took a minute to understand.

"What do you mean?"

The cop looked at me, saying nothing, meaning nothing good.

"No, really, officer, what are you saying?"

Then, in my head, I heard it all. Heard the precinct commander pleased to clear the latest arson case with the perfectly credible arrest of a longhaired fuckup. Heard them finding out about all the drugs, not to mention the FBI pictures of me with Jerry's Blue Boxes. Heard a hard-bitten city judge, up from a real neighborhood, more than happy to dispatch a rich kid, with or without portfolio, to Rikers.

I backed away, disgusted, spluttering.

" . . . Burn down my own place?" I gasped. "When I'm *in it???*"

From his jacket pocket the cop flipped his ace: a half-burned piece of junk mail with my name on the front.

"Ohhh!" I said, hand to temple. In a rush, I told him about the wastebasket. Then showed him. Explained how maybe I didn't get everything out before I filled it with water.

"See?"

I reached into the bottom, pulled out a pulpy fragment of a poem, mimed tipping the basket and started to tell the story all over again. And got the feeling that, though the cop didn't believe it, or didn't want to, and would have been fine to keep fucking with me, in the end the nightshift was over, and it was time to head home to Jersey.

"I'll be in touch," he said, a thin smile confirming that it was a threat and a prompt exit that he'd be too lazy.

By the time the fire department arrived to check the fire was truly out, it was daylight. Though the cops had radioed that the situation was in hand, procedure demanded the firemen see for themselves, clomping in boots, helmets and canvas coats up the rope-bridge stairway.

Arriving at the second-floor scene of the crime, the captain jerked a thumb at the stairs and said, without even a forensic trace of amusement: "You oughta get that fixed . . . "

Then one of his men, plucking a brown paper towel from the burned box, called him over. The captain looked, without expression.

"It was arson!" I busted in. "Arson—it had to be!"

The captain would not respond, even when I asked if there'd been other suspicious fires in the neighborhood. Unlike the cop, by now halfway to Hackensack, he was a serious man. All he said was arsonists do it for kicks. And when the firetrucks roll, they're usually watching.

* * *

IT WAS ARSON. THERE WAS NO doubt. Who and why, I refused to guess. It struck me as strange that no one else talked about it, ever. That no one outside of that small circle of witnesses seemed to even know it happened. Our little secret. Keep it in the family. As if we were protecting someone. Or protecting our scene. Or as if they were protecting someone from me. When I was feeling especially trembly—and I was after that, waiting for the firebug to come finish the job—I'd sometimes wonder if it wasn't just another bad trip, if really it had happened at all. Then I'd pop a couple of Valium, huff an amy, and it would all be better. Better, not perfect. So the party didn't end with the fire. Neither did the affair. Still, something gnawed.

I didn't even talk about the fire to Abby. She was freaky enough to say something in response that I didn't want to hear. I wanted to believe what I wanted to believe. And wanted to keep the party going. Anyway, Abby and I had broken up, three or four times over the previous year. Although, judging by the increasing frequency of her visits, before and after the fire, it didn't seem to matter much. It mattered to Jackie, who told me I had to buck up, be a man, tell her it's over, and take back the damn keys.

If you love me, she added.

Well, I did love Jackie. Loved her enough that I wanted to make her my bride if she ever broke up with her husband. And I certainly wanted to be a man. A month or so after the arson I was ardently making that case to Jackie, when Abby walked in on us. If our past breakups had been too namby-pamby to achieve a permanent effect, I had a sense this fleshy tableau might finally do the trick. After the frenzied scramble from the bedroom—with me yanking on jeans and Jackie clutching clothes to her front as her bare butt descended the wobbly stairs—Abby and I sat at either end of my couch, just the two of us, listening to her blubber and snuffle.

From time to time, Abby would pull on a pint of vodka that she extracted from her tote bag or throw back some pills from her purse—but not before catching her own crying face in the living room mirror and wailing all over again. The sadness seemed so bottomless I began to wonder about the biology of it. And it went on so long that, along with feeling horrified, I started to feel flattered: all this for me? Then I felt guilty. Then, the sliding down the couch to offer an arm around (any human being would). The wet cheek on my shoulder. The hugs. The bourbon. Eventually there were the poppers. Soon, as will happen at the perilous intersection of love and hate, there was the fucking. On the couch, half on the couch, on the floor. Fierce, desperate, exhausting breakup sex, *final* breakup sex—which, as the blubbering kicked up again and Abby, astride, splashed her fists, harder and harder, in the tears and sweat on my chest, threatened to turn into something else—before it swerved back, the deep crying, amid the pelvic bashing, now head-back, fully feral, until Abby howled us into nirvana. We fell asleep, naked and tender and entwined on the living room floor—until Roger came home. Amid the comprehensive, catastrophic, humbling, profoundly soggy and ultimate collapse of our bond, it suddenly seemed like we were some kind of back together.

* * *

MORE TRICK BIRTHDAY CANDLE THAN CAMPFIRE, our thing had once again flared. Jackie didn't like it. But I'd started to think Jackie was on shaky ground. On the other hand, the doc thought it was fine, and welcomed my old girlfriend back into the fold. More amazing—in a shift that made my stomach feel funny, when it should have made my heart soar—Abby thought it was fine. As if embracing my new thing—new friends, new kinks, even a new girl, an extra girl—might be just what we needed. Or maybe it was a plan for revenge. Or—the thought didn't occur till later—her turn?

Abby was full-time at Caroline Ward. Her mother had convinced her that, rather than that free-floating la-di-da of a four-year liberal arts college—which they could ill afford—a girl like Abby needed practical money-making skills, a way to get along in the world until she got married and then a way to get along if that husband turned out to be as much of a drunken bum as Abby's father. She sent her to the venerable New York secretarial school for a two-year intensive in typing, shorthand, bookkeeping and personal grooming. With Abby's intelligence and prodigious reading, it seemed a waste. Leave it to Abby to like it. Not the personal grooming, which she hated—but which explains why she was wearing a giant bowtie and tweed suit when she opened the bedroom door on me and Jackie naked. The rest of it, especially the shorthand, she loved, frequently whipping out her special notebook to transcribe our conversations, overheard bar chat, even *The Mary Tyler Moore Show* into the scribble-scrabble of Pitman Shorthand. It was weird—a mixture of surreal and square—and funny, with a tinge of sad. Which largely describes Abby.

Who was very much back.

Temporarily, she said. Commuting daily to Caroline Ward, she stuffed my closet with her dowdy Caroline Ward clothes and my living room with her cheery Caroline Ward books. At night, she'd ditch the suit, tie and stockings and head downstairs to party. I didn't know how she did it—up late, up early—until I saw the vodka in the tote bag. But Abby was so back, so much throwing herself into it that, one late night, when I left the party, Abby stayed. This wasn't normal. Nothing was normal then, but this wasn't how it had ever gone before. I was the guy who stayed, no matter what, no matter who was bugging me to do otherwise. I was the guy: didn't stop, didn't go.

Until—one time—I did.

Still don't know why. Except, being there in that room with those people—my new friends and my old friend—looking at it all through Abby's squinty blues, in the context of Abby, the innocence we'd shared and, in collaboration, shed, in the context of her and of that, and in the context of something that definitely *continued to gnaw*, it started to seem like the doc's new rising sun might be headed for a total eclipse. What could I do, in my condition? And, after all, this was the new thing, not the easy thing. No room for sentimentality in a revolution (we learned that from Chairman Mao). I looked into her eyes. I wanted to say to Abby this wasn't high school: badly rolled joints in Central Park, dad's pain pills at the Who, shitfaced at the junior dance and just-the-tip with her party dress on. This was different. I was different. I was part of this now. And different as she was, she wasn't. Anyway, we were kaput. She wasn't mine anymore. She wasn't me. In fact, at a time of no-limit and no-judgment, I was getting too used to thinking of her—cruelly, cravenly—as my one and only embarrassment. Wasn't this a case in point? Leaning on the doorjamb downstairs in his shades at four am, one bracelet-spangled arm slung around a crookedly grinning Abby—*who definitely wanted to stay*—Jerry the Producer taunted that, at 18, I must be getting old.

"Abby . . . ?" I said.

"We'll take care of her," the washed-up star-maker pledged, with the cackle that was actually his regular laugh. Later, he loaded a needle-less syringe with a preparation of vodka and tuinals and shot it—here was a theme—up Abby's ass.

* * *

I WAS STILL A MESS—STILL DRUNK, high, wrung out, torn up, suspended in a distant and dreamless nod—when I found myself summoned back by an inexplicable, and inescapable, refrain. A mechanical *thump* followed in dirge-tempo by a reedy mechanical *squeak.* I didn't want to answer. I turned over, writing off the noise to Con Ed in the street or the landlord's incompetent contractor in the cellar, until the relentless stupidity of the rhythm—penetrating not just my chemical stupidity, but the bathroom wall—finally demanded attention, from someone. I felt around the bed for Abby.

No Abby.

Opened my eyes. No Abby.

Thump . . . squeak . . .

Snapping aside the sheet, I stumbled forth. Not to find my sometime ex-girlfriend. To stop the goddamn noise.

Down the hall, in the gritty brown bathroom with the crumbly beige and brown tiles, I found both. She was naked, propped on the toilet, eyes rolled back, blue, her freckled Irish face caked in thick, cracked mud.

"Abby?"

I rubbed her cheek and checked my fingertips. No mud.

"What's on your face?" I yelled, thinking somehow that might be the answer. "*What's on your face, Abby?!*"

No Abby.

The realization came slowly, but no time to wait for it. The thump was Abby's head banging the wall behind. The reedy squeak, her dimming breath. The ashy, mud-like masque, simply the bloodless and expiring layers of epidermis on Abby's expiring face. And slapping that face and shouting loudly, I dragged the girl who saved me to and fro past dawn to return the favor.

CHAPTER 14
Captain

I WROTE SANDY. IT HAD BEEN a long time, but that didn't matter. I didn't know what I wanted to say or ask, but that didn't matter either. Because he'd know. I told him New York had gotten too depraved. A girl had almost died. And I wasn't feeling too good myself. I wasn't so sure about my new friends. I wasn't so sure about my new girlfriend either. Or her husband. Did I tell you the band broke up? I wish you could have seen us. It was Sandy first got me out to San Francisco. It was Sandy—a civilian now, but working out of Travis Air Force Base and living in Vacaville—who'd first driven me across the great, orange bridge to Sausalito and a friend's house high above Richardson Bay. And it was there, overcome by the panorama of hillside houses tumbling willy-nilly to the water and the tips of the city poking from the fog in the background, that I'd vowed—like every Sausalito sightseer—a permanent return. Anyway, isn't California where you go to start over? I told him the time had come. I was 19. He was 29. Sandy wrote back.

* * *

AFTER FOUR YEARS PLYING THE WORLD in the belly of an aircraft carrier, Sandy was now flying the world in the nose of an aircraft. It was still astonishing to me how my big brother had changed in the Navy: the surly punk flayed away, revealing underneath a man of—dare I say?—Ghandiesque empathy. Yet somehow the loving, responsible, generous—not to mention dogged and hardworking—Sandy was still the same fun guy.

Going to college year-round on the GI Bill, he plowed through the academic requirements to qualify as a professional pilot, while at the same time, working nights, weekends and every spare minute, sailing through his FAA certifications. After less than two years, he'd picked up his first steady gig, ferrying crop-dusters from the Allentown manufacturer to the burgeoning industrial farms of South America. The pilots generally flew in pairs, delivering two planes at a time. Once, confronting the mighty Andes, another young pilot balked. Sandy flew his own biplane over the hump and returned, by Peruvian bus, for the second. Two trips over the Andes in two days, in an open cockpit, and he would wake up the next morning in agony—all-over cramps and the worst headache ever (before he knew from headaches). Turned out the bends is not just for deep-sea-divers. But, in a region all about altitude, the Cusco hotel doc knew exactly what to do. And, in a twist that was nothing less than typical, became my brother's fast friend.

Having survived crop-dusters and nitrogen poisoning, the unsinkable Sandy progressed to Flying Tigers, the World War II outfit, heroes of the China theater, that had turned into America's first scheduled cargo airline—and sometime CIA front—delivering Minnesota grain and Langley spooks to Bangkok, Kuala Lumpur, Katmandu and other preposterous beyonds. After a few years building more hours, if not his bank account, he got his big break with Western Air, the LA-based passenger carrier. He started as flight engineer, third seat, and worked his way up to second seat, co-pilot, on one of the new 707s, the Latin route, including Cusco, where he'd catch up with the doc. Lately, Western had him flying out of Travis as part of a troop transport contract, shuttling soldiers in and out of Saigon, Da Nang and Cam Ranh Bay, sometimes under fire. Among flight crews and managers alike, he came to be admired as a highly skilled, highly conscientious pilot and all-around nice guy who was climbing fast. The union even drafted him as his local's shop steward.

Would've made captain, no problem.

* * *

IF, WITH HIS DEADLY CARS, AUTOMATIC weapons and simmering rage, Sandy had seemed like a boy who was doomed—in a different way than he was—I sometimes wonder if the hardening of his youth, that immersive childhood instruction in not giving a shit, served to block the more corrosive, chip-on-your-shoulder cynicism of adulthood. In any event, as his paycheck grew—along with a superbly un-Ghandiesque Buddha belly, its fur baked golden in the poolside sun—so did his heart. In the most dexterous feat, he managed to flip the standard keeping-up-with-the-Jones condo-consumerism into a joyous and entirely non-standard sharing-everything-with-the-Jones condo-communism. Everyone west of Suisun City knew that at Sandy's there'd always be something crass they'd never seen before—the first outdoor gas grill, first car phone, first ATV—and a half-dozen folks enjoying the shit out of it, which was a mere sampling of his worldwide cast of characters. Any balmy night in and around Sandy's unprepossessing condoplex might find the Goodyear Tire scion from Belvedere chatting with the crane operator from Rio Vista, while the Napa portrait painter, in rakish red kerchief, turned T-bones over the propane, and Sandy's Reno friend, Bambi, a fulltime bartender, part-time hooker and proud skipper of a baby-blue T-bird ragtop (Nevada plates: B-A-M-B-I), measured another round of Salty Dogs. Somewhere in the mix might be a fire captain from Lodi, a cashier from the Nut Tree, a self-employed Vallejo tax attorney and, on the occasion, a rumpled doctor from Peru. It was a cast of characters Sandy loved so sincerely he never saw them as characters. And there were more and more of them as the intrepid adventurer rolled into his most exotic adventure of all.

I had written Sandy about a trip to California. He wrote me back about a trip to a union clinic, where, out of the wild blue, a headache was diagnosed as brain cancer.

* * *

TUMORS. WE ALWAYS CALLED THE RAGING cancer "tumors." Not cancer. Tumors is what the doc said, and we stuck to it. For a while, it seemed to help. What helped the most was when the chief of neurosurgery came out after six hours to report they'd got it all.

My big brother's amazing luck.

A few weeks after the successful surgery, Sandy and his girlfriend Dory, a stewardess for Delta, slipped down to Vacaville city hall and made it legal. With her stock-steady green-eyed stare and penetrating Georgia accent, Dory was exactly who you'd want at your side in a battle against tumors and insurance companies. She was also fun in bars.

Big brother's amazing luck.

A few weeks after the wedding, Dory called with an offer of a free plane ticket if I'd come keep an eye on things while she headed out on a five-day work trip. Sandy had protested that no babysitter was needed, but Dory stared him down. On the phone, I promised this babysitter would never make anyone drink root beer. He laughed. "Oh, we'll have some fun, Tom."

Though the operation had meant his pilot's certificate had been revoked (temporarily, he insisted), Sandy's spirits were high, and—when we weren't riding his new dirt bike or zipping around Lake Berryessa in his new ski boat—we enjoyed a series of brilliantly motley barbecues. One day, back of the *Vacaville Shopper,* came a blast from sister Connie's past. "*The 'Charlie of the MTA' boys!*" the ad whooped. "*One night only!*" Within that carefree interzone before the FAA restored Sandy's license to globetrot, the Kingston Trio, even thirty-five years past being "boys," qualified as some kind of adventure. We headed north to Cottonwood, on the outskirts of the outskirts. It was a big, barny dive my brother had favored when it was called the Dunk Tank, but which, looking to elevate its clientele, had been reconstituted, perhaps overenthusiastically, the King of California Steakhouse & Music Hall. Tonight, opening night, though the joint was barely one-third full, the porterhouse gristly and the Trio's show goofy—more comedy than harmony—the whiskey worked its reliable magic. When the band walked offstage, brother and I, brimming with 86-proof gratitude, followed. Unlike certain show biz snotnoses, these veteran troubadours—the red-and-white striped shirts of their first album cover matched now by the varicose stripes of their noses—were delighted for the company, more for the free drinks. Only after we'd exhausted our cash and their stash—comically redundant quantities of high-potency thai-stick—did we bid our new brothers fondest adieu, climb back in Sandy's silver Firebird, and, while negotiating our exit, professional pilot at the con, back full-throttle into a parked car. *Thunk.*

Rather: *THUNK!*

And it wasn't the drinking or drugs.

"Peripheral vision!" shouted Sandy with a wide-eyed grin, as if it weren't the accident or even the surgery that was the story here, but the miracle of human physiology. "The optic nerve, Tom! Had to take it out with the tumor."

Sitting behind the wheel at the scene of the crime, one blinker ticking pointlessly, he excitedly demonstrated how it worked.

"Here, put your hands on either side of your head, like blinders . . . "

Eventually we got around to the responsible thing, scuffing around in the dark trying to inspect the stranger's shattered taillight and crunched quarter-panel, before jumping back in the Firebird and peeling out.

Somehow we got the car home and into the garage—without toppling the dense stacks of storage boxes that included, somewhere, the refugee carton from Harkness with my NASSA helmet and Total Eclipse Theory. Then, at Sandy's insistence, despite my demurral, we shared his king bed.

"Why sleep on the couch when there's a perfectly good mattress?" said the man who'd slept on a hundred couches and, for four years, belowdecks, in the cramped, fragrant crew quarters of a carrier.

"Jeez, Tom, we're brothers."

* * *

One time, before the tumors, he invited me to fly "up front"—the cockpit jumpseat. The trip was short (SFO-LAX), but the thrill unlimited: watching a hot-rod angel in epaulets throw four throttles wide, his familiar voice crackling in the headset, to sling 140 mortal souls into the firmament, before—by solemn adjustments of thrust and attitude, the biggest passenger jet of its time responding with eerie precision—floating them lovingly back to Earth.

O captain, my captain.

Dedicated to motion—in cars, boats, planes, motorcycles and, as jobs and whims steered him from California to Nevada, Texas to Florida, moving trucks—Sandy set forces in motion, among drive-in waitresses, country-club princesses, jet jocks, crane ops, hotel docs, union bros, regular bros, hookers, bartenders, firemen and fops. Forces as impossible to trace as they are to resist, of sex, class, power, fun, pain, politics, money, love and aeronautics. I want to say he changed the world.

He did.

It was as easy for me to forget, as it would have been hard for his friends, lovers and shipmates to fathom, that this irrepressible man of the people, feral spawn of doormen and whores, was the scion of Midwestern aristocrats—his besotted mère heir to the Milwaukee-brand battery millions—that with the snap of his fingers he could have been someone else.

King of California.

* * *

UNDER A FIERCE FEDERAL EAGLE, HIS forearm scroll pledged allegiance to USN. Memento of a drunken sailor night in a drunken sailor town, Sandy's tattoo would come to have many meanings, only some skin-deep. If it would represent barely a drop in the bucket of the billions of gallons later pumped into the epidermises of everyone from teenage girls to their grandmas, when my brother embellished himself, the practice was strictly for swabbies, bikers and cons. Father, who'd come up from that, from grunt work for the railroad, didn't take it well. Mother, who looked down on it, manifested displeasure with the gift of both a long-sleeved dress shirt and snazzy blue blazer to double-cover what could only be—she confided to me and Roger—our big brother's profound shame.

Sandy came to think of the tattoo as his "shit detector," because it made some people, bent on the judgment that eluded him, flinch. And that was the game: catching the reproving flickers. Surely that detector was spewing sparks after the doctors sliced off a facet of his head and left Sandy's skull lopsided, festooned in irradiated frizz, and Mother proposed that, when attending club affairs, brother might augment the shirt and jacket with a wig.

A proposition he quietly declined.

So Mother quietly excluded Sandy from the club until after the funeral—from which she tried to exclude him by trying to exclude his designated eulogist, me—before she relented to include him in the burial.

CHAPTER 15

Bolos

I CAME TO DETROIT, AND THEN its suburb I'd never heard of, in deepest, darkest, freezingest, brokest, lost-my-brotherest January, enough of a hallucination in the living I can hardly tell where memory leaves off. The night Jim Morton and Lester Bangs picked me up at Detroit Metro I didn't know much more about "America's Only Rock 'n' Roll Magazine" than what I'd gleaned from scanning the newsstand in the Astor Place subway station, the only place in New York it seemed to be on sale. Awaiting my train home from NYU, eyeing the latest garish cover in the news kiosk, I'd still managed some authoritative conclusions.

MC5? Stooges? *Grand Funk Railroad*? Are they kidding???

Oh, and Alice Cooper. I mean, I liked all that gender-bendery—liked it in the Dolls and, before that, the Mothers and Stones. But when I saw Alice on channel 11's no-budget Labor Day festival trying to make a point about stardom by hypnotizing a crowd with a pocket watch, it was just embarrassing. To me, a New York chauvinist as only a midwestern *arriviste* can be, *Creem* wasn't about the music, any more than the music was about the notes.

Lester was the magazine's editorial supernova. He was brilliant, I could tell you later. I didn't know it then. I'm sure I'd seen his byline in *Rolling Stone*, but I'd paid little attention to the prose—probably because, though he lived in El Cajon, outside San Diego, about as far from Motor City as you could motor, any random Lester piece was likely to extoll the virtues of Michigan's Stooges or MC5. I was hardly a Lester acolyte. It didn't occur to me he would have acolytes. *Creem*—a hick rag about hick bands edited and in large part written, I would discover, by an irreducible hick—just didn't mean a lot to me.

Slinging a Great Pine duffel stuffed with everything of mine into a rat-trap, red Camaro stuffed with everything of Lester's—books, records, notebooks, shoes, t-shirts, greasy jumper cables, festering Jack-in-the-Box wrappers—I finally managed to contort into the back seat, and the three of us beelined to Pasquale's, the cheery family restaurant on Woodward, near 13 Mile, where, inexplicably, the brain trust of America's Only Rock 'n' Roll Magazine went after work to extend the party. In what would become a nightly rite, if not an opiate, I ordered the Special Spaghetti—noodles and red gloop in a mozzarella-topped casserole, pizza posing as pasta—and we all got bombed on super-sized goblets of beer called bolos, before stuffing back into the Camaro for the last mile to the communal *Creem* house in Birmingham, an eccentric little burg on Detroit's vanilla fringe.

I often found myself wondering, clomping through the foot-deep snow those strange first days in Greater Detroit: how did I get here? Especially since I'd been headed to California.

* * *

Some think California means giving up. My father thought so. "Lotus-eaters!" is what he liked to say about it—though I suspect Mother put that in his head, as I'm 100% certain he'd never read The Odyssey. Most who think California means giving up are people in New York. And once, I was among the loudest of them: not just strident, unequivocating, fanatical even; pro-soot, pro-overcrowding, pro-urine stench. After the heartpunch of Sandy, after the dismay of Romper Room, after almost losing Abby and never quite getting Jackie, after hitting the credit card ceiling for both cash advances and Travelers Checks and being shut out of a shrinking job market ("*Creem* . . . " the interviewer would ask. "Is that, um, porn?"), amid the thousand little things, some of them cockroaches, that New York does to test you, I was more than ready to give up.

I'd told my brother I wanted to come to California. I hadn't mentioned the ridiculous plan. I would trade a band career for one no less uncareer-like that could be pursued without band members. I'd be a writer—in my head, I *was* a writer—and I would follow the counsel to write what I knew. Which was not actually much. Definitely not as much as I thought. Rock 'n' roll I thought I knew. Maybe I'd be a rock critic. And maybe that would lead to a novel. Which would lead to becoming—presto, change-o—a rock star, back door. I knew it was dreamy and juvenile, unlikely as it was convoluted—especially since I had not a clue where to start.

Then came a man in black and another in blinding white.

Jim Morton was a famous writer nobody knew, who would later be hired as interim editor of a magazine called *Creem* not a lot of people knew ("interim," because to Morton a permanent job was nothing less than servitude). I'd first met him at Ted Hall's basement apartment in the way East Village, when that sooty, overcrowded, piss-stained neighborhood was a burbling caldron of arty, scary and cheap. Allen Ginsberg lived around the corner, Auden, three blocks west, next to the Electric Circus, the Hells Angels a block south, on Third Street. Two avenues over, at St. Mark's-in-the-Bowery, Patti Smith was trying out her poems over Lenny Kaye's Stratocaster. Jim was there for all of it.

Jim was an albino—or near enough—who'd emigrated from the high desert around Lancaster, California, which regularly records the hottest temperatures on the planet and has to be the single most unfortunate place to raise a snowy-skinned lad. He was the first journalist—Black or ridiculously white—to cover the DIY scene in the Bronx, where kids were declaiming over turntables, and the early punk happenings in Lower Manhattan. He was a cultural frontiersman who'd mapped uncharted genres in rock, country, gospel and R&B, who'd queried the musically renowned and championed their unsung antecedents, who'd cut and buffed copy for every meaningful US music publication and who, in liner notes that could make you laugh, cry or drool, had sketched the context for a dozen definitive box-sets, a low-slung, barrel-chested man devoted to music, stories and booze, not always in that order, with zero appetite for self-promotion.

Ted Hall, on the other hand, was a famous writer everybody knew. He was tall and hulking, in a black cowboy hat with silver hatband, black cowboy boots, snap-button shirt and dirty blue jeans. His hair was black and oily and lanked down to his shoulders. His eyes were frosty blue. Beneath his snaggle-toothed sneer was a black goatee that came to a Satanic point. More than a lost cowboy, he was a lost Hells Angel—misplaced perhaps by his fellow brutes at the Third Street clubhouse—and certainly not a middle-class Oberlin grad out of New Rochelle.

I know I met him on a Wednesday, because that's when the Voice came out. I was now on the hunt for my residential destiny: a place to live that might not be California—yet—but wasn't fucking Tiger's. Generally, in my range, there was nothing. Sometimes I'd spend an hour or two wandering, eyes mostly open. But on a side street in the way-east Village, I nearly missed the low-hanging sign: "For Rent. 1 BR, basement." As I trotted toward the entrance, a biker type, carrying a cardboard box, clomped in from the right.

"Forget it," Ted bellowed. "I got it."

I don't know why I asked if I could see the place anyway. But then, with my bank account, it was all just make-believe.

Ted allowed I could peek: "But don't get any ideas."

Long before he turned into a curmudgeon, Ted Hall was an asshole. Inside the living room that was almost too low for his high-crowned hat, he now put down the box, revealing a lanyard with a press pass.

"So," I said, surprised, pointing, "who do you write for?"

He started with *Rolling Stone, Esquire, Creem* and *Life* and didn't stop for a while.

* * *

TED HALL COULD SPOT A FATTED squab. Over the next few months, in return for him being my unofficial writing instructor, I got to be his unofficial dogwalker, secretary, last-minute coriander-shopper, dish washer, house-sitter and whipping boy. And, in my earnest way, his friend. Along with Morton, with whom he'd shared an office at *Rolling Stone*, I also became Ted's constant dinner companion. Turns out this heaping helping of pseudo-biker liked nothing more than to lace on the flowered apron and whip up a gourmet Americana feast—jambalaya, sweetbreads, a whole fish, head on—guaranteed to scare the shit out of a food baby like me. As he sliced, slurped and sniffed the kitchen bounty, he pontificated about the abysmal dearth of fresh, local ingredients and chefs who knew what to do with them.

Ted made me shut up and learn about food that wasn't curdled chocolate dishwater or laboratory-generated cherry pie. After dinner, over the black-and-tans he also taught me to enjoy, Hall and Morton would quarrel tartly, concur fractiously and conspire ardently to peel back the mysteries of popular song, cueing up a procession of obscure vinyl, from every label, genre and era, often arranged around a theme, extracted by the big guy with cotton-glove care from the crates that lined his basement and occupied his life.

Bless that asshole, he initiated me into the deepest joys of music—while vividly illustrating the prejudices of its professional appreciators—and went on to show me how to structure an interview, transcribe a tape, format a manuscript. Christ, he pretty much taught me to type. Then, as promised, he gave me an assignment, told me who to call and what to say and, afterwards, struck red through most of what I wrote. Point is, a few months later, Jim Morton—Ted's friend and now mine—moved to Detroit and called with a gig on the lowest rung of the editorial ladder. Which, from my vantage point, was an indisputable step up.

* * *

And here I was. Don't know what I expected, but Pasquale's was not it, and neither was the *Creem* house—preposterously normal, a white Cape Cod on a well-mowed street of them. The bedrooms were up a flight and, for now, fully occupied. Lester and Jim set me up on the couch and, somewhere after three in the morning, left me to whatever first-night jitters might have survived the bolos of beer. As it turned out, I'd only last a couple weeks at the *Creem* house. Which was another surprise, but shouldn't have been. Bank Street had taught me I wasn't really made for communal, and Lester wasn't made for communal with anyone who had independent ideas, maybe even about Lester. Just as I was starting to get comfy, he passed judgment that the new kid wasn't cool enough, reminded him of that other kid from New York they'd pushed out, and dutifully the communards pushed me out, too.

I won't say it wasn't painful, even if the reason remained veiled in practical excuses, even if in one sense it made sense. I won't say the whole living/working situation wasn't totally high school, if not a tad Jonestown. Mostly, I was terrified of losing my new job—a job I viewed, first and foremost, as a rung on the ladder to financial redemption, a paycheck. A month later when the lavishly opinionated high priest of *Creem* flip-flopped, as Lester was known to do, announcing to anyone and everyone that the new kid was not only cool, but—perhaps his highest accolade—funny ("as funny as *he* was," was how Lester put it, lavishly, to the Allman Brothers' flack), I was already ensconced in a solo 1-BR three blocks the other side of Woodward. But I took Lester's flattery as a kind of apology and tried to let it go. Tried. After all, I didn't lose my job, and suddenly, to go along with my secret grudges against them, I had a bunch of new friends. Then there was Detroit itself.

* * *

Now I have been to Schenectady (where I was Virgil'd around by a stumpy, strutty, muscleman friend from Harkness, who'd grown up there). In the city of Schenectady, it was such a fact of life that everyone worked for G.E. I finally stopped asking. But the human brain is equipped to comprehend a factory town of 70,000. Detroit, on the other hand, was a factory town of a million-five. One thing to know it from popular lore as the home of the U.S. auto industry; another to see that this was not just a Rotarian platitude, to bear witness on the ground. Because whether they clocked in at Ford's River Rouge plant or Campbell-Ewald, Ford's ad agency, everyone in the Motor City went to The Line.

The auto assembly line, that's what they called it: The Line. That was the syntax. Not *working* on it. Going to it. Submitting. Now the young people who'd watched their parents go to The

Line were refusing. The money was good—even more so, as the mid-Seventies recession took hold—but not so much the soul-destroying. And this new generation had the learning and leisure to think about such things as souls. This wasn't the Depression-era dad who'd lost the farm in the Upper Peninsula or the Jim Crow-era refugee from Memphis, each punching in, grateful and numb, to make it better for the kids.

And these were those kids.

White ones, who only wanted to be the MC5 or Stooges. Black ones who wanted to be Curtis Mayfield or Marvin Gaye. And a few who, in the meantime, worked at *Creem.*

* * *

NO ARGUMENT THAT I WENT SOFT and mushy for that hard-bitten factory town. With its inexorable tunes, guerrilla grit and bubblegum-sweet ginger ale, Detroit was a city unlike any I'd encountered—in every deeper way sui generis. After we got the hate out, I fell for Lester, too. And the days of *Creem* became all kinds of odd inebriation. More of it than you might imagine having to do with the work.

Seated at his typewriter, Lester faced the wall. Eight feet away, seated at my typewriter, I faced Lester's back. Among the things he could do better than me was type. As I struggled with a jury-rigged three-finger technique, stopping frequently to reach for whatever derisive nugget I might drop next about my beloved Todd Rundgren, Lester zoomed along, stopping never. Besides English, touch-typing must have been his best class in high school. We didn't have touch-typing at Harkness (they presumed there'd be Caroline Ward-trained secretaries for that), and if we'd had, I'm sure I wouldn't have had the patience. But if you think it might have been demoralizing to write next to Lester Bangs at the peak of his powers, you should try typing.

* * *

MAYBE AS A BOY, HELPING HIS mother spread the word of *The Watch Tower*, Lester had put on a suit and tie. Not since, I'd bet. Greasy, bagged-out jeans and a t-shirt fished from the pile replenished several times a week by record labels, were his ensemble of the day, every day. In the winter, in Detroit, he might also throw on a fleece-lined overcoat. Later, in New York, after he'd decided it might be time to be cool, it was a mandarin-collared black leather jacket, winter and summer alike. But on this Birmingham spring day, against all odds and way off type, Lester was wearing a tie and three-piece suit.

He'd met a girl he really liked. When Cindy invited him to a fancy wedding, I escorted him, at Cindy's request, to a fancy men's store. The suit we landed on—that I landed on, Lester had fully dissociated—was a green-yellow plaid thing that only sounds disgusting. The tailor fitted it nicely—mustachioed mannequin gazing silently skyward, St. Sebastian of the straight-pins—and the poker-faced salesman, pretending we were normal customers, accessorized it with a white button-down shirt, green striped tie and brown oxfords, and Lester arrived at the Episcopal High Mass looking not at all like himself. Not at all like himself, he enjoyed the punch in moderation and chatted amiably and his girlfriend beamed. Pulling away afterwards in the rattletrap Camaro that suggested there might be more to the story, he dropped Cindy at home, saying he had work at the office—which, by the time *Creem*'s hungover editors straggled in, was often busier at night than day. Taking the shortcut through the mailroom, he strode directly into the editorial department—proudly, it seemed to me—with tie knotted, vest buttoned, jacket on, and everybody in the room went: Aww!

As always, when getting down to business, Lester put a record on the turntable and turned it up. Whether it was post-bop, proto-punk, *Metal Machine Music* or—redeploying his assault from the sensory to the conceptual level—John Denver, I don't remember, probably because I tried not to hear. I do know it wasn't meant as an assault, or even a show. Caustic or treacly, the vibrations, for Lester, were all sympathetic. He was marshalling his instruments, tuning up. The goofy hick evaporated. Silent, tunnel-visioned—a man under the pressure of his ambition, his audience, real and imagined, and too much work neglected too long—Lester found the pill bottle on his cluttered desk, spilled a handful of yellow Valiums into his hand (tranquilizers, yes, not speed, not this time) and washed them down with warm beer. Without removing jacket or tie, he plopped his oversized self down at his undersized metal typing table—a grownup on a tricycle—toggled the black Selectric on and, for close to 30 seconds, as if in invocation, surveyed the shelves above him, perilously bulging with records, books and promotional tchotchkes.

Eight feet away, a hundred miles behind, I wrestled with Todd's newfound meatlessness as a metaphor for the sharp left in his career—about which, as a critic of a full year's experience, I was indignant—while my friend and co-editor spun god-knows-what about god-knows-who, an exegesis you knew would be hysterical, incisive, poetic and way too long. Around midnight, frustrated with my own efforts—especially compared to the clatter across the room—lying to myself that a break might replenish the critical bile, I grabbed our mutual friend Karwreck from the mailroom, issued a perfunctory invitation to the clatterer—who barely whispered a demurral—and headed out for the last couple hours at Pasquale's, followed by the quarter-to-two ritual where one guy would settle the bill and the other make the pre-curfew dash to 13-Mile for a 12-pack. It was almost four when we returned to the office with beer. Lester was alone now, but doing exactly what he'd been doing, wearing what he'd been wearing, not having moved anything but his absurdly nimble fingers.

I'd witnessed Lester on writing binges—that's how Lester wrote. It was also the way he drank and took drugs and fell in love and, for that matter, listened to music. Not a shock, always a marvel. But not enough to keep me from finally heading home. I arrived back at the office the next day bright and early at two pm. Sweat soaked the back of Lester's new suit jacket, and his hair looked like he'd taken a shower—except you knew he hadn't because he stunk. While he'd lowered the tie a couple inches and unbuttoned the vest, he seemed determined to wring every last drop of value from his now dripping, completely trashed purchase. Still, it made me feel good he'd so enthusiastically endorsed my selection. In the meantime, oblivious to anything but a gap in the noise, he continued banging the Selectric, becoming, if possible, faster, getting up only to flip the record or change it, until sometime after eight pm, 30 hours from when he started, he abruptly stopped, gathering up the inch-thick manuscript—it had to be thirty-thousand words, half a book—and thumping it on my desk.

"Take a look," he said. "I'm hungry."

That was Lester's work.

My work, part of it, was to try and machete through those inch-thick mega-blurts (because even in a sopping suit, on a fistful of Valium, the guy was good for 50% gold, if you were intrepid). This particular disgorgement became the cover story, "John Denver is God," for the 84-page holiday extravaganza, complete with an illustration of the bespectacled mophead in a manger. I finished my hit-piece on Todd for the issue, which also enclosed the first of many stories on Kiss and another on Iggy—or was it the MC5? On top of the feature stories, most written in-house, there were news items to concoct, record reviews to write or edit and monthly columnists—on drive-in movies, fashion, gadgetry—to cattle-prod. There were wiseass photo captions and headlines and a table of contents to make up, and there was subscription promo copy—a year of *Creem* gets you the too-small t-shirt our receptionist is wearing in this picture; two years, we'll throw in Suzi Quatro's greatest hits. And there were deadlines. Immutable deadlines. Because it didn't just have to be good, it had to be done. In a way, that was the most intoxicating part: all of us pulling together—no time for anyone's bullshit—to get the next number written, illustrated, typeset, laid out, packed up and delivered to the printer. Delivered personally, sometimes by me: hand-carrying mechanicals on a plane to Montreal and, thence, in a rented car, in the moonless night, in a Canadian blizzard, to the plant in Magog ("the hostile nations," the old testament translates—and what winter visitor would argue?). Inextricable sometimes from the play, the work was still work, and a lot of it got done every month, and some done well, and circulation—the name of the game for the folks the other side of the editorial department door—climbed.

But journalism and its sprints were just part of the fun of America's Only Rock 'n' Roll Magazine. Another, you tried not to admit, was meeting rock stars.

Like Jim Osterberg.

* * *

IT WASN'T LONG BEFORE I'D ACCEPTED Michigan's favorite son Iggy Pop—Jim, friends called him—as my lord and savior. When I say meeting him, I mean waiting around in a rock-star-dim Detroit hotel suite for David Bowie to show up for an interview and realizing after a few minutes that the platinum-haired pixie snoozing on the sofa, the only other person in the room, is Pop.

That was the kind of thing that happened.

Other things that happened: careening to Bobby Womack's for a late-night jam in the company of a Rolling Stone, the two of you tossed around with the empties every time Karwreck took a corner. Dropping the last of your cash at a comically stacked version of 21 called 22 in an after-hours "blind pig" with Mitch Ryder, the King of Blue-Eyed Soul. Discovering a postcard in your mailbox, handwritten and personal, from John Lennon, hero of your childhood guitar-case. There was a swig of Bowie's Cristal. Herb tea in Rob Tyner's kitchen—he of "Kick out the jams!" godhood. A peck from Dionne Warwick. Dinner with John Cale. A fist-shaking tantrum from the short guy in Chicago *in the city of Chicago.* And, among other road trips with Bruce, three days on a tight, ripe band bus through the cradle of the blues.

Sometimes we even traveled in style—though last I'd seen Ronnie Wood was the back of that rollicking van (a memorable night which, ever the most gracious of barbarians, he was now pretending to remember). This time I was on deadline for a story about Woody's and Keith's side project, the New Barbarians, and while the interview was yet to take place, the gemütlichkeit, at four in the morning, was flowing lushly. Woody assured me we would talk, soon, and I was inclined to believe him. But four seemed as good a time as any to let my hostess know I was going to miss last night's dinner. All I needed was a phone.

The night had started in the day, when we'd piled into a block-long parade of limos that thirty minutes later pulled up next to a 727, where I was invited to climb aboard and have a seat in the pub. With plaid carpeting, tufted-leather chairs and wood-grained tables, the pub on the plane looked as much like the terra firma variety as you could ask at 35,000 feet. Crowning the effect was an impeccable British barman, in bowtie and diamond-patterned vest, who, even before wheels-up, had delivered a perfectly assembled black-and-tan on a New Barbarians coaster. Sixty minutes more and a fresh convoy of Caddies roared onto the tarmac to take us the last five miles to a sold-out Chicago Arena, where the band hit the stage for a blistering set, three encores and, before the sweat was dry, a fast break for the hotel.

So here I am lounging in the presidential suite with Ronnie Wood, Ian McLagan and Keith Richards, who sauntered in, barefoot, clutching his squared-off fifth of Tennessee whiskey, every inch himself: swigging, puffing, snickering and doing this thing that was kind of like talking—demonstrably exuberant and thoroughly unintelligible. When Woody jumped up to answer the door, Keith glanced over and burst into wildly agitated, proto-primate vocalizing—even less intelligible, if possible—bouncing in the chair as though a hot ash had fallen down his open shirt. The visitor was turned away, and, as if I were just another mate, Woody confided she was an NME reporter of whom Keith was not at the moment overly fond.

"Hey," he added, tapping my knee, "we'll get to the interview later—definitely, promise."

Cool, cool, cool, I assured Ronnie Wood. "All I need is to make one quick call."

The feather-haired limey ushered me to the bedroom and, with a hospitable sweep of the wrist, indicated the bedside extension, before returning to his other guests. I sat down on the edge of the white bedcover and reached for the white telephone, which matched the walls, curtains, headboard, nightstand and wall-to-wall shag rug. White on white on white. I slid the phone close, picked up the receiver and had just finished poking buttons when Woody stepped back in, tapped a finger to his temple to indicate *Duh,* and said softly, so as not to disturb:

"Pardon . . . "

Pinning the cigarette in his straight-cut, marionette mouth, he reached over and lifted the base of the phone. While I watched, dumbly holding the handset to my cheek, he gathered from the white surface of the white nightstand beneath where the white phone had rested what was left of a white mound of powder I had snowplowed onto the white shag.

White on white on white. On white.

I sputtered apologies. Unfazed and unfailingly polite, grinning around the cig, the good Mr. Wood raked what remained of the powder into a folded slice of paper.

"Naahh," he whispered. "No problem, mate."

And left me to my quizzical caller.

* * *

I NEVER SAID I WAS COOL. Nobody at *Creem* was cool. Nobody—back-door or any way—was a rock star. Not even Lester, in his unselfconsciously galumphing, self-consciously anti-cool way. Not then. It was *the thing* that was cool. Within the punch-drunk culture of that overinflated factory town, working for a national rock 'n' roll magazine—for sale as far away as the subways of New York—when rock 'n' roll was the center of culture, carried a full measure of glam. Even the radio guys looked up to *Creem*. To settle a bet, scratch an itch or demonstrate his dominion, Lester from time to time would call the jock on the air and tell him to put on the Velvets. The *Creem* crew were hometown heroes, with their own fan mail and groupies. In almost any Motor City venue, many bars and most of late-night Greektown, your business card was good as cash. Free kebabs, free shots, not to mention, backstage—whether at giant Cobo or tiny Frenchman's—bottomless free beer.

The only thing you couldn't use it on was the phone bill.

* * *

THIS WAS A PROBLEM, AMID A sudden cascade of them. They were draining my building of tenants, in preparation for its demolition. Before long the population was down to me and the guy I called the streetwalking cheetah—a chiseled, shirtless sociopath (living breathing model for Iggy Pop—I mean, Jim), who, until he vanished, lived in the attic. It was the cheetah, who otherwise didn't talk much, told me the end was nigh. Saw it as further proof, as if any were needed, of his unified field theory: rich real estate bastards + CIA mind-controllers = stuck-up Birmingham bitches who wouldn't give him the time of day. Weeks later when I stopped by with the rent, the building's agent made a big point of calling me Tom and confided what I already knew. He added I was welcome to live out my lease. Or they'd be happy to pay me off, give me 500 bucks, cash, now.

"But if you don't want that kind of money, *Tom* . . . " The ellipsis being the threat.

I was broke, and I was tempted. I was also comfortable and knew it would be impossible to find anything near as cheap. Based on my New York training, I was pretty sure the threat was hollow.

"Suit yourself," said the agent. I could tell what he was thinking: *Dirtbag. Like that attic dirtbag.*

Of course, I was always broke. This time I was broke because my girlfriend lived in New York. When I say girlfriend, I should reiterate she was another guy's wife. But we'd get that sorted. Until then, Jackie and I would talk on the phone while the doc was at work.

They charged a lot for long distance. And it had gotten to the point where it wasn't rent or Pasquale's bolos that were busting my budget, but the phone. After taking longer and longer to pay the bills, I stopped. The collections lady, never less than compassionate on our Saturday morning calls, let me slide three months, and then, without further notice, not a minute more.

No more compassion. No more collections lady. No more phone. And no more long-distance girlfriend.

Then it struck me that, as 47 Purdy's sole remaining tenant, I might be able to bust through the living room closet into the closet of the unit next door and order a new phone in a new name at a new apartment number—what would appear to the phone company as a whole new customer at a whole new address. The new me living at the new address, I decided, would go by the moniker Fred Halstead, after a graphically outspoken gay porn star recently profiled in the *Voice,* whose specialty was beating the living shit out of consenting partners on 16-millimeter. It was a different kind of love, Halstead argued, combatively. I hadn't caught his oeuvre—and hoped Michigan Bell hadn't either—but Fred had piqued my imagination. Meaning I made a lot of naive S&M jokes around the *Creem* office. Credit was loose—if you were willing to tell a few white lies—and the phone company cheerfully scheduled an appointment. I set myself up with a lawn chair and TV table in the purloined flat, and a nice installer guy came, saying not a word about my reduced circumstances (down to just a lawn chair and TV table), and put in the new phone, and I said:

"By the way, I'm going to need a really long cord."

After he left, I dragged it through the hole, closed the closet door and dialed long distance.

Jackie was telling me she had cancer.

CHAPTER 16

Biff

NOT JUST CANCER, LADY CANCER. SOME test had come back iffy, and she had a bad feeling. My girlfriend, the wife of a doctor.

Lady cancer was all the excuse I needed. I hung up Fred Halstead's phone, slung my duffel bag into my $65 car and, in the middle of the night, without ceremony or even the common courtesy of two-weeks' notice, motored out of Motown.

Not sure why I needed that excuse. I loved my job—the paycheck wasn't much, but a lot more than nothing, and I was young. It was a lot of freedom—sometimes, usually, I didn't roll into the office till well past noon. And the editorial strictures—well, there weren't any, except for the occasional eruption from the Jewish publisher when some goy writer dropped a Holocaust joke.

"I don't wanna be a lampshade," Barry would say, gesturing with the galley and making his own Holocaust joke, "but does he have to drag dead Jews into a fucking Captain and Tennille review?"

For a chronically late, semi-irresponsible, intermittently sensitive college dropout, it became, as I rose from editorial assistant to managing editor, a spectacular volume of responsibility, pretty much the definition of a great job. What's more, in Lester and Karwreck I had great friends. And I'd come to love the beautiful-loser town—Detroit, but Birmingham, too. All that was lacking in the great state of Michigan was a girl to love, a real one, a warm one, as opposed to the disembodied Brooklyn accent on a porn star's pilfered line.

It wasn't that I couldn't get a girl. I did. Once. Had sex with the magazine's typesetter. She couldn't have been sweeter. But the fact was, I already had a steady girl, Jackie, to whom—with this one tiny exception over eighteen months—I had remained steadfast.

That was another stupid thing I learned in Catholic school. Being faithful. Though Jackie was married—unfaithful, de facto—I told myself that wasn't her fault. In a grotesque accommodation with the jealousy that had bedeviled me since Abby went to Mexico, I reasoned if I could refrain from fucking around, maybe she could refrain from fucking around even more. *Even more*—I was actually willing to give her that. And when she told me she had cancer of the lady part—*probably* had cancer of the lady part—it struck me as urgent to get back to New York and rescue that insatiable fair maiden before someone else did.

The $65 car made it to the block where Jackie was now living, but not a block further. Like a faithful nag, the faded green Fury that had carried me from Woodward Avenue to Hudson Street faded to black. I extracted my duffel from the trunk and paperwork from the glove compartment, unscrewed the Michigan plates and abandoned Ol' Paint to the car maggots, those ubiquitous New York parts thieves.

Then I pushed Jackie's buzzer. Three times.

"Hey, I'm here," I said into the microphone, trying, in view of the lady-cancer, to keep it light.

I could hear she'd pressed the talk button, but all that followed was crackle and hiss.

"Hey," I said, with a laugh, "buzz me in!"

My gut tightened. My brain told my gut relax. Then, after 600 frantic interstate miles, burning bridges—and $65 Plymouth Furys—all the way, the crackle and hiss parted and my damsel-in-distress, main squeeze and number one girl at long last spoke.

"You can't come up now."

* * *

"You can't come up now."

OK, she didn't have to repeat it. Or maybe she did—frankly, I did find it hard to hear over the cerebral hemorrhage now in progress. Mostly, after I'd so abruptly discarded work and friends and future—and, lately, sleep—I found it hard to believe.

You can't come up now.

It wasn't so much I found it hard to believe in the here and now. I found it hard to believe in the there and then. Hard to believe that, in the entire dismal chronicle of our noble genus, written and unwritten, there had been any interaction more treacherous, more cold, more cruel.

But hold on. Maybe what was coming out of the intercom was the fear. Or the sadness. Or the cancer itself.

Or.

Or maybe while I was death-racing to milady's rescue, she was already at the upper end of that intercom getting milady's itch scratched. Maybe she was getting it right now. Not even by her trial-separated husband. By her boyfriend. One of them. Biff.

You can't come up now.

* * *

By some ignoble combination of my thespian skills, which are not insubstantial, and her gall, which outstripped even mine, I was finally able to persuade her it was cool. That I was cool, she was cool, everything was cool. And the damsel let me in.

I shouldn't have been surprised. But, as a lifelong member of the church of blind faith, I always am. Sitting solicitously near my girlfriend on her couch—but not so near as to amplify the insult and further hurt my feelings—was none other than Biff, there to white-knight her from her white knight.

I'm sure when they'd heard the buzzer he'd asked if she wanted him to run up to the roof or climb down the fire escape. I'm also sure she'd waved it off, said don't bother, that I was a loudmouth who was, ultimately, a pussy. Now, inside the apartment, as if to confirm, I unleashed on him in a loud, pussy way. Told Biff to do us all a favor and split, and, when he didn't, when he tried to answer soothingly, saying it was probably better he stayed, I went on to make fun of his manner of speaking, his haircut, his IQ, his shirt, shoes and name. His stupid, fucking name.

"Biff, Biff, Biff," I singsonged satirically, as I ran out of real insults.

Of course, I went on some more, getting ugly in every freakish way my exhausted mind could conjure. Maybe scare Biff into believing I was just crazy enough. When none of it made my girlfriend break down, and my girlfriend's boyfriend turned out to be as Dudley Do-Right as a damsel might dream, I pulled out the pathos: threatening to destroy myself in various gruesome ways—plucking out my eyes or ripping off my jaw—vowing to leave them as emotionally mutilated as I was. In the end, my overwrought Grand Guignol turned so ridiculous I actually saw loverboy stifle a laugh. But it wasn't the laugh that killed me, it was the motherfucker trying to spare me.

CHAPTER 17
Conk

AN IDIOT WOULD HAVE KNOWN IT was over. And beneath my innate inability to let anything go—visions of a neighbor girl in a Minnesota sprinkler, no less than the glint of a kitchen knife on New Year's—I'm guessing I really did want it to be done. But that doesn't mean I gave up. Not surprising. What *was* surprising is that eventually I did. After a few days of mad despair, of calling and, when she stopped answering the phone, stopping by the vestibule to try and talk over the intercom, even after she unexpectedly buzzed me in and greeted me at the door half-naked to tell me the tests had come back negative—"No cancer!" she said—and tried to seduce me into makeup sex, I walked away. It was kind of like that Sam Andrew thing, where the offer was enough. I never saw or spoke to her again. Never wanted to. And underneath the loneliness, I felt the stirring of something I'd always thought I wanted to be:

Free.

Free of love and sex and jealousy. Free of Mother and Father and the torments of family. Free of church and school, of landlords and rent and exorbitant telephone bills. Free of the daily grind—bosses and deadlines. Free, like Dean Moriarty (but without the car), to go where I wanted, do what I wanted, to fashion a whole new life, if I wanted. Free, like Dylan, to paint my masterpiece. Unencumbered, save for a Great Pine duffel full of dirty clothes.

I stumbled around Manhattan in a state of "free" for a couple months, more than once spending the afternoon on a bench in City Hall Park, opposite the Army recruiting office, in somber consideration of 11% unemployment, 14% inflation, round-the-block gas lines, and how I'd look in a private's uniform. There wasn't much else available. And it was still a kind of freedom, in that it would shatter expectations and completely blow minds—while proving this hippie faggot was a real American after all. As I failed to turn myself over to Uncle Sam and hunted alternative ways to pay for my glorious freedom, I slept on couches, floors, in closets and in borrowed studios and, when I got sick of it, or they of me, took a room from a man in a bulletproof cage in an infamous downtown fleabag, where the all-night fighting, yelling, sobbing, and stiletto-heel-clomping, just a 3/8-inch drywall from my head, was real as America gets. A few nights cowering in the Alfred—out of my depth and free from nothing but sleep—I ran sniffling to Tiger.

My grade-school chum was wrestling demons of his own—more or less literally, having embarked on a crazy boxing kick, accompanied by a maniacal exercise kick, a self-lacerating discipline kick and a vicious mean streak. Besides he was still fuming I'd left the last time without paying. More to the point, he was mad that a kid from the mean streets of the Lower East Side, whose laboriously maintained persona was founded on Lower East Side savvy, had been had. Finally he calculated if he bullied me enough—and, for a white boxer who went to private school (albeit on scholarship), the six-three, 220 southpaw could be an imposing bully—I'd beg it out of mom and dad (whom I hadn't talked to in a year). Going for the angle, my childhood pal finally welcomed me back to the cat-piss railroad flat, thinking his angle was me.

The rent was steep, for a hairball-slimed couch with no privacy, but Tiger assured me, with relish, he had to charge me more because of "bad credit." Even more, he added, because the deal was "week-to-week." And every one of those weeks, the minute the rent was due, my old pal, jacked on early-morning muscle-building, would shake me awake and wave a speckled account book in my face. When I'd groggily tell him, not yet—"Promise, Tiger, soon as I get a check"—he would spin into a frenetic shadow-boxing war-dance, at the end of which, proffering an enlarged, fist-capped bicep to my nose, he'd make me write I.O.U in his ledger and, locking me in a stare less scary than fucking rude, jog backwards out the door on a ten-mile run.

I think Tiger enjoyed the company. I really do. But I put out the word to anyone and everyone that I was in search of more amenable accommodations, and, while trying to squirrel away a few bucks for my exit west, took any and every writing assignment I could scrape up: profiles of Aerosmith, ZZ Top, Nazareth and other groups I didn't give a shit about and, because I was both a devoted fabulist (no cumbersome interviews necessary) and born-again cynic—but mostly because at that moment, in those rags, there was no subject more in-demand—Kiss. When, months later, I got the call—from a friend of a friend of a distant acquaintance—about a suddenly available apartment "in my price range," I hit up my other old friend, the rich one, Sean, for one last loan.

One last.

* * *

IT WAS NIGHT, MIDDLE OF A blackout—an historic one, with historic traffic jams, subway shutdowns, looting and fires—when the tip came in about the historically cheapest apartment in New York City: 1-BR, Sixth Avenue and 14th, half-a-block from the Village. I scrambled downtown, heedless of any peril except having to continue living on Tiger's couch. The current tenant, a thirtyish actor retreating to Baltimore after a thwarted Manhattan decade, was planning to break his lease, but needed to deliver an upstanding replacement—played, against type, by me—in order to save his deposit. By the yellowed beam of a reluctant silver flashlight—that he slammed against his palm with much outscale cursing—it was impossible to tell if the place was dark, filthy, falling down, heatless, roach- and mouse-infested, subway-rattled, if it had cracked fun-house floors, a slanted swampy tub and, through a dense weave of burglar gates and fire escape, looked across a narrow, sooty airshaft at an army of stowaway Asian women, toiling solemnly, under low fluorescent tubes, to sew zippers into American jeans. All of which it was and had and did. Though the actor invited me to come back in daylight, I knew that in this market, in this town, at this price, there was no waiting for cleaner, warmer, smoother, better, let alone morning or the restoration of the Northeast power grid. I took it on the spot, in the dark.

* * *

BY WHATEVER DAYLIGHT MANAGED TO PENETRATE the airshaft and manifest through the steel girding of the window, it was still clear that the fifth-floor walkup was an infested, disintegrating mess. It was also clear, from my long experience of the neighborhood, that the apartment was just a block-and-a-half north of the drinking establishment that would render it, for all intents and purposes, ceremonial. Because my real home was the Bells.

More than just living or dining room, the Bells of Hell was office, bank, clinic, church, concert hall, hideout, prison, fort and bedroom of last resort (there was, for a time, a freshly divorced guy sleeping on a cot in the drippy basement). And because the bar's management allowed any barely known deadbeat to run a tab—within entirely unenforced caps and disastrously flexible payment plans—the rent, on my real home, was basically free. When, after a half-decade of its customers' unearned high-living, the bar's cash-flow trickled to a halt, the Bells purchased a full-page ad in the *Voice* offering a half-off sale on tabs. Which failed dismally as financial stratagem, but—to the nihilistic proprietors, no less than their deadbeat beneficiaries—succeeded delightfully as farce.

It wasn't much of a business model, but that wasn't the point. It was owned and operated by a pair of journeyman butchers from Wordsworth's Lake District, endearingly dubious Brits who enjoyed it far more than any businessman should. Behind the bar was a broke-down sportswriter-turned-unpublished-novelist, whose alcohol-related osteoporosis made him limp like a pirate captain and who was so deeply and authentically crusty no one would ever mistake it for lovable. As recounted in a notorious letter of complaint—which carefully identified the offending bartender as "the one with the limp"—Ben had responded to a tourist's bleat about a cockroach in his beer with a confirming peek in the man's mug, followed by an acid glance into his eyes—as if a customer was far the worse pestilential insect—before snapping the infested brew through the air in the general direction of the sink and pronouncing, just above a mutter: "I wouldn't drink at a place with cockroaches." Of course, had the aggrieved correspondent believed in forgiveness as much as retribution, he might have returned to discover his crisply typed missive framed and hung in a place of honor above the jukebox. Which is not to suggest the Bells wasn't serious about its bug problems. On the counsel of a household hints columnist in the *Daily News*, one co-owner ducked down to the pet store for a gekko. The scaly, foot-long predator, touted as nature's most dogged roach exterminator, instead occupied most shifts lolling under the lights of the bar's bottom shelf amidst the little-used bottles of Bols—"slob" spelled backwards, an introspective evening once revealed to me—as his prey frolicked and fornicated amidst the beer mugs.

On the other side of the bar from the caustic barkeep and his trusty reptile was an egregiously incongruous set of young, old and prematurely old journalists, novelists, screenwriters, critics—"Drinkers with writing problems," in Ben's nicked trope—mixed with after-shift restaurant types and between-tour musicians—from the composer and Kerouac cohort David Amram, in layers of beads and ocarina necklace, to the miniature guitar god Rick Derringer, of "Hang on Sloopy" and Johnny Winter renown, to the all-day burger-serving, all-night piano-banging Edwin Eldridge Neil. Or, as he would proclaim, in a slightly exasperated run-on exhalation of rich baritone phlegm with full, impatient stop:

"Eddie-Neil-the-Village-Legend!"

* * *

I MUST HAVE ASKED, AND HE must have answered, a dozen times. It was called kerosene. That's kerosene—longer than a bark, grittier than a growl, accent on the ultimate:

"Ker-o-*SENE*!"

Or was it the initial?

"*KER*-o-sene*!*"

Either way, keep the tempo stately, but—to underscore the pitifully obvious point that any fool with a lick of sophistication knows kerosene—punctuate with a yelp. All this particular fool knows is the drink was mixed, very mixed, something to do with Triple Sec, vodka and two or three other distilled ingredients, cloudy-white in color and served on the rocks in a beer stein, all night, every night, to a single enormously thirsty customer.

Considering just the perils of kerosene—setting aside the perils of being drunk and brown and a cuckolding gigolo—it was a miracle Eddie survived as long as he did. No less a miracle that he raised his pickled noggin from a pillow every weekday, pomaded his salt-and-pepper conk, drew a razor across his thick café-con-leche mug, polished his great, gapped smile, spritzed his breath—for the first of ten-dozen times a day—clipped his regulation black bowtie onto his regulation white shirt and made it, Village to midtown to his locker of 30 years and into the starched white coat that carried his red-scripted name, promptly at 11. In that venerable New York establishment, named Prime Burger and founded in 1938, this connoisseur of the offbeat cocktail, shoulder-to-shoulder with a dozen other natty Black men time-traveled from a 1938 Pullman car or the Cab Calloway band merrily peddled beef patties on sesame buns, topped with lettuce, tomato, onions, side of fries, to Bermuda-clad vacationers from Outer Bumfuck, TV stars from across the avenue at 30 Rock, East Side ladies-who-lunch and chattering shop girls from Saks around the corner, each, regardless of age, status, income, creed, race, national origin or girth, snapped into her own built-in dining unit behind a swiveling oak tray—a kind of low-rise adult high-chair—attached at the flank to dozens of others arrayed around the perimeter of the wood-paneled, grease-darkened room, like daycare toddlers at snack time.

It was a day job. And though he performed it with a cheeky ebullience that never came off as fraud—no more than any other aspect of Eddie's hammy existence—his real work, he assured fellow barflies, what his god and public demanded, was music. Thanks to the music-smitten partner, Tim (who, to be clear, never actually hired him), the Bells was his gig.

* * *

A THIRTY-YEAR-OLD IMP IN BEATLE BANGS, Tim, the younger butcher, was a mad music fan and it showed in the Bells' record machine, stocked, for starters, with the very latest punk and new wave shipped weekly by a mate in Blighty. The fresh sides were duly installed alongside the classic efforts of Steeleye Span, the Chieftains, Pentangle and other Anglo-Celtics that, as a Celto-Gaelic limey, he was powerless to resist, and cheek-by-jowl with

America's finest Anglo-Celtic inheritors: Waylon, Willie, Johnny Cash, George Jones. There were obscure new American singles that Tim had unearthed at Bleecker Bob's ("Little Johnny Jewel" by Television) or that an industrious indie proprietor had trotted by (Patti Smith's "Piss Factory"). There was Frankie and the drunk national anthem, "One for the Road," but also a Mozart etude by synth—and transgender—pioneer Wendy Carlos. When it came to music, Tim loved whatever. And, as a poker-faced Brit, expressed it the only way he could: through a blinking, whirring box of gears. At a time of the next tectonic shift in pop, that moment when Tim the Butcher unlocked the glass and fed his vinyl-sorting robot "Anarchy in the UK"—which no one in the States had heard of, let alone heard—it reinforced the impression that the tectonics were shifting here first, that the Bells of Hell had the best jukebox in New York.

And in the back—spritz-spritz—had Eddie Neil the Village Legend. Who played a mean 12 minutes of piano.

Kerosene stein a-hand, Eddie would gravely mount the stage, take a seat on the bench, rotate his shoulders like a power hitter—Harmon Killebrew?—and rip into the sour upright. The scrunched concentration of the face and passionately disheveled conk were Beethoven, but the music—ornate, eddying glissandos, with the Legend's nubby digits first stumbling up the keys, away from all meter and sense and then down into a fatal pileup of a turn-around—was strictly Liberace. "Champagne Music" on kerosene. Not so much theme and variation as intro and more intro and more. Oh, the tune might segue briefly into a woozy oompah take on some jazz standard—or what you could imagine, if you imagined hard, was a jazz standard. It might even turn into "Happy Birthday"—that is, Eddie's multi-movement, oompah-ragtime "Happy Birthday Concerto," all 90 seconds of it—before scrambling back to loopy fanfare. And after ten more minutes—a span that represented either the total running time of his repertoire or capacity of his stein—without further fanfare, musical, verbal or otherwise, the Legend would abruptly stop.

And float away.

* * *

Between the rare records, rude characters and wry bonhomie—despite the magnanimous mismanagement—the Bells of Hell faced a rapidly growing risk of success. No doubt this drunken orphans home was always, in its inattentive way, cool. And you could see the forces of fashion—the downtown scene-makers dubbed, in the downtown papers, PIBs, People in Black—assembling on the wire. But I shuddered that Judgment Day had dawned when the call came in from Terry.

Despite the black-hatted, -shirted, -booted and, round-the-clock, indoors and out, -sunglassed demeanor that signaled his status as a prince among PIBs—while taunting the world's customs officials into snapping on the latex gloves—Terry Landsman didn't make, take or sell illegal drugs. He didn't drink. Not a drop, ever. Nor, for that matter, did he play piano. Neither did the new band he was working with. (Neither—it shall soon become relevant—did I.) Terry was a friend—a decent one when he deigned to lower the shades—but a friend you took on his own terms. A onetime *Creem* contributor turned controversial record producer, he was controversially overseeing the first American recording by a British band called the Clash. And tonight, Terry informed me on the phone, he and the band's brain-trust were en route, for purposes yet undisclosed, to the only bar in America with the Clash on the jukebox.

The Mick and Keith of their generation—the Joe and Mick of their band—strolled in around midnight, unremarked by the assembled Yanks to whom their music (D5 on the Select-o-matic) might have been familiar, but whose still-smooth English faces were not. In his ironically polite way, Terry introduced the Brits, who seemed to immediately take me for a specimen, staring when I spoke—even when, for chrissakes, I was offering drinks—and speaking little in reply. It was hard to tell if this was new-gen rock-star aloofness, a populist punk take on old-gen rock-star condescension, or if, after being pop gods in Britain for a whole 12 months, it was a well-earned disinterest in the to-ing and fro-ing of mortals. Or did it bespeak a more pointed distaste for the Bells' bourgie clientele? Maybe I misunderstood the evening's mission. I took it to be play—let's get drunk in downtown America—when it turned out to be work: hiring a pianist (studio clock's a-ticking, mate), and, if possible, for the composers of "(White Man) in Hammersmith Palais," a Black one. When I returned with a half-dozen embossed green bottles of Western Pennsylvania's finest hops-water, Terry took me aside and said, "The guys want to check out Eddie."

All I could say was: "Are you sure?"

I had the fearsome knowledge, as unavailable to Terry, Joe or Mick as to the drunks who tumbled through the backroom's swinging doors looking for the john or tourist couples who tiptoed in for the romantic "Jazz Piano" they'd read about on the chalkboard. If I knew too well that Eddie was miserable at music, I also knew he was masterful at art. Performance art. The Village Legend—who decidedly wasn't—performing as the gifted pianist he also wasn't. Not to mention the gifted raconteur or ladies' man—actually, ladies' man is another story. But at the piano level, it was no good. Not at all. And I alone in this august company and fraught moment was possessed of the awful truth: The Village Legend was a 12-minute loop.

* * *

EDDIE'S PIANO-PLAYING—IF NOT MOST OF HIS Earthly endeavors—might best be characterized by a term that, on the punctilious page, I'm forced to spell phonetically:

YOK-a-may.

It was a made-up word, made up by Eddie. While there's a soundalike term—Yaka mein—for a New Orleans noodle specialty, Eddie's simply meant bullshit (as in: "Don't give me none of that yok-a-may, Randy!"). And this fateful night, with the Village Legend somehow deeper into his cups—or steins—than usual, the yok-a-may was at flood tide.

"I'll find him," I said to Terry.

Eddie had sleepwalked to the bar and was waiting, in suspended animation, at the service end, where, as house band, self-appointed, and a 30-year member of the serving fraternity, he surely felt he belonged. He didn't have to say he wanted another kerosene. All he had to do was stay upright. It took a while for me to retrieve his attention.

"Eddie . . . ? Hey, Ed!"

He looked at me, and through me, through the wall and stratosphere and somewhere past the Chuck Berry satellite before the jack-o'-lantern grin finally opened and Eddie grabbed my shoulders in warm recognition, showering me in my name:

"Tom Randy!"

My Eddie name.

"Listen, Eddie," I said, dodging left and right to evade the spray and lock in to his drifting gaze. "There's a famous band here, from England, and they want you to play a little piano, maybe even play on their record."

After I repeated the theme, with variations, two or three times, Eddie paused to process—or keel over dead—but eventually did something far more remarkable: snuffed the jack-o'-lantern, smoothed his do, spritzed his cavernous yap, and pulled what I imagined was the same string that reassembled him every morning for Prime Burger.

Snap, the Village Legend was sober.

* * *

THE BACKROOM FELT LIKE A MEETING of the Five Families, as the guys from the Clash stood up and Terry stood up and I stood up, and we all soberly shook hands. Eddie, too. Steady, focused, urbane—even legendary—Eddie remembered the name of the band, like I'd told him at the bar. And after we went around the table, the names of the band members and their producer. For a few sublime moments Eddie poured on the Eddie charm, busting out autobiographical tidbits from the days of bongos around Washington Square fountain and Trane downstairs at the Gate—until the producer jumped in.

"You know what?" Terry said, twisting his sunglassed head into an awkward, but familiar, pose, a skeptical tilt that suggested graciousness and enthusiasm might actually be satire. "I'd really like to hear the Legend play."

Thus did Eddie Neil and his cloudy beer stein climb the stage and, in effect, audition for "The Only Band that Matters."

They weren't the Only Band that Matters then. That was coming, as part of the album's ad campaign. (Coming, by the way, from the typewriter of our old pal Eric Lasker, back when he was a copywriter at Athena Records, not yet a musical paragon in his own right.) Nonetheless, months away from release, you could already sense the buzz.

Then, as magically as he had pulled himself together, Eddie Neil fell apart.

* * *

I THINK EDDIE WAS FROM SOMEWHERE else. Atlanta, I want to say. Or New Orleans. He wasn't one to dwell. At some point, I know, he was a respectably married dad. Many times—many, many times—he told me the story of how when he was casting about for names for his first-born, he came upon the package for a fancy French beauty product. On the front, in big letters, it said "Savon," and Eddie was struck by how perfect a word for his pretty precious—exotic, romantic, musical. Only later did he discover—and here he'd start slapping his thigh and screaming—it was French for soap.

"Soap!" he would howl. "I named my baby girl soap!"

Another night Eddie hooked my arm and asked would I go with him to see his son.

"You didn't know I had a son!" he laughed, adding: "Doesn't want nothing to do with me."

Eddie explained that his baby boy was a singer, composer and keyboard player—like dad, kinda—and already in his 20s a big disco star, about to headline New York's most renowned disco inferno. As a straight, white rock critic in good standing, I knew shit about dance music. I did know the claim that his son was a star had to be Eddie's most outlandish yok-a-may yet. In fact, I had not a scintilla of doubt all the way up to the moment we stood among the shimmering multitudes outside Palazzo and stared up at the marquee. Where, in irrefutable caps, the bright lights confirmed:

"EDDIE NEIL, JR."

Eddie the elder spritzed his breath, elbowed his way to the velvet rope and threw his head back.

"Eddie Neil—SENIOR—the Village Legend!" he announced. "I'm here to see my son."

The dark, hulking tower of power at the door was unimpressed. He rotated his starkly cropped head first left, then right—slowly, as if on precision motors—adjusted his earphone, scrutinized the crowd spilling into the street, barked at any ticketholder who dared dab a toe inside the ropes, and, still not certain he'd deflated Eddie enough, asked him to repeat his name. Only after a few more officious rotations did he finally drag a single, oversized finger down the front of his clipboard.

"No Senior on my list."

"Now, listen here, brother," Eddie declared, with a distinctly streetward shift in dialect. "This here's my son, and he don't wanna have nothing to do with me. But I've never seen him play."

The listmaster said nothing, acknowledged nothing, but eventually—having waited long enough to imply that whatever he did or didn't do would have nothing to do with whatever Eddie did or didn't want—mumbled into his walkie-talkie. After many minutes more, while proud papa flashed his jack-o'-lantern at shiny streams of disco girls, every one younger than Savon, the walkie-talkie returned a crackly answer. Without bothering to make eye contact, or raise his volume to audible, the bouncer delivered the breaking news to Eddie, who judging by the change in expression managed to hear it loud and clear:

"He don't want to see you, man."

* * *

NOT RIGHT, NOT EVEN FOR A guy like Eddie, who with his outthrust chin and relentless cheek always seemed to be daring you to. Not cool. After all, going along—with Eddie, as with any rock star—was half the fun. Believing that the implausible figure in front of you is exactly the hero he says he is—that eensy-weensy Prince is the hog-riding bad-ass of *Purple Rain*—is part of the fun and essential to an audience's love. When a guy like Eddie, a Village Legend, gets mistreated—in the Village, of all places—it hurts you, too. Not that sometimes you didn't want to crack him on the jaw yourself.

"Bertie! Bertie! Bertie!" he'd woof into the phone. "I wanna talk to Randy!"

But my girlfriend's name was Rebecca—Becky—not Bertie, just as mine wasn't Randy. And the call had electroshocked both of us awake at 4:55 am.

Like a lot of the strangers I've stumbled upon over the years, Eddie had my phone number. I gave it to him, as I generally do, way too early in the relationship. It seems to be part of how I make friends—that reckless gesture of trust. Because while everybody makes promises in bars, I pride myself on keeping them, and mostly do. It's how I've managed to accumulate all the weirdos and waste-cases (and they, me) that have—in the end, if not always in the early-morning—made my lifes [sic] pageant so rich: the parking attendants, chefs, welterweights, museum guards, civil engineers, cabbies, waiters, sales managers, merchant mariners, janitors, fire-fighters, special ed teachers, one millionaire playwright—another Ed, as in Albee, who accepted a drink from a brokeass, but didn't return the favor—and, of course, the many writers and hundreds of musicians—the rich and famous and mostly the poor and unknown. And I liked to tell myself I learned it all from my big brother, that we were that close.

In any case, Eddie had my number—and used it with alarming frequency—but I also had his. At nine the morning after his unofficial Clash audition, a Saturday, Eddie's essential day of rest from pulling that damn Prime Burger string, I used it.

"Eddie," I said to the catarrhal drowning noises on the other end, "we gotta talk."

I wondered if his terrible, drunken performance had helped mask the terrible, sober incompetence—no matter how charming—at its core. In other words, did his abject drunkenness allow Joe, Mick, and Terry to write off the ineptitude to a bad night? Whatever the explanation, the band wanted Eddie at Studio C—Athena Records' storied temple of recording on 52nd Street, where Dylan, Bruce, Miles, and Sinatra had cut historic sides—by two to play.

Which meant that, by two, Eddie had to learn how.

CHAPTER 18

Yok-a-may

I'M SORRY I GOT FRUSTRATED. EVEN when he called at five in the morning, Eddie was a gift. More than magisterial performance art, he was a living, barking Rushmore of human hope, of the possibility that the average shmoe, you and me, with a little pluck—or a lot—can rise, not just above, but high.

Case in point: the piano-beating burger man was also a first-class gigolo. He was kept in a manner befitting by a rich German-born émigré he called Mommy, who was married to a dentist in some tony North Jersey suburb. Or so Eddie said. I assumed again, sensibly, it was the kerosene talking. Then, early that Saturday, I stood before a long green awning on the coziest, tree-lined section of West 12th Street, in front of a handsome pre-war, red-brick. I fumbled to check another scrap in my pocket. Before I could, a smiling doorman hurried from the entrance. When I asked for Eddie Neil, instead of looking quizzically or shaking his head disgustedly, he escorted me into the castle-like lobby and formally, via house phone, announced my arrival—saying "Yes, sir. Very good" into the handset—before ushering me to the speckle-mirrored elevator, which ascended to the tenth floor, where, in plush robe, slippers and partly unsprung hair, my late-night friend opened his too-early door and beckoned with a demitasse for me to follow him past the view of the Empire State to the Steinway baby grand. Later I'd meet the mythic Mommy, who turned out to be a raven-haired vamp of 45, alarmingly sexy, entirely real.

No yok-a-may.

But with 120 minutes to teach him how to play his instrument, there was no time to marvel at the true life of a guy who severely understated the case when he called himself a legend.

To reiterate, I didn't know how to play piano either. But I had listened to enough rock 'n' roll keyboard that, when Eddie started in with the Liberace and oompah, playing the same dopey stuff sober as he did drunk, I could say, "No, not really." And, by way of demonstration, bang out sixteenth notes on the high keys with my fist.

"You know Little Richard? Jerry Lee Lewis?"

Eddie would start into a halting imitation of my primitive banging for 20 seconds, before backsliding. For him, rock 'n' roll wasn't just a different language, it was a language, period, with logic and rules, all of which substantiated my suspicions that the Village Legend wasn't a piano player so much as a player-piano, with a 12-minute roll. For two whole hours in Mommy's love nest overlooking the heart of Greenwich Village, side by side on the bench, we tried. Eventually having made, if you squinted your ears, slight progress—but most of all not wanting to destroy Eddie's most potent musical weapon, his balls—I, who didn't play piano, reassured my piano pupil:

"You're gonna kill."

There were moments in Studio C when I thought he was. When I thought *we* were. Because by the time the lesson was over and we got ourselves up to the famous music studio on the famous music street, I was fully invested. Over-invested. There were fond greetings all around, and then the assistant led Eddie into that eerily muted, orchestra-sized room and sat him in front of the full-sized Steinway and adjusted the seat and carefully fitted the cans over his conk and checked the levels were to his liking, and Terry the producer—ensconced behind glass with Joe, Mick and me—told the engineer to roll tape, and a stupefied Village Legend seemed to register only that something was happening—as Bob Dylan had put it *in that very room*—but he didn't know what it was.

The tune was a three-chord shuffle about a drug snitch, written by Strummer in an ironically bouncy Fifties style. It's easy to say, when it's not your ass on the line, that it couldn't have been easier. Fair to say that plenty of big stars—Dylan or Bruce or Frank maybe—have lost it when the engineer, in those flat engineer tones, says over the headphones: *And we're rolling* . . . It's a phenomenon so common they even have a name for it. Redlight Fever—after the crimson lamp that illuminates when the machine is listening for the ages. There were a million excuses for Eddie's abysmal first passes, and the young limeys, it must be recorded for the ages, gave him the full benefit of the doubt. After half-a-dozen attempts in which the only consistency was the Village Legend's lapse from driving sixteenth notes into oompah, the righteous bard of punk announced to the control room:

"I'm going out there."

Joe Strummer stretched out on the floor of the performance room to keep Eddie company and called for a new series of takes. Which Eddie continued to blow. Two or three times, Joe shed his headphones, popped up from the floor and, in a scene that felt oddly déjà vu, joined Eddie on the piano bench to demonstrate sixteenth notes. Then, careful to give the Village Legend a reassuring rub on the shoulder, he'd sprawl back on the linoleum and fire up a fag. After another hour of Eddie utterly failing to improve, Joe signaled for a break and, returning to the control room, asked

Terry and Mick to step into the hall. When they came back, Joe leaned over the engineer's shoulder and pressed a button and spoke into the talkback mic, the news shooting straight from his snaggle-teeth to the keyboardist's headphoned ears:

"Great, Eddie, I think we got it."

What Joe Strummer had got, I knew, was the awful truth.

* * *

AT A PRESS PARTY IN THE Time-Life building for Ozzy Osbourne—where the guest of honor could be found, with difficulty (even if you were his publicist), chin to chest, in a dark, back corner—a producer acquaintance, yet another of that hard-hustling breed, palmed me the number of an editor looking for an unauthorized biography of Kiss. And the next day I called that number. For a few zlotys down and a pitiful percent down the road, I readily agreed to prostitute what I viewed as my considerable, yet virginal, talents. And if writing a Kiss book might seem far from the most dishonorable thing, for me trying to be a *real* writer—in order to be a rock star—it wasn't far from shitting yourself in a St. Olaf's classroom. It exponentially compounded the agony when the first printing arrived and the publisher's marketing department booked me as an exhibitor at the First Annual Rock Flea Market and Collectors Fair in the ballroom of the Roosevelt Hotel.

Directly opposite Penn Station, the Roosevelt had once teemed with real armies in transit home from real war, the ballroom floor pulsing into dawn with straight whiskey, syncopated horns, hair-flying Lindy Hoppers and undiagnosed post-traumatic stress. Now those hallowed cedar planks were swirled in must and crawling with the Kiss Army—allied forces of the round-shouldered, the inhaler-dependent and the pre-pubescent, a white-faced band's even paler disciples and not coincidentally my best shot at a dime of royalties. It was exactly the kind of place a rock snob would not be caught dead. For my sins, the publisher had shipped in a dozen cartons of product and commanded me to get out and sell. Wedged between the Satanist belt-buckle kiosk and a stoney scammer's-apprentice peddling crates of illicit promo records—possibly the selfsame crap I was peddling to this guy Benny ("No last names!"), the illicit record-buyer who, twice a month, lumbered up to the fifth floor with cash—I sat at a card table, counting the minutes till closing and doing my damnedest to hide behind an improvised duck blind of my own disgraceful books. Which is why it took a minute for me to note the arrival of the new scourge of the bourgeoisie, torch-bearer of the rebel spirit, savior-in-waiting of modern youth and leader of the Only Band that Matters.

It had been two months since I had slunk from Athena studios with a dazed and confused Eddie. Terry called a week later to let me know they'd got the Blue Öyster Cult's keyboardist to bang out the piano part in less than 20 minutes, and, since the ever gracious Allen Lanier had also agreed to forego credit, the Village Legend would never have to know.

"Eddie," Terry said with a snort, "can go on dreaming."

It was kind and cruel at the same time. I decided the kind part was Joe's idea. The cruel part—making sure I knew they'd formally nuked my "protégé" and effectively putting the fiasco on me—was just what you'd expect from a guy in indoor shades.

In the meantime, our friend Lasker had tagged the Clash the Only Band that Matters, and the record company had airlifted Lester into the middle of their UK tour, enabling a week-long bender and slobbering multi-part hagiography, and a legion of premature ejaculators were stroking their Selectrics over the impending disk.

In the US, in other words, the Clash had advanced beyond buzz.

"Oh, hey," I said to Strummer, as I raised my head above the paperbacks.

He nodded and fingered the volume.

Then along came Jones.

"Oh, hey," I repeated.

Mick nodded and turned the book over and back, and over again, like he wasn't quite sure where to begin. I hemmed and hawed:

"Yeah, well, kind of a joke, you know . . . "

But I was too hot-faced to pull it off. And once more Joe stared.

This time it wasn't wariness. Worse, it wasn't judgment. This time at the Rock Flea Market in the smelly belly of the Roosevelt Hotel, Joe Strummer looked at me with pity.

As if to confirm, he shrugged and said, "We've all got to make a living . . . "

Agonizing later, I told myself that, rather than a whore and rock Judas, I had been joined, in Strummer's mind, with the lumpen youth he was bent on redeeming, that the pity I had read in his black gaze was actually sympathy—"We've all got to make a living"—and brotherly commiseration on the state of the Clampdown.

It wasn't like the Clash hadn't compromised. The debate about whether you could be beholden to a media conglomerate and still be revolutionary—the Only Band that Matters—fueled half their publicity.

We . . . Strummer had said. *All* . . . he'd appended.

I had to write shitty Kiss books, and he had to suck up to the suits at Athena. Same prison, different cells.

CHAPTER 19
Killebrew

I SOMETIMES WONDER IF, AS A fervent convert, I didn't learn New York too well. I'd arrived in fourth grade rooting for Harmon Killebrew and the feckless Twins, even as my new town was transfixed by Mantle and Maris dueling for Ruth's home-run mark and the best-ever Bronx Bombers headed—again—for the Series. To one S.I. bully, the red TC (for Twin Cities) on my navy-blue cap was more than an index of profound disloyalty. And the kind of thing that, as prisoners and private school boys know, can lead to accidents—especially when the little Twins fan, a funny-talking new boy, is threading his way between cafeteria tables, balancing a half-pint of milk.

So that was the first lesson.

Within a few months, having gotten over spilled milk—not to mention the shock of moving from amber plains of grain to plains amber with piss and landmined with shit and battled over by clamorous cars and hellbent pedestrians—I found myself wanting so badly to fit in that I systematically taught myself the tricks. To swallow my vowels, flatten my grin, harden my gaze, snort derisively at friendliness and inject a little strut in my gait. A year later, on our one and only return trip to Minnesota, old friends and neighbors—even Kristin, I was pleased to note—could hardly get over the transformation, especially the accent.

I bring it up because there were a few more things I learned as a new boy in Gotham: keep your strut brisk, wallet in front, eyes ahead. When someone calls you out on a dark stretch of Eighth Street, pay no attention.

"Walk tall," Bruce himself admonished, back when a Jersey boy was still just peeping in. "Or, brother, don't walk at all."

Sure enough, someone on Eighth Street was calling me out.

"Guy over there's talking to you," insisted my date, a Coney Island hardass who should've known better.

As a slight scruff with a wisp of beard, knit cap, peacoat and black high-tops shuffled from the shadows, my peripheral vision mashed the "This is not a drill" button.

But wait.

"Bruce?"

* * *

I'D MET HIM IN DETROIT—*CREEM*, OF course—and, as sparsely social as he might have been, we kept running into each other at unexpected intervals in New York: other people's shows, other people's press parties, and one time in the dark on Eighth Street.

We just seemed to hit it off. He was a hick, too, and fundamentally shy, with spotty skin, instead of bucky teeth, and came from a province that, no matter how physically near, was still—like Minnesota, but like any place *not New York*—far away.

I say, we *seemed* to hit it off, because, again, I don't trust those kinds of friendships. For all our affinities and overlaps, Bruce and I were still worlds apart. He was the kind who'd stuck with the guitar, who'd studied the canon, who'd practiced, not just his hair in the mirror, but his scales in his room, while I, from the age of 14, was hanging out in bars. Well, he was hanging out in bars, too, but it was because he had a gig. The boy who'd got The Sickness and then, incredibly, The Cure—the transubstantiation that unsure types had daydreamed since first scrabbling their tennis rackets to *Ed Sullivan*. Or as Bruce would later put it, offering the overprotected daughter of a skeptical dad a powerful new reason why:

"Because a record company, Rosie, just gave me a big advance."

Now what did a guy like that want from me?

* * *

BACK FROM DETROIT, INSTALLED AMONG THE cockroaches of Sixth Avenue, I was working on the Kiss book and a slowly expanding freelance trade, thinking the winds had shifted. But I was bedeviled by an insecurity I didn't know then was an occupational hazard. Even after two whole years of publishing, I had to constantly reassure myself—harking back to an A+ on a ninth-grade composition or encouraging words from a freshman-year NYU professor—that the talent was really there. And it was. I think. What was missing, for better or worse, was something I might have struggled to describe as craft. It didn't come fast, and it wasn't often fun. But I was learning: the rudiments of telling stories on paper, not just in bars. And the assignments were getting juicier, with this the juiciest of all: shadowing a new crown prince of rock 'n' roll through the Mississippi Delta, not a hundred miles from Tupelo, birthplace of the recently departed King, and not six feet, on the vertical, from the ebony gods who'd blazed the trail for both (and whose graves, I'm afraid, were not kept clean).

It was nicknamed the "Darkness" tour, after the album, and I was on the bus for four days, which was three or four more than usual. Unlike many of his peers, Bruce wasn't wired or drunk, or drunk on the distilled juices of his own ego, so you could have a real conversation. And every Bruce show was a cathartic delight, a soaring cathedral of down-to-earth communion. It was exhilarating, as a writer, to be up-close and inside. Outside, beyond the rushing bus windows—everyone asleep but me—and in the streets and auditorium parking lots, in the hotel lobbies, po-boy shops and at Lee Dorsey's hospitably down-and-out Ya-Ya Lounge, it was summer and the parboiling South. Before we even got to the interview, I stuffed several sweaty pockets full of notes:

—Six o'clock news. *Local TV-hair asks coach about quarterback's new contract: "Did you Jew him down?"*

—Hotel lobby. *Cabbie ducks in for a hit of AC. Notes three agitated girls out front. "Who y'all got in here?" "Boy from . . . ," says day manager, pointing up, meaning north, adding with effort: "Bruce Spring-stein."*

—Royal near Toulouse. *Out for pre-soundcheck stroll, me and large Black man are stopped. "Waitress says you walked out on the bill," says cop to Clarence. No bill, no sir, didn't even walk in. Unconscionable amount of time later: the large Black man, known to audiences worldwide as the King of the World, Emperor of Everything, is finally tucking license back in wallet, free to go (after a fashion), when I notice his big eyes are full.*

—Sign, store window. *"Big Easy Oldies—Biggest in N.O.!" Middle-aged, white proprietor, turning red, doesn't want to know from Professor Longhair or Fats. "It was me! I invented Black music!" Except he didn't say Black.*

* * *

Municipal Auditorium. In a fluorescent-harsh back room opposite Congo Square—where enslaved Africans invented American music—Bruce was shaping a sentence with his hands, trying to explain about saving kids. He didn't mean orphans or the starving—though there was that, too.

"There's always a kid with no shirt in front of the PA," he confided, more awe-struck than amused. "You know, *that* guy. And that guy has come to get saved." And this night, opposite Congo Square, and the next, up Highway 61 in Jackson, sure enough, arms wide at the woofer, there that guy was.

I told Bruce it put me in mind of Holden Caulfield, that preppie who'd dreamed of rescuing falling children, of being "the catcher in the rye." Then I worried I was giving myself away—though doesn't everybody read *Catcher*? Even Catholic school kids in Jersey? No, he said. And it didn't seem to wreck anything, not even when he courteously rubbed his chin (for this incarnation, clean shaven) and replied, "Interesting . . . " But after a couple hours trading shovels—burrowing through fathers, mothers, nuns, New York, the Swingin' Medallions, Mitch Ryder, Sam the Sham, punks, malaise and a future that, like the future tends to, offered distinct portents of apocalypse (Johnny Rotten's "no future"; Bruce's own "Darkness on the Edge of Town")—bullshitting in the back room and, on and off, in back rooms in Houston and Jackson, as well as aboard the cramped bus, I wrote a long story for *Creem*, and, for the first time, felt I really had a grip. A few months later, after his first Garden gig, his official New York homecoming, he threaded through a backstage cafeteria full of movie stars, rock stars, and rich folks beyond saving and sat at a distant table, our table, where he told me that not since the story where Jon Landau called him "rock 'n' roll's future"—the one helped make him just that—had there been better.

I didn't trust those kinds of friendships. But as a token of mine, I gave him a copy of *Catcher in the Rye*. As a token of his, he invited me down the shore.

* * *

BRUCE WAS A ROCK STAR HIMSELF now, a condition about which I—a nobody, nothing—could offer little insight. He didn't drink, not really, an activity which seemed integral to my entertainment value. And something fundamentally unnerving about the son of a bus driver hitting it off with the son of a hatchet man. As to swaying "critics," he'd already captured the undying devotion of all the big ones—among them the rave-reviewer Landau, now his manager. And while I was pretty sure I was more fun than those nerds, did Bruce even know?

I didn't trust those kinds of friendships. Then Bruce called—as he did about Cleveland—to say he wasn't kidding. I don't recall what I said. I know I didn't tell him I was short car fare, because that might have sounded like begging. I didn't talk about journalistic integrity, about getting too cozy to be mean—Lester's knock on his friend Cameron, the *Rolling Stone* wunderkind—because that might have sounded like a pompous ass. I certainly didn't go into the evolution of my abnormal psychology (didn't yet know about his), how my childhood hobgoblins—fear of the dark, of wetting the bed, of strangers' strange food—had morphed into a distressing array of adult hobgoblins—fear of running out of cigarettes, of running out of booze, of strangers' strange food. Not a peep about acid flashbacks—though there was that hobgoblin, too. Told Bruce I had an appointment. Had a deadline. Had a cough. Something rickety. It occurs to me now that maybe, deep down, I wanted to put another rock star in his place.

Whether it was envy that won the day or nerves, I didn't actually have the car or train fare. Having foregone a steady gig in the City of Motors for an unsteady one in the City that Never Sleeps—as a penny-a-word mocker and ranter in the rock 'n' roll pulps—I was broke again. The favorable winds had died. And for all-of-the-above and whatever other gossamer excuse, I had turned down Bruce, like I'd turned down Sam. Then the more broke I got and the more famous I did not become and the more I toiled, for the less and less, as the tick did mercilessly tock (already, at 22, three years past

George Harrison on *Sullivan*), I found myself consumed by the road not taken. And consumed, speaking of abnormal psych, is not an exaggeration. The longer I didn't hear from Bruce and the bigger he got—going from big as anyone could imagine, simultaneous covers of *Time* and *Newsweek*, to just ridiculous—the smaller I felt. Bruce in his success was the measure of my failure. Wasn't he also the Holden Caulfield? Didn't I have it on tape? A few years later when he sang that line about being "sick of sitting 'round here trying to write this book," and I was doing just that. I thought it was a signal. He was on his way.

Bruce with his own damn problems.

CHAPTER 20

Gomorrah

THREE MONTHS AFTER I MOVED INTO the Sixth Avenue place, the old lithographer in the mirror-image floorplan next door keeled over, and I pleaded with the landlord to let me call Lester's bluff.

"Hey," I said into the phone to the Big Fish of Birmingham, "you're always talking about moving to New York . . . "

Six weeks later, there he was. There we were. Writers, artists, drinkers, pals, and now, gloriously, next-door neighbors, toiling side-by-side, five stories above the fondest fantasy of a Jehovah's Witness refugee from El Cajon, California, by way of Metropolitan Detroit:

Gomorrah, just like I pictured it.

* * *

NO SURPRISE THAT MOVING TO NEW York, consecrated stomping grounds of Ayler, Monk, Miles, the Velvet Underground—and, of course, Satan—was long the greatest fear and greatest aspiration of a clever, driven hayseed like Lester. The mythic city was a thread through both his starry-eyed chatter at Pasquale's and credulous rants at the office, often touching on something he'd read in the *Voice*—a story about S&M star Fred Halstead, my phone-fraud alias, engendered a week-long jag—or had just heard from a New York freelancer on the phone (Lester loved to gab on the phone). As only an innocent abroad, he constantly lamented the latest dire New York fashion—for heroin or swastikas or disco—and the nullity of Andy Warhol. Above all, he bewailed a certain murder-porn movie that had recently premiered, to a forest of scandalized press, on 42nd Street. *Snuff*, which purported to show an actual murder, had sent the big galoot into apocalyptic sugar-shock. After it was exposed as a hoax, a mere porn-*horror* movie, his lamentations only escalated—to Lester, even dreaming up a scam like that was the end of the world. And the end of the world was his beat, as he rapturously teased every vile thread into a grand thesis about Terminal Decadence, Final Decline, Death of Love, of Art, of Tribe (but not rock—he'd killed that years before), sometimes wrapped around a profile of Lou Reed or John Denver, a review of John Coltrane or Anne Murray, his end-times rhetoric as much a sublimation of his own apprehension and lust, as it was moral outrage. Because there was no city more morally outrageous, he always had a boner for New York.

In Detroit when a New York band passed through, Lester would barge backstage and, after running down the good, bad and Stooges-like aspects of their performance, pump them, in his gosh-golly way, for breaking news of Downtown Manhattan. At first, they wouldn't know what to make of him. The larger-than-life barger would overrun their bafflement with urgent verdicts, theories, wet dreams, homilies and harangues about a city, *their* city, he'd only ever visited, about its music, players and milieu, delivered behind an unwavering mustache-stare that, from time to time, would crack for a self-deprecating laugh. Meanwhile, the band—skinny, spiky and chain-smoking—would cycle through reactions: asshole, nut, drunk, druggie, hick, confounding, exhausting, outrageous, hilarious, brilliant. All of which Lester most inextricably was.

That uncut outsiderness (not to be confused with cluelessness) was in many ways the engine of his wonder, fundamental to his honesty, if not his dishonesty, and all tangled up in his artistry and charm. This was no New York vampire. That was made clear, however unwittingly, in the mustache—the bushy appurtenance Lester held onto well into the clean-shaven era—and the gut. In a landscape of undernourished rock stars, he would always stand out for a bouncing belly that seemed to pull his shoulders down and pitch his body forward and behind which, in promo tee and grimy jeans, he clomped through the world like an overfed Groucho, El Cajon to his core.

Part of what spooked Lester about continuing his journey all the way east, after five years in Michigan, were his own appetites, which came to him far too naturally from a father whose appetites had been his fiery undoing. Part was Lester's conscience, shaped by boyhood missions with his fervent mom. Mostly he was afraid a kid from the San Diego sticks would be just another passing chump: not good enough for the city. And it wasn't about being good enough as a rock critic—he was already celebrated, even in New York, as Detroit's icon-smashing, critical fauve. It was about, one day, becoming a lion of literature—the Burroughs of his generation—stepping up to the next field of glory. In the meantime, he wallowed in the glory he had.

"I'm Lester Bangs!" he'd exclaim, with a big, hick grin, eyebrows high in anticipation. He was genuinely excited for you to meet him.

I'd wince. I'd wince because a hick was what I'd worked so hard not to be—not to talk hick, be hick-dumb or, for that matter, hang with a hick who didn't know a Twins cap from a Yankees. No doubt mine was also a wince of envy. Because while he might have been a yokel, he was also "Lester Bangs." It was amazing how many people, in the hippest precincts—of New York, Detroit, Austin, Paris—were excited to meet him.

Turned out to be all the fame he needed.

* * *

We shared our perch above the byways of Gomorrah with a Cantonese restaurant left over from the Fifties: red leather booths, long green awning and grand neon sign that in a pseudo-Chinese font heralded the joint's name: Gum Joy. The words were a botched translation none of my Chinese-speaking friends could figure—Happy Mouth was the best guess and that was mine. But thirty years on—red leather patched with red tape, a triangle of torn awning flapping in the breeze, plastic letters punched out, and a new generation of mouths getting happy on Szechuan and Hunan elsewhere—it surely meant irony. I started to slug my dispatches with the dateline "Gum Joy Towers"—a coinage which in the communal euphoria Lester was quick to borrow.

Which was great and fine. I guess. Sharing bon mots. Because another thing we shared was: everything. Since the streetside door to our building was double-bolted and well-armored and we didn't have a lot to steal, Lester and I, far away on the top floor, decided why bother locking our apartment doors? *Mi shithole es su shithole* was the idea—in the communal euphoria of the moment.

I can't remember how long the communal euphoria lasted. I can say that togetherness was less complicated in Birmingham. The circle of people you could make sick jokes with was small, precious—you could never afford to lose one. Not so in New York. If we arrived as closest of friends, if Lester inspired and instructed me and helped open doors to editors, writers, music folk who might otherwise have kept them closed and if I, a Bucky Beaver from Minnesota who'd spent just enough time in New York to be pompous about it, helped him become less of a Gomer from the sticks of Greater San Diego and opened the door to the other cheapest apartment in New York City, if we were competitors—in an unspoken way—each determined to conquer the culture, while the city, with its bottomless diversions and shameless sycophants, was always trying to pry us apart, we remained closest of friends for a long time. Which only made it worse.

* * *

LESTER HAD BEEN DATING CINDY FOR a year, and now, satisfied with his vow to do his darnedest, she'd come along to New York to try living together. An aspiring actress—theater, not Hollywood, with a low, mellifluous theatrical voice—Cindy was a levelheaded young Michigander and brought a large measure of calm, restraint and, judging by his googly eyes, puppy love to the case of Lester Bangs. It seemed like he really would do anything for her—even quit booze.

I remembered when he tried to do it without her.

"I'm not drinking," he'd announced, as we piled into the booth at Pasquale's. He'd decided to lose weight, get healthy (it happened from time to time). When Wanda came for the orders, she stopped writing and stared when he said: "Just a white wine with dinner."

Then, while the rest of us guzzled beer, Lester matched us ounce for ounce with wine—twelve percent alcohol to our four—until the guy who wasn't drinking also couldn't speak.

Lately, however, things had been sunny and clear—if to my jaundiced view a tad candy. Still, no one doubted a bout of abstinence would be good for Lester. And it may have been a mark of how far I'd fallen that *I* was judged the basketcase now, having lost those favorable winds, along with a semi-steady girl, and promptly reverted to form: junk pies, chocolate Donettes, Slim Jims, Yoo-Hoo and Coca-Cola, washed down with Marlboros and every night, by the grace of the Bells of Hell, gallon upon gallon of Rolling Rock beer. The happy, shiny Lester confided in a friend that I'd always been the basketcase anyway.

* * *

His theory gained credence the night I ventured uptown for a friendly visit with Tiger. If my old friend had been a dick, he'd also been a boon—his cat-piss accommodations saving me, as I saw it, from a subway grate. When he phoned around to see if any of his old S.I. crew—Bob or Sean or me—wanted to have drinks at the pad with a long-lost classmate, I was the only one to bite. It probably pissed him off that I was the only one. I'm sure it pissed him off that I'd managed to quickly come up with the money to rent the Gum Joy place, but another year to come up with the back rent for him. Somewhere in there he was also pissed he wasn't a rich and famous painter. Pissed his girlfriend was bugging to move in. Pissed because being pissed was part of his training, the effort to expand his capacity for brutality, en route to his becoming a rich and famous boxer. One who painted on the side. This on top of still being pissed that, before puberty made him big, he was little and scrawny, a scholarship kid who showed up in sixth grade and insisted on calling himself by that ridiculous name—Tiger—ensuring he'd instantly become an object of ridicule. Then the long-lost classmate, now a big-shot-in-training on Wall Street, just to ratchet the resentment up another click, arrived in a fancy suit with a fancy bottle of Cuervo. Add beer, whatever odd liquor was hiding in the cabinets and his loudmouth friend slobbering about the girl who wanted to move in—the sharp, sexy college girlfriend Tiger worried was too good for him anyway—and you get a situation preordained to send a Marciano-meets-Modigliani over the turnbuckle and his loudmouth friend, me—in a ferocious flurry of left-right-lefts I could hardly process, let alone fend off—to the hospital.

Three busted ribs and a punctured lung.

"You're lucky I didn't do your pretty face," he said to my gulping ruins on the kitchen floor.

Except I didn't go to the hospital. Bent, twisted, bruised where I wasn't broken, protectively floating spread fingers above an agonizing right flank, wheezing and grimacing the whole way, I managed to Quasimodo myself half the length of Manhattan, Yorkville to the Village, where I didn't go to St. Vincent's, not then or later, but to the Bells.

I derived little satisfaction that a few weeks later instant karma, in the guise of a two-ton, sixteen-year-old son of Bed-Stuy—the old Bed-Stuy that knew how to tangle (they tell me)—caught up with Tiger at Golden Gloves, delivering a definitive first-minute K.O. and sending my childhood friend on his own trip to the E.R., where a quixotic boxing career expired despite no one's heroic attempts to resuscitate it.

* * *

CURIOUSLY, TIGER'S FIGHTING PHASE COINCIDED WITH what I came to think of as my fighting phase. It was way more unlikely and far from formal—no rules or rings or ambulances standing by—and, with that much beer and junk food, it had nothing to do with fitness. I'm sure it all started with that silly overbite, with me proving—before it was too late—that I was no longer daddy's little disappointment or, for that matter, mommy's punching bag. The results were not pretty. Along with getting the shit beat out of me by Tiger, they encompassed: getting the shit beat out of me by a bouncer and tossed down two flights at Max's Kansas City; shoving Alex Chilton, the flyweight power-pop star, into Sixth Avenue traffic; body-slamming an incredulous *Creem* photographer at a show in Kansas City (an attempted flirtation with, by way of defense of, the girl he was flirting with first); and, perhaps most noteworthy, a bumbling rumble with an old friend from Detroit.

That was later. For now, I was 0-1 on a bench in the booth in the front room of the Bells. Which is where Archie and Veronica—aka

Lester and Cindy—popping in for a sarsaparilla after the picture show, found me balled up awaiting sleep or death.

Oh, was I happy—if too wounded to fully express it.

Oh, were they surprised.

Lester hurried to raise me upright. But soon decided, with all that awful gasping and screeching, to let me be. He and Cindy sat together sipping their sodas on the other side of the table, while, like a wraith from *The Odyssey*—or Monty Python—I told my tale from a prone position below. I was openly weeping. From pain. Maybe from shame. Certainly from relief at being with real friends who really cared. Mostly, I told myself—and, at great aggrieved length, them—I was crying over the injustice.

"I'm not a boxer," I declared. "I'm a writer. You don't see me beating him up with, you know, words."

Of course, words—about his girlfriend and who-knows-what—were exactly what I was beating Tiger up with. Words were what finally made him—and not a few others over the years—snap. But Lester, another dedicated non-combatant full of fighting words, couldn't have been more sympathetic, humoring me in ways he never did—Ah, yes, the sword's ineffable injustice to the pen!—while Cindy, looking down at a red-eyed, defensively-curled armadillo-man, reflexively slapped a hand on her heart. I'm not sure she'd ever seen a human being so brokedown, and she was the girlfriend of *that* guy.

It took forever to get me standing—to a soundtrack of "AHH! AHH! EE! EE! NAH-NAH-NAH . . . NO!"—and infinity to get me to Sixth Avenue near 14th Street, two blocks further. Not sure how they got me up five flights. At the top, Cindy told me later, they couldn't find my keys. Since we weren't locking apartments, I'm pretty sure she was trying to help me save face. Maybe I was still crying. Maybe—shudder to think—I said I didn't want to be alone.

Because the next morning I woke up with sunshine on that face in a strange and wondrous chamber, sunny and white as heaven (or a Rolling Stone's hotel bedroom): white walls, white sheets, white-painted brass bed, diaphanous white curtains and, next to me, in white, in the bed—to my blackest horror—a honey-voiced, level-headed angel. It took five seconds, maybe six. But they were long seconds—hours, on the emotional chronometer. Finally, amid stabbing pain and throbbing terror, I summoned the strength yet remaining in the muscles of my own bouncing abdomen and sat up, one inch—a mile, on the broken-bones odometer—and there, on the far side of Cindy, was a bushy black mustache.

* * *

IF HIS PROSE HAD SHED THE jagged, trippier edges of the *Creem* days, it may have gained its most poignant expression when a few months later Elvis died.

"So I won't bother saying goodbye to him," Lester wrote, in a eulogy that, without a shred of mawkishness, invoked the vast, multi-generational, multi-national community that knew the man from Memphis, via Tupelo, as their King. "I will say goodbye to you."

It was indelible before the ink was even dry. And that first post-Presley afternoon when, with a catch, I put down the *Village Voice*, I had no doubt my friend had done what he'd set out to. It started good for Lester in New York.

Then Cindy got sick.

And they carried her out on a stretcher (first of two times I'd see paramedics on the fifth floor).

And Gum Joy Towers began to crumble—metaphorically (having long ago crumbled for real)—before collapsing into the subway pit below.

That is, Cindy left.

Having packed Lester's wounds with all the love she had, she got sick and got gone. Had to. Doctor's orders. No shame, no blame. If it was anyone's fault, it was mine. I was the one who'd called his bluff.

After that, it's on New York. The hype, the bullshit, the yok-a-may that Lester, who loved to see through, should've seen through. Instead he horked it all down, got too drunk or too high, too distracted by downtown and seduced by creeping fame, and was devoured by what he would have been the first to call a stupid cliché. Banal, contemptible, beneath him.

After that, it's on his dead drunken dad and Armageddon-cheering mom—who still regularly phoned her "Les" in Babylon—and on the wrathful god that, whether Lester knew it or not, was his, too.

CHAPTER 21

(Patterson)

SEVEN BLOCKS SOUTH OF THE BELLS, smack in the middle of Dylan's Positively Fourth Street, is where it began, in a perfectly ordinary dive opposite the Stonewall Inn, the historic dive that a couple years prior had been the site of the gay revolution's Boston Tea Party: the Stonewall Riots. But with that revolution still in ferocious flower all around me, Deacon's was the one joint I knew in the Village where a fella might get drunk without getting hit on by a fella. Loud, filthy, towel-snappingly butch, Deacon's was a gay bar for straight guys, with Schlitz, Schaefer and Rheingold on the taps and, high on the walls, the latest cathode-ray marvel: a 27-inch color TV. Three, in fact, one for each network. I didn't give a shit about sports. But, I calculated, neither did the gays. Delicious irony, in supremely gay Greenwich Village, at the peak of glam, heyday of the New York Dolls, Queen, Roxy Music, Bowie, Alice Cooper, Lou Reed (who, Lester posited in *Creem*, had turned an entire generation into "faggot junkies"), that heady era when rock performance turned into a preening dance of gender veils and singers (like me) pretended to be cool by pretending to be gay—even while hiding out from the real thing at Deacon's.

* * *

In that miraculously elastic daypart called Happy Hour—that can run from noon to midnight, depending how bad business is—three preppies walk into a bar. They've come to listen to another preppie mewl and moan. First, it's for real—seeing as, in the last six months, I'd lost my job, my ride and my neighbor's wife—and, later, turns into a drinking game, every burst of bellyaching an excuse for "Shots!" It was Greg Carter, my old Harkness roommate, in from his cattle breeding operation in Pennsylvania, who drew on the practical wisdom of animal husbandry to provide the evening with a mission.

"You know what you need?" he said. "No, listen to me, Tom. You know what you need?"

Freshman year, Carter was a chirping soprano and the shortest kid in class. Now I had to look north of the giant TVs, as my ex-pipsqueak roomie, retooled as a radioactively overgrown basso profundo, leaned down to clamp my shoulder and lecture with barroom solemnity.

"Tom, you need a girl."

It so happened, at that moment, just past Deacon's front window, on Positively Fourth Street, USA, two strolled by.

Taking the sperm farmer's counsel to heart, I ran outside. It was a gentle grab, a "Don't I know you . . . ?" grasp of a chastely covered patch of upper biceps, but a grab nonetheless. I should've known better—though I like to think I knew full well.

"Get your hands off me!" she said.

I was wearing the salt-stained red Smirnoff cap that had turned up in the couch after someone's going-away party, the crumpled yellow button-down, shirttails a-flapping, that had turned up in the laundry pile, and shredded black jeans with the *Post* sticking out the back pocket—a mashup of hillbilly drunk, ebbing preppie and standard creep on the street. While I promptly removed my hand, I did not remove me, backpedaling as they marched purposefully east, purposefully paying me not a shred of attention.

"Buy you girls a drink? One drink. On me . . . "

I rattled on, wheedling and wise-cracking, for three or four blocks—well beyond what was sensible, polite or, by all rights, persuasive.

"Where you girls going? Seriously, where?"

The one girl was short and muscled, in sleeveless denim vest, with a freshly etched phoenix, shiny in antiseptic grease, cuffing her forearm. She commanded attention, this strongwoman, inked by an underground tattooist at a time when the craft, in New York City, was a felony. But my eyes were drawn to the other. Skinny, gangly, still not used to being the tallest girl in the room, she rounded her shoulders as she rushed, with a syncopated lope, in flower-embroidered Greek blouse and skinpaint jeans of emergency-red. Her eyes were azure, her smile, on the rare occasion it arrived, crooked and spare, and above it all the most joyous eruption of chestnut curls.

"We're going to the Bottom Line," she said, looking up.

For all her Brooklyn-bred, Q-train-honed glower and inked-up accomplice, something else.

"Who you going to see?"

(Kindness?)

She turned her azure lights back to the sidewalk and kept walking.

(Honesty?)

Pastel ribbons trailed from her wrist in spirals, echoing the curls on her head.

(Something else.)

Then she looked again and answered:

"Elliot Murphy."

* * *

SOME ROCK-CRITICAL CONTEXT:

After Dylan's metaphorical death in the motorcycle accident, and then his musical death in the dismal *Self-Portrait,* before his resurrection in *Blood on the Tracks*—and before the folky run-on Dylanism of Bruce's first album—Elliot Murphy was anointed "New Dylan," the folk-rock savior foretold to pen the next "Positively Fourth Street" and shepherd disreputable pop back to—ironically—literary respectability. Not only did I know Murphy's songs from post-prandial listening sessions with Jim Morton and Ted Hall, I knew his publicist. With unchecked exultation, I swooped in for the kill:

"Hey, I can get you in free!"

* * *

WITH MORE THAN A HINT OF touché, the curly-headed girl proffered a cockeyed smile—her first—and crowed back:

"We're already getting in free."

(I get it: nerve! What they call in New York chutzpah.)

I'm not sure how much of it showed on the outside, but inside I was sinking fast. Much as I'd asked Ted Hall to see the basement he'd already rented, I couldn't resist the moot point here:

"So, why are you getting in free?"

Nodding at the tough girl, the tender one replied:

"She's a singer. I'm a photographer."

Only in my backwards-jogging, never-say-die church of blind faith could such a humble tidbit—*I'm a photographer*—register as a candle. I mean, of all the blocks, all the Five Boroughs and all the eight million, more than half women, a third photographers, what were the odds? I pressed.

"What's your name . . . ?"

After a beat, she said it. And from Battery to Bronx, Christopher Street to Coney Island and throughout the ganglia of my brain, bells did peal and illegally purchased skyrockets did fly.

"Rebecca Holtzman?! I'm Ransom. From *Creem.*" I said. "I sent you a check last week!"

I escorted my new friends back to Deacon's, striking doubting preppies dumb. After we all shared a celebratory swig, some of us went to Elliot Murphy. Later one of us went home with the tough chick—who taught one of us a thing or two about "animal husbandry"—and another with the tender, who was pretty damn nervy. Though her name was Holtzman, Rebecca Holtzman, this being New York and the golden age of illegal sublets, she made sure to append to the ripped-out notebook scrap with her vitals the different name on the buzzer:

"(Patterson)," she wrote.

Next morning, at the onetime West Village 1-BR of cult filmmaker Ray Jacob Patterson, we were awakened by a call from what turned out to be a mutual friend, who'd moved back to New York the year before. Jim Morton said to Rebecca Holtzman, "Hey, I want you to meet an old buddy who just got back to town."

And (Patterson) said: "He's right here."

CHAPTER 22

Bop

AT A FINANCIAL LOW EBB, I received an opulent mailing from the American Express company concerning the wonders of plastic. I didn't receive a lot of mail on this topic, certainly not from this level of correspondent. As other solicitations did not, this caught my eye and fired my imagination. I didn't have any credit cards and didn't imagine anyone in their right mind would ever offer me one. But, with the help of this junk mail—with which I engaged to a pathological degree—I began to grasp how one might alleviate my situation. I dialed the number to inquire, discreetly, what it might take, in comprehensive detail, to gain admittance to this polyvinyl El Dorado and then set about precisely satisfying every one of the criteria, no matter how niggling. With the help of a confederate in the *Creem* finance department, and the nearby copy shop, I was able to document, in crisply Xeroxed black-and-white, that I had not foolishly given up my job and raced east at midnight in a $65 car, only to end up homeless as well as jobless. To the contrary: as a top executive, I had been transferred from Detroit to the magazine's "New York office," where I remained gainfully and importantly employed, as I had for the previous three years, knocking down the princely sum of forty grand a year (when, in reality, I was barely knocking down four). Ten days later, to my astonishment, an embossed rectangle of acetate arrived. Not green American Express plastic, but gold. I'd done my job too well. As I contemplated the penalties for federal fraud, my pulse accelerated. But having no clue—along with no money—I signed my name on the back and took Holtzman out for Mexican. Halfway through our third margarita, we agreed she must move in, stat. I was exultant. She was kind and honest and beautiful and loyal. But she was also nervy and full of mystery. It felt like love.

If, post-Cindy, my friend and neighbor was teetering, I was now on a roll.

* * *

To me, he was teetering. To him, he was on a roll. At this point, Lester had been in New York long enough to meet everybody, and everybody him, and not so long that everybody noticed he was teetering and started to back off. He was meeting new people, as well as people who knew him from his writing, correspondence or from the phone. He was meeting magazine editors, book editors, agents, other writers, photographers, musicians—most of whom were fans—as well as fans who worked in sales for their father's sweater company (and, every visit, brought Lester a new cardigan), fans who were still in high school and took the bus from Jersey to do an interview for a report, fans who managed a brothel, one who owned a TV repair shop and others who were starry-eyed girls, who wanted to sleep with him, no matter how stinky. Along with sweaters and sex and other tangential goodies, some of those fans gave him writing assignments and book contracts and invited him to join in their video or photo shoots and gave in when he wanted to sing in front of their band. Lester had been in New York, HQ of the American culture industry, just long enough to have become just what he imagined he was: the toast of the town.

My town. Roll or no roll, I wasn't anywhere near that. But if jealousy figured in what happened next, so did proximity. I'd been around Lester long enough and close enough to know that the scales were tipping, way tipping. As alarming as it was, it was also tiresome. So when I rolled home one dawn and reached in the fridge, only to discover that a Lester fan—hanging next door and acting on the master's directive—had taken advantage of our open-door policy and made off with my last six-pack, I teetered, too. Actually, I tumbled headlong into a molten pit of rage, grabbed the nearest heavy object—the five-foot iron pole that was the wedge part of the unused police-lock—and, with a loudmouth war-cry about motherfuckers stealing my motherfucking beer, motherfucker, flung it like a javelin. Not a lot of forethought, but I'd guess it was intended to make a fearsome racket and convey a visceral message of profound indignation. Instead, the spear neatly penetrated the old tenement wall between my kitchen and Lester's and sproinged there, half in one apartment, half in the other, for a cartoonishly long time.

It didn't kill Lester, and was not—I don't think—meant to. But imagine his surprise. Imagine mine. In textbook cartoon timing, there was no response for three, two, one . . .

Then my neighbor exploded into the hall, roaring. Nothing so inarticulate as writerly words—just roaring, like a great horned beast (or homicidal Southern mother), bashing his fists on the door I'd leapt to deadbolt and that bowed alarmingly beneath the barrage. Out of fear, disdain and massive instant regret, I let the bashing go on, 10-20-30 unrelenting seconds, before bracing myself and throwing the door wide.

What ensued had to be the least elegant combat in the entire history of hand-to-hand: two unfit drunken spazzes—amid the shouts and cries of a kind, clearheaded girlfriend—trying to push, punch, crush, kick, bend, toss and slap each other, upending chairs, tables and the aforementioned fridge, sputtering, cursing, puffing, sweating and soon wearing completely out.

As a wrestler, my father's son was a passable writer.

Puddled on the cracked linoleum, gasping, spent—not just like onetime bed-sharers, but fervid lovers—Lester and I finally shook hands and tried to laugh it off. He even said something about what terrible fighters we were, both of us. Which only irritated me all over again.

Still, we made up. Made a show of it. Sharing a drink when someone from *Creem* or a favorite freelancer was in town, sharing a gripe among the ever-griping scribes of the Bells, sharing a moment when someone in the circle died—I remember getting the call about *Creem*'s publisher, Barry Kramer, Lester's benefactor and bête noire, and stepping down the hall to knock. Because now Lester's door was locked. Like mine. Though I would still read his stuff (and vice-versa, he said) and took a subway to see his band and couldn't help but keep an eye out, though there was clearly an ache, it was never the same.

* * *

WITH HIS HEAVY, FORWARD-LEANING GAIT, LESTER produced a signature sound effect as he fell up the five flights of stairs. It could have been a bit from a Jerry Lewis movie, and it was distinct from the sound of Lester falling down, which, miraculously, almost never happened. I would hear Lester falling up our stairs three or four times a day: when he'd return from picking up the promo records in the vestibule or making a beer-run to Smiler's or escorting a visitor up, because the downstairs was locked and there was no buzzer system (our doorbell was the payphone across the street). Late night, his tempo might downshift, but the rhythm was still unmistakable. And the sound of Lester ascending became part of the texture of life in Gum Joy Towers—for me and Holtzman, no less than the dozen other tenants, who seemed to have grown fond of the jolly émigré from Geewhizland. I saw it in the closeted young landlord, Umberto, and his panicked *No-English!* mom; the persnickety typist who'd retyped (and tried to re-edit) the Kiss manuscript; the giggly Puerto Rican-Chinese sisters on two who ran that PR-Chinese café on Ninth Avenue; and the retired accounts receivable clerk, a fastidious classical music devotee, who somehow managed to live directly under Lester (who when he wasn't falling up was clomping around, blasting Public Image). In the communal era, the signature sound might have inspired me to stick my head out and ask him in. No doubt, in our sitcom of a New York tenement, that falling-up paradiddle would have been the theme song.

But the charm of the falling-up faded in light of the post-Cindy spiraling-down. It hit a new low during the reign of the Sixth Avenue Slicer, the latest of the *New York Post*'s circulation-pumping sewer monsters. This one was a maniac slashing citizens' jugulars—dozens, you might think, though it was only two—up and down the city's streets of blood. Arriving home one night to find Lester sprawled in the Sixth Avenue gutter, it seemed like keeping an eye out was no longer enough. Unable to rouse our corpulent neighbor, Holtzman and I, lifting and tugging at the limits of drunk physics, eventually managed to leverage Lester's inertial ass into the locked vestibule, where at least he wouldn't be butchered by a tabloid psycho. Or run over by the Sixth Avenue bus. At this point, Lester and I had mostly stopped talking. The next day, out of an unsavory combination of love and contempt, I told Jim Morton—who I'd come to think of as our go-between—that he really had to tell our friend to cool it, that we'd just dragged Lester's body in and one day would be dragging it out.

It seemed a little hypocritical, if not icy, coming from a guy whose busted hulk Lester and Cindy had once dragged in, but the spiraling-down had by now been going on for so long it had become routine. Not just hopeless, boring—except when it was terrifying. Morton, who wrestled beverage demons of his own, dismissed all concern as hooey.

"Nahhh . . . " was the sum-total of his reply.

It was about a year after the fight of the century when Umberto knocked on my door. Despite the agita, or maybe because of it, the twenty-something landlord was clearly fond of Lester. It made some sense. Saddled with this white elephant of a rundown property when his immigrant father died prematurely, Umberto was crowded into a second-floor 1-BR with a sour-faced sister, a mother who pretended to speak only Italian so she wouldn't have to deal with tenants, and a jumbo disco ball, hung from the living room ceiling and plainly visible from the street. Sometimes he'd sneak out to gay bars—we had an awkward encounter on Christopher Street one night—but mostly, chary and close-mouthed, he carried on the life's work of his virulently old-world papà: making stopgap repairs and trying to outsmart the local government. Lester and his sprawling openness—*Lester's* loudmouth ways—were a glimpse of another dimension. Lester liked Umberto back. We all did. And found it an odd comfort—if a cold one—that when the steam was off in winter, because he couldn't afford heating oil, he was freezing in his apartment just like we were. Even more comfort that when we were broke, he'd let us slide, one time for six months. In my book, Umberto was A-OK.

"Something's wrong with Lester," he said.

* * *

"So what was this guy, a musician?"

All around, to the cop's amazement, on the gray metal shelving Lester and I had schlepped from Ninth Avenue—as well as on the floor, chair, desk, bed, windowsills, under beer cans, t-shirts, *Voices* and *Creems*—were thousands of the records, in sleeves and mostly out, that Lester couldn't bear to sell to Benny. In front of us, lounging on the couch, eyes casually pondering a spot high on the wall, was their owner.

The smell of death filled the air. Not because Lester was dead—he'd smelled like death for years, no more, no less now. This time he was. Only minutes before, he'd been alive, and we'd heard the familiar sound effects of him falling up the stairs—not obviously drunk or high, but obviously Lester.

I picked up his hand, because that's what they did on TV. It was no colder than a living hand. The eyes were staring, but lifelike. As with Abby before him, I started in immediately with the loudmouth CPR.

"Lester! Lester! Lester!" I yelled.

And when the paramedics arrived, I yelled some more: "Shock him! Shock him! Please shock him!"

I kept on yelling until a paramedic snapped.

"I can't!" he yelled back. "*I can't!*" And bounced up from his crouch next to the sofa to face me, nose to nose. "If I start his heart now, he'll be fucking brain dead."

"Brain dead!" he spat. "You know what *that* is?!?"

I tried to argue. I told him it had only been a few minutes. I told him Lester was young. I told him Lester was important. Famous, I said. I cajoled, harangued, wheedled and desperately tried. I was impossible—and insisting on it.

Until, finally, I wasn't. Didn't. Couldn't.

Soon, the life-savers had packed up and left the irredeemable to the city department that deals with it. I stayed—to understand, to bear witness, and because, in Lester's absence (and ongoing presence), I felt an obligation. Maybe a Southern thing: because the host was indisposed.

I don't know when the cops arrived. There were two of them at first. The cop that stayed was a short, Black man in his late 30s, serene and unassuming. He was waiting. That was his job, for the moment. Waiting. And in the gaps of my less than lively repartee, he occupied himself by casually sorting through the gray shelves.

"I'm a jazz buff," he offered, by way of explanation. After a ten-minute browse, in his unassuming way, he held up a battered album and asked: "OK if I take this?"

But it was Lester's, I thought. Not mine. Not mine to say.

I knew the record. Anyone who knew Lester knew the record. *Spiritual Unity*. Albert Ayler—the tenor saxophonist and young suicide whose urgent squall may have scoffed at the pussyfooting of words, but seemed a perfect match for the inside of my wordy friend's knobby head. Still, mild as the request might have been, mildly submitted, it took me by surprise and, a moment later, turned my stomach. It confirmed Lester was dead, like the EMT had already confirmed. What's more, it confirmed that after you're dead—and I mean *right* after—you're dead, period, end of story, and any random stranger can fuck with your shit.

At least this guy had the love. Soon a flock of vultures would descend—Benny the snarling record fatso would pant up five flights to descend—and the love would be picked as clean as the Plymouth I'd left outside Jackie's. And, in the end, this was Lester's end, and he would have wanted the bop cop to have it.

CHAPTER 23

Voicemail

GREEN HOTDOGS WERE THE FINAL NAIL. It was like: *Now I gotta kill somebody.*

The emergency fund was two brown socks full of silver quarters that Rebecca's dear daddy had collected over six decades servicing refrigerated vending machines. He gave them to her when she was the first in the family to graduate from college and first of the women not to go straight into babies and the Kosher kitchen. It wasn't so much that he approved. But it wasn't so much that he disapproved, not fully, not wholeheartedly. There was a part of his heart that admired his brave, smart baby girl, ever the black sheep. But it was new territory, and he was scared. The silver quarters were the best he could do by way of hoisting her into his arms in case of trouble. It was not an easy decision to cash them in. When we spent a chunk of the proceeds on groceries that turned out to include moldy hotdogs, something snapped.

The brown socks netted only 900 bucks, but, I calculated, that might be enough to keep us going another month or two—long as we didn't pay the back rent. As to the Kiss book, my queasy attempt at selling out, the first royalty statement arrived after six months registering goose-eggs. Holtzman had officially abandoned her longtime apartment and moved into Gum Joy Towers with me. If the place was smaller and many flights of walk-up higher, it was a lot cheaper (especially when you didn't pay). But, we soon discovered—as the Reagan recession dried up work and an American Express abyss yawned at our feet—none of that made much of a difference. Broke is broke.

Cue the landlord: "Thomas, I just can't carry you anymore. I'm going to need the whole six months."

* * *

By one of the miracles bestowed too sparingly on the sufferers, that apocalypse was followed—I want to say days later, but I no longer believe in miracles and may be suppressing a dark month or two—by a phone call from Los Angeles. A stranger named Gus Dunn was calling to say he was a fan of *Creem* and a big fan of Bruce.

"The Boss!" he'd shouted into the phone, as if bruiting about the widely known nickname would certify his bona-fides.

Gus had been doing research (actually, Gus had never done a spot of research in all his 37 years, which means his latest brainstorm was the work of an unpaid intern harangued into finding something/anything to give Gus leverage). Gus, via his intern, had run across my story about Bruce in the Delta. He wasn't just calling to express admiration. He wanted to hire me as what he called a "secret weapon," because I was "buds with Bruce." More than a fan, of me or anyone, Gus was a lifelong hustler, a scheme machine. And me selling out my sometime, would-be friend was his latest. The thing was, Gus had a budget.

A former high school wrestler—like Father—given to his own strain of drunken overenthusiasm, often accompanied by headlocks and noogies, he was marketing chief for the rock 'n' roll-themed hotel and restaurant chain called Big Beat (and "rock 'n' roll-themed" is all you need to know about where rock 'n' roll was heading). What Gus wanted most in the world (until tomorrow or the next day) was for Bruce to play the opening of Big Beat's flagship eatery in Times Square (and, not coincidentally, demonstrate that the real boss was Gus).

"I want you to write a little note to your pal," he said.

There was other stuff he wanted—other connections, other copy, other counsel—related to my vast experience in "the biz" (as he liked to call music), among them a bit of cultural halo for his overpriced chain of tourist traps. I wasn't sure how much glory a woebegone ex-*Creem* guy could reflect, but I wasn't going to argue with the retainer, which was substantially more than six decades of silver quarters, every month.

It would have taken a much stronger man—and a wealthier one—to not write Bruce that nauseating letter. But the check cleared. And after a snootful at the Big Beat launch bash, where "the Boss" did not, and would not in a thousand years, perform (after he would not, and never did, reply to the note)—I slipped away to meet Sean and Bob in the Village, where we talked until a fiendish bartender turned up the lights. They flagged cabs for home, and I set out via my favorite transit system, the high-top sneaker, for somewhere incredibly far and surprisingly well-hidden. I couldn't tell what part of my navigation issues was about being trashed and what was about having been holed up in my apartment long enough for some joker to re-shuffle the grid. To make it fully impossible, Gus had insisted on putting me up, alongside him and his interns, at the bankrupt hipster hotel his company had just purchased off Times Square. "Gotta sample the product, Tommy!" he said. Really, he just wanted a drinking companion.

Besides: *who the fuck stays in Times Square?*

I didn't notice that my fancy new flip-phone—made possible by my fancy new credit card—was squawking "Kick Out the Jams."

The MC5 anthem, once the object of my derision, was now my ringtone. After 30 or 40 minutes traveling in a diabolical circle, flummoxed and fatigued, I decided it was time to take a breather at my favorite transit station: a stranger's stoop. And it was there on the steps of a random brownstone, on a random block, in a neighborhood I didn't know and a city from which I was now in retreat, that I pulled the sleek communicator from my pocket—idly, reflexively, proudly—to discover I'd missed a call and received a message.

* * *

"THOMAS!" THE VOICEMAIL SAID, LOUDLY. "YOUR father's dead!"

Only Mother could make it sound unsympathetic. Juiced. Like when she called to say my big brother had succumbed to the tumors that she, alone among us, always called cancer.

I snapped the phone shut. Nothing about it was right. With Mother, nothing ever was. Of course, the real message of her message—this one, every one—was she wanted to tell you how to react. More product demo than emotional news flash, the call was designed to deliver marching orders for the etiquette of the occasion: how to emotionally dress. Though detailed instructions on what clothes to wear, you could be sure, would be coming soon.

Since there was never much correlation with actual rules or customs—other than the rules she invented, often on the spot—that etiquette could vary crazily. For instance, assuming her mantle as the sworn foe of sentiment, Mother might enact stoicism, like she did when brother Sandy died. Or she might do Arab-funeral freak-out, like when the Peruvian maid quit—or was it the Swede? Judging by the voicemail, I'd have to locate this performance at the blacker end of the spectrum, closer to servant-quitting than brother-tumors. It appeared that somewhere under the show-grief, Mother was genuinely shook.

Still, though you may have cared deeply—did—that your father had died or your brother, you always tried to hold back. Because when you didn't—much the same as when you did—the Queen of Correct was there to nail you:

Too much.

Too little.

Too unemotional.

Too unmanly.

Anyway, too late to call back now and too blotto. I called Holtzman.

* * *

I HAD TO PEE. I WAS walking north again, northerly, talking and walking. But I really had to pee. She pleaded with me to flag a cab. I told her I'd call back and looked around for privacy. I'm not sure I ever envisioned my father's dying day, but I wouldn't have envisioned this. His eldest son—me now, with Sandy gone—lost, wasted, wedged between two parked cars, pissing in the street. Like the 14-year-old me on malt liquor. "Like a good-for-nothing!" Father would have said.

What to make of this pissing?

What to make of this pissing from the eyes? A busted flush-lever of teardrops. I mean, I didn't care that much about Father. Besides, I resented him for not stopping Mother (except once). Resented him for going along with her bullshit, following her lead. She'd say to us, dress like this, or eat like that, or don't do a eulogy at your brother's funeral, I forbid it, and Father would say sternly, Listen to your mother.

For a strong, silent type, he could be quite the candy-ass.

But fathers didn't have to be involved then. And they weren't, and he wasn't, running off to Elmira, Des Moines, Shreveport or any of the half-dozen remote, off-axis destinations where he did his best work and felt most at home. Not for Father Newport or Beverly Hills or even Coconut Island, where Mother eventually, permanently, dragged him, the place from which he was always running off. Not New York—with its mystifying preppies and aesthetes and Chinese—where Mother dragged him first, when he thought he was dragging her. Father wanted the towns others didn't. The no-frills towns, ugly towns, towns a hundred miles from a symphony orchestra. Useful places that meant nothing but business. Father got excited about factories, railyards, forklifts, drill-presses, acrid smoke, about dangerous banging, clanking and hissing. He lit up about loading docks, corrugated roofs, concrete floors with big, bolted-down machines. And preferred the company of short-sleeved plant managers with hardhats and clipboards, hairy-armed guys without irony, two steps up from the stevedore he used to be, two decades on from high-school wrestling themselves, guys who had their own way of doing things and never backed down—unless the boss said.

That boss was Father. And these were his towns.

* * *

FATHER, WHO TOLD US ABOUT PAYING two bits at the Pima County Fair in Tucson to go one round with a traveling wrestler—a "pro," when the only certification was the circumference of your biceps and ferocity of your lumpy face—in the hope of winning a sawbuck, which no one ever did.

"Came close," said Father.

Who you knew wasn't lying. To Father with his heavy brows and hooded stare, intimidation was just a dare. Father, who started in factories and climbed, from busting his knuckles loading boxcars to a clipboard of his own, before marrying the boss' daughter. My man-sized old man, who approved of man-sized men—even as he disapproved of slack-shouldered "fags," like Sam Andrew. Who approved of Barry Quinn—if only because, my six-six eighth-grade pal, ex of Abby, was superman-sized. Approved of Barry until that day our iceballs hit a shiny new car on First Avenue, and the driver slammed it into park, and my giant friend took off running. A perfectly legit reaction—Barry may have been big, but he wasn't actually grown. Still, it left me on my own. Afraid of looking back to see if the guy was really coming and afraid of not being fast enough if he was, I put my faith in guile and ambled toward the East River and the gunmetal span of Simon & Garfunkel, an innocent boy out for a mid-winter stroll.

"Me???" I protested.

The volcanic little driver clenched my shirt and smacked me across the face, cursed and smacked, viciously and long enough I wasn't sure how it would end and, without realizing it, had pissed myself. What to make of that? What to make of it was that this sweet new ride of his meant a lot more than transportation. It meant vindication for years of being a shrimp, for getting smacked around himself—on the playground, in the cafeteria, at the kitchen table—and he reveled in every blow. There was a dot of me that didn't blame him.

Suddenly, here comes Father. Not running, marching. Big, tall, son of a cowboy cop marching—strolling—to flick a flea. By the time the driver turned, it was too late. He was dead—good as. With his hands flapping a semaphore of excuses, a classic B-movie coward, he immediately started backing up. And with the kind of contempt you can only convey by not conveying any, Father—a B-movie sheriff, of sorts, himself—without raising a fist or in any pitifully blatant way menacing, delivered the coup de grace that sent a stranger running away as fast as an eighth-grade best friend:

"Why don't you pick on someone your own size?"

* * *

I WON'T SAY FATHER WAS FULL of surprises. But for a pokerfaced cowpuncher, he had a few. Now that he was safely gone—available to be whatever I wanted him to be—I could safely tell.

After the war—and the war of his divorce—Father's old boss invited him to work on the Marshall Plan in Rome, where he moved in with four other Yanks in a grand hillside villa that cost, total, sixty-five bucks a month. Italy was where he met Mother, evacuating from her marital disaster and accompanying her father, a war hero with secret orders from the State Department who was secretly trying to evacuate from a domestic disaster of his own. It happened on the Via Veneto, main drag of Fellini's Dolce Vita. Taking pity on two American girls outside the Hotel Excelsior, Father jogged into the rainy-day traffic and snagged a cab for Mother and her sister. Then lured them to a party at the villa.

"You could hire a dozen musicians for twenty bucks!" said Father.

He and the boys threw a lot of parties and met a lot of girls. Post-war, the Eternal City, for a young American with twenty bucks, turned out to be *molto buono.*

Among the things my future father picked up—along with my mother, shoes, suits, an Alfa Romeo and what seemed to be fluent Italian (but may have been an Eddie Neil-style loop)—was the unexpected habit of kissing his kids, just a peck, on the lips.

"Why does he *do* that?" we'd ask Mother, mortified.

"He saw the fathers do it in Italy," she'd say, "and thought it was nice."

Painful to think *nice* was Father underneath. More painful to think *nice* was the father underneath I refused to see. The father who saved his kid from B-movie cowards. The father who insisted I have some self-respect and shut my mouth. The father who trudged off to Elmira to bring home the bacon, so the son of a son of a sheriff could sit at the feet of great men like George Norman Hardy.

The father who, before he kissed us, liked to rub our faces rosy.

If ever a man more manly, never a more manly beard—with a five o'clock shadow that showed up early for lunch. When he was home, he shaved again before dinner. By way of greeting, after a long day on the road, away from a razor, charcoal-cheeked dad liked to raise us up by the armpits and, with a growl, buff our tender young faces with the wire-brush of his. And it was on a rare family Christmas, when Sandy, Connie, Roger and I—all his children, all grown, all still here, and all together—got to comparing notes about that exceptional pain, and I felt, as if for the first time, the pulse among us.

"Nothing feels better than blood on blood" is how Bruce put it.

* * *

By the time I tried to call Holtzman back, the fancy flip-phone had run out of juice. My eyes had not. And here at this inane crossroads of gullible strangers, the void was closing fast. I'd walked a million miles—probably a half-million more than I needed to—and was trying again, amid the seizure-inducing whirligig of lights, sound, and video, to find my bearings. I thought of another whirligig moment in this neighborhood—with Johnny, Bob and Maria—but the tears rolled on. The tough guy son of a sheriff—who, with bristly cheek and leather belt, had tried to pass that grit on to his children—would have disapproved. But my reptile brain had seized control. My good-for-nothing gekko brain—and certainly not anything recognizable as me—was balling for not anything recognizable as Father. Still, for all the precipitation, not to mention fog, I eventually managed to find my way up the right avenue onto the right cross-street and almost to the door of the right bankrupt hotel.

And who at that moment should be staggering from the opposite direction?

I was torn.

I was high.

Better him than a bartender, I thought, and blurted the news right there on the sidewalk. And my new friend, old fan and part-time employer threw a thick arm around my neck—just this side of headlock—and offered the most heartfelt condolences he could muster:

"Let's get a drink."

I wanted more from him. I always wanted more—no affection was ever enough. Though I protested I had to go home and pack, sleep, fly, I wanted more. And bellied-up to the bar with Gus to get it.

Then, instead of bereavement, how he'd never forget the day his old daddy died, my new friend started talking business. Even if it was only your reptile brain grieving, Gus talking business—chain-store cheeseburger business—not only violated the etiquette of grief, it violated the etiquette of drunkenness.

I waved him off. He pressed.

"The letter to your buddy Bruce didn't work," he said, half-taunting, half-accusing. "Maybe we can get him to London? Kick off summer with the Boss in Blighty? And maybe"—grinning, poking—"you can write a better letter!"

The cracked actor toting the checks tossed something over his shoulder about last call. I wanted more. Always. And ordered it. And got up to find an indoor place to pee. When I returned, I was dumbstruck to discover my companion—my friend, patron and torturer—had picked up the bill. It was a small gesture, tiny, but in its tenderness—when tenderness was needed—huge.

Then I saw.

Even weeping and stupid and one-eyed, I saw. Rather than sign his own name and room number, Gus had signed mine. Once I figured out he hadn't undergone a catastrophic identity crisis, cerebral thrombosis, while I was in the john, I figured out he'd inscribed Tom Ransom, not Gus Dunn, to keep one more yok-a-may charge off his Greek myth of a Norse saga of an Irish hustler's bullshit expense account. At Father's expense, in a sense. Which meant—in a sense—that my old man, a rank heathen of monkish habits, who venerated the almighty dollar and lived by the strictest Christian dog-eat-dog principles, had died for somebody's sins.

CHAPTER 24

Pome

Loud. Quiet.
Manhattan. Brooklyn.
Private school. Public.
Public. Private.
Catholic. Jew.
Fat. Skinny.
Rich. Poor.
Writer. Painter.
Poodle. Parrot.
Straight. Curly.
Drinker. Jew.
Earth. Other.

Twins so uncanny it could only have been fated, we were married on the first day of spring—just like John and Yoko—under a drizzle that, for a few minutes, turned into snow and then a blizzard of banal wedding-reception commentary on meteorological ironies. The ceremony, strictly godless, took place in the living room of her parents' cottage off Mermaid Avenue, in Coney Island, where Holtzman grew up, in the Son of Sam year, presided over by the Son of Sam judge, attended by a delightfully indecorous sampling of Bells of Hellions, *Creem*sters, artists, writers and punks, among them both the Village Legend and the Blue Öyster Cult keyboardist who had secretly replaced him on the Clash record. I see Rebecca's tattooed sidekick, the mighty Ayla, from Fourth Street. There's Lamps lead guitarist Sean, Romper Room rhythm guitarist Adam, and my taciturn partner-in-crime Bob. Tiger was there, as was Greg the sperm farmer. And Holtzman's favorite uncle, Mel, who in his salt-and-pepper toupee really did look like Sinatra and with the most glancing encouragement belted a not-bad "Come Fly with Me." There was big sister Connie, husband Gunnar, little brother Roger, girlfriend Frances, and four-dozen other friends and fam from both sides. We invited Bruce, but he was playing New Haven and, instead, dedicated "Born to Run." Which was almost as good.

* * *

If it took us 16 months to get from 4th Street to Mermaid Avenue, the tickets were already bought and paid for the morning after the Bottom Line. As she slipped the first of the day's nonstop records on the turntable and padded off to fry, peel, squeeze and scramble an unduly generous hangover breakfast, I pored over her astounding album cover of an apartment—filed somewhere between the deadpan anti-graphics of the *Music from Big Pink* gatefold and the nightmare surrealism of *Trout Mask Replica*. In the bedroom, under the screaming red poster for the women's-prison flick *Caged*, I'd already had a vivid encounter with the ribbon-bedecked brass bed that collapsed if you weren't careful (and you never could be enough). And I wobbled now in the doorway to the living room, studying the mantelpiece mirror whose mahogany frame had been gnawed to Brancusi curves and dripped Ab-Ex white by the squawking, shitting cockatoo. At my feet, tattered souvenir rugs memorialized cartoon couples—Minnie and Mickey, Rocky and Bullwinkle, Pokey and Gumby. Strewn around the room were various parodies of furniture and decor: a third of a sectional sofa in plaid, a third of another in stripes, a bicycle bent in two, a painting on the back of a canvas and a musty Monument Valley of piled-high books. Scotchtaped to the walls, in no apparent pattern (unless the pattern was none): magazine and newspaper pictures of pigs; a pressed bouquet; fanciful swizzle sticks—especially ones with animals; a tuft of lichen; a Chinese map of French Quebec; novelty handkerchiefs embroidered with grinning mascots for far-flung sports teams. Meanwhile, shelves and cabinets overflowed with commemorative plates ditched at thrift shops by heirs who could not believe the corny crap granny had left behind.

The rock 'n' roll in this sleeve, to be clear, was not. It was country. Wall-to-wall through the day. Her contrapuntal soundtrack—with cockatoo chorus—of Willie and Waylon, Dolly and Porter, Hank, Haggard, Conway, Buck—all the major gods of Nashville, Austin, Bakersfield, the best of the rural tradition in the heart of urban Sodom. Turn it up—no big deal—when the boys the other side of the kitchen wall start in with the sex howling, as they liked to do around dinnertime. Supper of tempeh and tabbouleh and tahini and other unpronounceables—not from any King Kullen I'd known. And, all around, the cockroaches she could no longer bring herself to kill—not after that heavy metal dude brought a studded boot down on "Reddy," her russet-colored favorite—the wildly proliferating cockroaches who'd earned way too much of her affection, now tipping digits inside her space-age flip-clock, Earth's inheritors trifling with mere human time.

* * *

LONG BEFORE WE MET, I'D HEARD about a crazy New York artist, with a crazy New York apartment. Which had instantly put me in mind of the Cedar Tavern—that romantic high-point of American art and alcoholism—and lodged, like a stray ceremonial bullet, in my imagination. I didn't remember the artist's name—I'm not sure anyone said it—but I did, somehow, have a picture of ribbons. She was a friend of just about everyone in this and every other artistic New York scene. Friend of my friends, Lester, Morton, Hall, but also friend of my favorite new band, with my favorite new band name: The Dictators.

They were teenagers from New York—from the Bronx and Queens, they'd adamantly correct—and, with their sawtooth edges and heavily accented bluster, fully sounded like it. On the first decent Detroit day in a long, cold time, I'd put on my advance copy of their debut album, the perfectly titled *The Dictators Go Girl Crazy*, thrown open the window and, over a six-pack of the Motor City's fire-brewingest, contemplated the majesty of their mordant pop and the gritty glories of the town they mocked, celebrated and stood for and which, after a Michigan winter without a girlfriend, I found myself missing. I didn't know the Dictators were the first salvo of punk. No mistaking the songs were punkish. But by every indication—dismissive reviews to record label dismay—there would never be a movement behind them. Still, I loved that record—the words, music, attitude. The whiny singer set against the gruff one, the windmilled ta-da guitars—an outer-borough Who. I loved the sublimation of stupid—with ardent anthems to recreational sleeping pills, cheap beer and that desiccated, all-night grease-square White Castle called a burger. And I was transfixed by the cover.

On the front, glint-toothed and Jewfro'ed, in black Spandex, was Handsome Dick Manitoba—a wrestling bad-guy in a grimy bad-guy locker room. On the back were transcendently trashy portraits of each band member in his teenage bedroom, every detail reaffirming their bratty nasal taunt: "I'm the one not to let your son become." Not too long past teenage myself, I gloried in the pubescent nihilism, in the rock posters on the walls and records scattered on the floors and in the guy in white sunglasses reaching his tongue out to a handful of plastic dog poop. I memorized the credits.

One was for the intrepid producer who'd managed to wangle these snot-nosed wisenheimers a deal, and who would become my friend Terry.

One was for the photographer, portraitist to the pimply stars, who would become my friend, too.

* * *

AN ARTIST SHE WAS, BUT CRAZY only by comparison. Rebecca Holtzman was a polymath of the peculiar. Not only did she like to ponder the weird, she liked to ponder the ordinary to a depth that—like a word repeated over and over—could make anything seem weird.

"A pome fruit. Fleshy outside, with a tough core. That's the seed. Part of the rose family," she said, without stopping. "Bosc, Bartlett, Red Anjou, Green Anjou, Forelle, Starkrimson, Concorde, Comice, Seckel."

"Above all," she said, "Seckel."

"Crispy," she continued, "and sweet, but not too."

"Then there are the European varieties. Blake's Pride, Packham's Triumph, Vicar of Winkfield—yes, great names—and the Asian varieties, some of which are round . . . "

When my baby brother Roger married the wide-eyed baby sis of tightlipped Bob, and they came to visit us on their honeymoon, it was this performance—which was not actually a performance, not from Holtzman—that freaked out Frances the most.

"How does she know so much about pears?" she whispered to Roger across our breakfast table, by way of banging on the silent alarm.

How?

Holtzman contained multitudes. But she would only tell you every living thing there was to know about pears—or the sex organs of pigs or hiccups—if you brought it up first. Rebecca was slicing a reddish one for the salad when Frances asked what was likely an idle question, maybe just a polite one.

"How many kinds of pears are there?"

If her answers tended to be more dilatory and multifaceted than the less multifaceted among us could comfortably accommodate, well, most of the time you could count on Holtzman not to talk at all. Which makes it either ironic she married a loudmouth or proves again a cliché.

* * *

In addition to the cockatoo, Rebecca owned a turtle named Ghidra—after the nemesis of Godzilla—who hibernated under the striped fragment of couch and would emerge on occasion to eat lettuce and sliced grapes, often with a sad tumbleweed of dust hooked to her spiny shell. Ghidra reflected not only Holtzman's love of critters, but movies. Imported black-and-white monster movies, but also Hollywood movies, art movies, animated movies, documentaries, silents, shorts and *Phantom India*, a film she watched at the Museum of Modern Art that went on all day. (Did I mention she was patient?) Made sure to pack an eggplant sandwich, with honey and olive oil, on a multigrain loaf she'd baked herself. It was hippie—that's definitely a part, a proud part—but, with Holtzman, never dippie.

She was a trend-setter, too, in her offhand, untrendy way. It may sound ridiculous to say she was the first to wear her purse across her chest, but I remember when the squares made fun. Certainly she was first to wear electric-blue plastic shoes—I remember when her new brother-in-law threatened to eject her from his reception due to disrespectful footwear (and a year later begged to know where she got them, so he could stock his boutique). First to wear ugly glasses—found a cat-eye pair with green argyle pattern at a junk shop and got an optician to turn them into shades. In case you'd wondered who started that whole thing, she was first to cut the collars off her t-shirts—tourist tees friends sent her from Mount Rushmore, Six Flags and Pismo Beach Pier, as well as spoofs of tourist tees from her trippy pals at the Rhode Island School of Design.

That's another thing. Rebecca knew strange people, other strange people. Painters, troublemakers, funlovers, a goatherd. Some I'd even heard of. She'd been to Allen Ginsberg's East Village walkup for his 50th birthday party. And Charlie Mingus's West Village walkup for his Christmas party—where between ladling out sangria and playing Christmas carols at the piano, he'd pressed on her his mimeographed magnum opus about toilet-training your cat. At 16, in her first group show, one of the three other artists was Yoko Ono—before she was half of John. And Rebecca's relentless childhood suitor, a biker, AWOL Marine and poet known as Coney Tony, once stashed the original *On the Road* scroll under her bed after conning it out of a drunken Jack. Who a few days later came by her parents' house, in a snit, possibly with Cassady at the wheel, to retrieve it. There was dinner with Lou Reed at Sissy Spacek's. A joint with Nico and Jim Morrison at the Dom. Hanging with Jimmy James at Salvation—a tiny basement club between the Stonewall and Deacon's—before he was Jimi Hendrix. Chit-chatting in the art supply store with Mark Rothko. And backstage—when the rest of the Nation was stuck in the mud—at Woodstock. Woodstock! To Holtzman—open to anything, unimpressed by anyone, honest in a way that surpassed mere truth-telling—just a day in the life. Most of it she never bothered to mention to me. I found the cat-training manual tucked into *The Natural History of Vacant Lots.*

* * *

In the vinyl purse with the penguins, she carried a compact camera that served as her sketchpad. To me, it also served as proof of the unquenchable perversity of her gaze. On a stroll along the Hudson, presented with the red-orange horizon of Hoboken at sunset, I'd say something awestruck and turn for her reaction. She'd be in the gutter photographing a pigeon eating raw chicken. She took a lot of landscapes with that camera, but the plants were always dead and gardens ruined. In the grandeur of Gaudi's Barcelona cathedral, where I just assumed a husband and wife on a long delayed honeymoon would marvel together at the mad, soaring altar, I turned to find her scrutinizing a broken shoelace on the floor—"Is that . . . " she asked, edging closer, "a rat tail?" It was the kind of thing that happened often enough that my answer could simply be a quote from the title of her painting: "Mouse or Moose Toe?"

Somewhere along the line Rebecca had contentedly floated off from convention. It made you realize how much our lives are fenced in by it. Sometimes she seemed to even float away from time. She operated by a different clock anyway—the Hebrew calendar of clocks (did I mention she was raised Orthodox?). Though, paradoxically, she was never late. The alt-timing factor meant we were constantly crashing into each other at the door to the bedroom or bathroom, even in the wide-open spaces of the living room (maybe that was the fun?). And when we were anxiously hurrying to an appointment across town, she'd still have to stop time if there was a pile of dog shit that looked like a flattened squirrel.

She never closed cabinet doors—kitchen, bathroom, any cabinet, anywhere. I guessed it signified something psychological, maybe about openness. It could be she was showing off the thrift shop crockery inside or her incredible Band-Aid collection. Still, it was so specifically odd, so uniquely Holtzman, I never said anything—even when those doors whacked me in the face—and she never asked why I was slamming cabinets.

If we were always running into each other in the house, we could never seem to do it in the world. Ask her to meet you on the corner by the florist shop, stipulating a familiar corner and familiar shop—even if you methodically spelled out Alfonsi's Flowers, northeast corner 8th Street, intersection 6th Avenue, directly across from Papaya King—you could count on her not being there. She'd be somewhere, promptly. Just not there. She'd be three blocks away and have a perfectly logical, technically flawless, splendidly contorted reason why, an argument that might brilliantly marshal elements of linguistics, math, physics and history, and leave you wondering if *you* were in the right place. Much as my voice was stuck on loud, her sense of invention was stuck in overdrive. When it came to seeing the possibilities that would never occur to anyone else, that no one else could see, she had the real x-ray eyes. You could count on her to see through, zoom in, find the oblique angle and underlying pattern and to never accept the accepted usage. And it wasn't easy to keep up.

She contained worlds. And those worlds contained gravities, and those gravities jostled my axis. Beyond new ways of seeing and hearing, a new sense of taste. Holtzman took a guy not just ignorant of culinary cosmopolitanism, but proudly disdainful, habituated to the most egregious dietary simulacra—the chocolate Donettes and cherry pies of 7-Eleven—and somehow caused the beast to crave Indian, Chinese, Thai, Ethiopian, Japanese—raw sea urchin!—matzo ball soup and other unthinkable comestibles, along with all manner of things that were fresh. Like fruit. Like pears. Then she held my hand and manipulated my fat fingers and eventually accomplished the impossible task of teaching the white and terminally impatient to operate chopsticks.

She was the Queen of Boheme. An outsider and free-thinker, off-kilter and out-of-sync in her most fundamental mechanism. In other words, an artist. And along the way—as a sidelight, a lark that started as a favor to a writer friend—she took pictures for magazines. Muddy and Jerry Lee and Screamin' Jay, Garcia on the Hells Angels boat ride, Big Star at the Rock Writers' Convention, Patti's first reading at St. Mark's, Elvis's first show at the Garden. Did it and moved on. After all, there were broken shoelaces to ponder. And if that uninflected openness could be hard to read, it was all worth it. Like a Seckel.

* * *

THE NIGHT AFTER THE MORNING AFTER Elliot Murphy—after I'd slunk home to Gum Joy Towers and was trying not to call too soon—Rebecca Holtzman answered the phone at midnight. And as if a slurred call from a near stranger was plenty to go on, ventured out to an old sailors' dive in a dim corner of the way-west Village. I glimpsed her big curly halo floating past the gun-slot window. A moment later, trailing pastel ribbons, she stepped in and looked around without giving away a thing.

And we were on.

And on.

CHAPTER 25

Andy

"THEY'RE CUTTING MY BUDGET, TOMMY-BOY!" GUS barked into the phone, before asking me to do something for free. Who didn't know this day was coming? But, against all odds, Rebecca and I had managed to hold onto a chunk of the handsome sums Gus had already paid. And we'd sold the Kiss book to a Japanese publisher for a few grand. And though I was anticipating goose-eggs again, figuring the fix was in, the latest royalty statement for the US edition actually delivered a few grand more. We paid off Umberto. And American Express. Tried to pay the tab at the Bells of Hell, but Tim couldn't find it, bought us another round instead. Even paid Tiger, who seemed disappointed to give up an excuse to be bitter. Before it was all gone, I said to Holtzman, let's get the fuck out of New York. Make a run for it—finally—before the baby.

* * *

AH, THE BABY: THAT BRIGHT RED dividing line between your childhood and someone else's.

We'd spent a few years agreeing it was not the right time—until the day we realized it's never the right time. So we were still pretty broke when we told my mother, who pounded a pillow and asked, through gritted teeth, "How're you going to take care of this child!?" We didn't understand then that it's the child who takes care of you. Makes you do what you have to. Even makes you want to. "You'll have to move," Mother said. "Follow the jobs, like they did in the Depression." Holtzman and I looked at each other.

Holtzman, who'd never lived any place else, whose whole aesthetic and métier was the dirty streets of New York and whose whole family, generations, was clustered in a ten-block square of eastern Brooklyn, wasn't so sure about this California dreamin'. Oddly, it was Terry Landsman—whose prescription shades, it turns out, concealed not only his science-fair myopia, but an unforeseen reservoir of sentimentality—who showed the way. Terry put me in touch with a rock star's girlfriend who managed a sub-department of a California-based in-house ad unit of an intergalactic mega-bank holding company that was looking for a writer. It was my first real lead in a year. We scraped together money for plane fare, and I flew out for the interview. I told the interviewer, as he stared down at the word *Creem* on my resumé, that we were having a girl and—manic energy surging—that she was going to be the first ever woman boxing champion. I got the job anyway. Afterwards, I raced around San Francisco for a day-and-a-half looking at apartments, finding no one who would rent to a guy without "local references." Terry's reservoir fixed that, too.

Two months later, at lunch hour in the downtown San Francisco complex where I worked, amid the shelves of the ground-floor newsstand that had become my refuge from the sub-departmental cubicle maze above, feeling a distinct sense of flaming youth en route to gray-flannel senescence, I picked up the latest issue of a teenybopper rag to which, once upon an hallucination, I'd been a contributor. It wasn't a publication a grown man, new father and gold-card member in good standing brings back to the office. I was taking a minute to peruse it in the store. Paying conspicuously casual attention—in case anyone was looking, in case everyone was staring—I quickly flipped through the flimsy pages of cavorting celebs until something in the periphery made me flip back: a photo of Debbie Harry, Joey Ramone, an up-and-comer who called herself Madonna and Andy Warhol backstage at the Academy of Music. In the middle of that modish summit, at its white-hot center, arms encircling them, theirs encircling back, best friends and geniuses together, was an older, browner gentleman with a gray conk and jack-o'-lantern grin. In an offhand way meant to suggest there was no one in the rock scene *Rock Scene* didn't know, the caption identified the graying gent as "Eddie Neil the Village Legend," adding, for the benefit of us squares: "Clash piano player."

CHAPTER 00

Hudson

I DON'T KNOW WHAT BRUCE DID with his bullet. Mine I put in the nearest metal place—the black Rolodex with the pebbly matte finish and roll-top cover at the corner of my desk. Stolid emblem of adulthood and sophistication and my first real job, the Rolodex was what I was most excited to order when Creem *said order all the supplies you want. And over many years, through many desks, on the cards inside, I inscribed an unlikely memoir in the phone numbers and addresses of friends, business friends, itinerant family members, pizza places, rib joints, writers, bass players, fake piano players, real piano players, record dealers, editors, publishers, flacks, hacks, geniuses, the famous (I can see the card marked Bob Dylan) and their minders (the number was really Dylan's manager), people in Detroit, New York, California and one in Cleveland.*

This is how we'll remember, Charlie had said. And I did. Mostly because, knowing nothing about guns or ammo, the bullet scared the shit out of me. When I needed to conjure a distraction from bashing out the news, reviews, profiles and books that had become my marginal living, I'd fret over Charlie's bullet, concerned, without resort to chemistry, physics or, for that matter, reason, that the aging gunpowder was becoming unstable, festering, and one day would spontaneously combust—with the roll-top box pathetically inadequate to its containment.

But I remembered.

I remembered Cleveland, and Bruce when he was scrawny and unguarded. I remembered Charlie, songster, poet, tour-guide and mama's boy, who went to sleep at his mama's, at 24, and didn't remember to wake up. From river to flaming river, through all the fast-flipping cards of this Rolodex life, even when I thought I didn't, Charlie, I did. I remembered. It wasn't until the curly-crowned space traveler presented us with a bump—an invention as beautiful and terrifying as time itself—that I knew I had to forget.

What if the bullet shot the baby? Killed the baby? Killed the mother?

I snapped off the Selectric and, scratching around like Charlie in the glove compartment, dug the ammo from the box, and at six in the morning of the summer of the ripening bride—the last New York summer—climbed down five flights, hurried to the pier and hucked it in the river as far as I could.

Acknowledgments

Can't say one thing before offering up my immeasurable gratitude to the immeasurably patient friend who read the manuscript in its entirety three times, listened to it aloud four times and then read and listened to it again, in fragments, at odd moments, in odd locations, infinity times, every one of those times proving again her uncanny editing skills, her insight and her nerve, even in the face of the most ardent foot-stamping. I'm talking, of course, about my longtime partner-in-crime: soulmate-number-one Roni Hoffman. I'd also like to give massive credit to the editorial counsel of Jay Schaefer, who pointed the way out of a five-year thicket of words, paragraphs, and pages, more than once. Big thanks to Eileen Gittins, the very first reader and a fount of encouragement early on, and to my fake son, Max Werner, whose belief was as contagious as it was appreciated. Slobbering bear hugs to my longtime brother-in-arms Jeremy Koch and sister-in-arms Kitty Humpstone, the most generous friends in the world. And to my longtime "Sam" (aka Nick Rorick) (aka Toledo Shorty), who doesn't know how much his yabbering has meant, thanks for the photo on the front. All my love to *il mio gemello*, Big Kev, and our brother Ned. Hickeys to Lance. Major props to Josey Duncan and Hardie Duncan for their intergenerational wisdom. And big ups to Mike Lemme, Jen Kellogg, Shannon Burns, Jen "Moe" Moe, Alexandra Camacho, Michelle Mirasol and the whole Duncan Channon design combine for an astounding panoply of visual invention, resulting in one killer cover. Can't forget my pal at the Center of the Universe, Wendy Fitz, the enchanting songstress who one night, in the back room, said you gotta meet my friends Kat and Peter. Finally, to Kat Georges and Peter Carlaftes at Three Rooms Press for taking a long shot. To all of them and all I've forgotten and the friends, family and passers-by who've lent bits and pieces of their real lives to this fiction: *mea maxima culpa.*

—Robert Duncan, Fairfax, CA, March 2020

About the Author

At 22, Robert Duncan was managing editor of the renowned *Creem* magazine, working in Detroit alongside Lester Bangs. He has contributed to *Rolling Stone, Circus, Life* and dozens of publications and been singer, songwriter and producer for several semi-obscure bands, including 3DayBig&Tall. He is author of *The Noise: Notes from a Rock 'n' Roll Era*; *Kiss*, a tongue-in-cheek bio; and *Only the Good Die Young*, profiles of dead rock stars. He was story consultant and interview subject for the documentary, *Creem: America's Only Rock 'n' Roll Magazine*, which premiered at SXSW in 2019, and appears in public TV's *Ticket to Write*. He is anthologized in *Springsteen on Springsteen*. His poems have been published in *Maintenant: A Journal of Contemporary Dada Writing and Art* (Three Rooms Press), and Patti Smith gave him a shout-out in *Year of the Monkey*. He is founder of the advertising and design firm Duncan Channon and its Tip Records subsidiary. He was raised in a Southern family displaced to New York City and lives now with his wife, the artist and rock photographer Roni Hoffman, near San Francisco. *Loudmouth* is his first novel. https://www.duncanwrites.com.